Carter-Krall Publishing

Changing the world a word at a time.

Carter-Krall Publishers
42155 Rue Saint Dominique, Suite 207
Stone Mountain, GA 30083

Printed in the United States of America
Published by Carter-Krall Publishers. First Edition

Cover art by CKP Staff
Typesetting by CKP Staff

Edited by Jennifer Carsen

The Big Money Match/Brian Egeston
ISBN 0-9675505-6-4
Paperback

Library Of Congress Catalog Number
2003091131
First Edition June 2003

The
Big Money
Match

Brian Egeston
www.brianwrites.com

Dedication

For my friend and nemesis, Geoffrey Royal.
Here, ya happy now?
Wait until *I* win.

Other Works by Brian Egeston

ⳗ

<u>Novels</u>

Crossing Bridges

Whippins, Switches & Peach Cobbler

Granddaddy's Dirt

Catfish Quesadillas

<u>Anthologies</u>

After Hours

Acknowledgments

God, thank you for giving me signs when I was playing too much golf instead of working. You always know just when to take my golf swing.

This list can't be compiled without a very special acknowledgment to the most wonderful woman in the world. My beautiful wife, Latise, who caddied for me on my birthday, doesn't mind me playing golf until dark, congratulates me when I shoot low scores, encourages me when I'm terrible, and understands that my love for the game will never surpass my love for her. I'm sure divorce lawyers all over the country are lobbying against the cloning of your DNA as we speak.

Special thanks to Frank Archer from Scranton, PA who practically begged me to take his club to the driving range and learn this wonderful game. People are placed in each others' lives for a reason and at just the right time.

Thanks to my golf buddies who have allowed me to tag along for eighteen holes or more. In an amazing feat I will now try to list you chronologically:

The TCE Scranton plant golf league—thanks for letting me show up in jogging pants, basketball shoes, T-shirt, and not kicking me off the course. Oh, and thanks for not laughing at me when during my second shot of my first ever round of golf, I teed my ball up in the middle of the fairway. Hey, how was I supposed to know?

Clay Batts—thanks for the lessons in just getting it in the hole.

Thanks to Ken Kavanaugh, my first golf instructor. I still tell the story about how you wouldn't take my money because I was so bad.

My old and trusted Motorola cronies. Norbert Williams, Marc Riley, Dave Thibodeau, Dan Myers, Todd Smith, Wayne Wiggins, RC Covington, Jerry Lessin, Scott Mays, Patrick Pillette, Mike Robinson, Yasser Mauhmud, Portia Lewis, Stephen Benoit, Edwin Crespo, Ramon Martinez, Rolando Sosa...wait a minute. This could take forever. Let me just thank all the members, past and present, of the Motorola Golf League. Thanks for putting up with my antics and my two-hour PowerPoint presentations. I miss you all more than you'll ever know.

Thanks to the business partners I met while in the corporate world. Mike Rooney and Barry from Mar-Tech. Sorry I stunk it up so bad.

Thanks to the Ques who taught me another way of taking it to the greens—Marcus Shute, Len Starks, Rob Morrell, Willie Ivery, Ralph West, and the other golfers of the word's finest fraternity.

Thanks to Sam Puryear and Nyre Williams. I'm sorry we laughed at you guys when you were playing college golf before it was cool. Now that you're both shooting in the sixties, could I get five strokes a side?

Thanks to the wonderful Bellsouth Classics volunteers, especially the Black Hawk Down crew of player escorts, Skip, Bill Stout, Bob, and the rest of the gang. Watch those ropes.

I'd also like to thank PGA tour caddie Tony Terry, Charles Howell III, and Charles Howell II for a wonderful afternoon of cordial conversation during your 2002 practice round at the Bellsouth.

Thanks to Hidden Hills, Mystery Valley, Sugar Creek, Sugar Hill, The Hooch, Providence Club, Brown's Mill, Tup Holmes, Candler Park, Hamilton Mills, Apalachee Farms, and the other great courses in Georgia. I appreciate you allowing me to till your fairways with my clubs.

Thanks to my church golfing buddies. It's great fun to watch grown men bite their lips to avoid cursing on a golf course. Bob Williams, Tim Berry, Wendell Robinson, Frank Rudd, Tracy Young, Joe Montgomery. I am blessed by your mere presence.

A special thanks to the master of golf fiction, Troon McAllister (aka Lee Greunfeld). Thanks for crafting *The Green* and showing that golf books and good fiction are a wonderful combination.

Thanks to the strangers who have shared their lives with me for eighteen holes and have shaken my hand as a friend after the last putt dropped.

I offer to each and everyone on this list, and ones I omitted, a tip of the hat and a pat on the back.

Hit 'em good.

DeKalb County, Georgia

2002

Chapter 1
Jeff King

Three Handicap (Even on a bad day).
Strength: Hits the ball to Jupiter.

In this damp and dark room, lives had short expiration dates. On one visit, a life might be spared; on another it might be snatched so suddenly that a family's shock besieged their grief, leaving depression as the only available emotion. Another life trying to beat the odds had just entered the room, trying to reach in a monster's mouth and pull from its throat the words that would offer a reprieve. Jeff King was here to bargain with the man they called Nagga.

What you sayin' is, you wanna eat the bullet instead of me feedin' it to him?" Nagga asked.

"I never liked the taste of lead," said Jeff with a smirk.

"Don't matter to me. Lead, copper, wood, steel--

whatever hurt taste like to you. I 'on't care. But you bedda get ready for a feast if you gon' try to be a man all up in my face. Don't try to act like you tough and got it all together! I'll break yo' brain right now and forget about all this drama. You feel me!"

The man's booming voice forced a heavy silence. Suddenly, Jeff could hear the humming of a small refrigerator pushed against a wall in this stockroom-turned-office. He could hear water escaping above, swirling and splashing inside the rusty, corroded cast-iron pipes. Faint sounds of video games crept in from the next room through openings that the barrier of walls could not contain. Jeff could easily die here. There were, in fact, several rumors of people attending meetings in this office and never being heard from or seen again. Yet for some strange reason, he'd thought it necessary to face this self-made demon to solve his dilemma.

"My bad. I crossed the line a little bit there," said Jeff humbly.

"You damn right!" Nagga rose from his desk. He towered toward the ceiling and hit his head against a hanging light, causing it to cast sporadic swaying spotlights about the room. A poster of Sugar Ray Leonard was illuminated, then a poster of Mike Tyson. A poster of Calvin Pete caught the light, then a poster of Tiger Woods. As the swinging light lost momentum and began its course to become motionless, Nagga sat on the corner of his desk, an arm's length and a chokehold away from his visitor. Jeff was visibly nervous.

"All I'm sayin' is, if there's another way out, then that's what I wanna do," said Jeff.

"Why?"

"What chu mean, why?"

"Why you wanna help this clown? He headed straight for an express casket no matter what. It might not even be

me, but that fool got a death wish. You talkin' about somebody who not only gon' steal my product, but sell it and
buy another stash from my enemy and sell it on one of my
corners. Then he gon' take it to the extreme and use some
of the money I loaned him months ago to try and open up
his own corner. Is he crazy or just stupid? I mean, the juice
on the loan by itself is automatically one family member
put in critical condition by my policies. But theft and trea-
son? Bruh, that's a contract on his life worth five grand
easy right there. And now I hear this punk tryin' to be a
paid informant. Why the hell you wanna help him? He
don't wanna help hisself. You ain't even like him.

"Everybody on the West Side was behind you goin' to
college and playing golf. A brother from our neighborhood
playin' *golf*. And winnin' too. Just walk away from him,
bruh. Get married. Have yo' own kids. Yo' brother, he
headed for nowhere."

Jeff was immune to the words. He'd heard the warnings
numerous times from several different people. School offi-
cials, family members, therapists, police officers—and now
a professional thug. Even this admonition would not make
him take heed.

"Look, I know he jacked up the creed of the streets or
whateva, but it's deeper than I can explain. Nagga, I ain't
got nobody but my little brother. If he's a crook then he's a
crook. If he's in the dope game, then that's his life. But
he's all I got for family. I know you got to do what you got
to do and I can't stop that. What I wanna know is, is there
somethin' I can do?"

Nagga sighed, predicting how the story would end. A
broken heart and a bullet to the skull. Looking over at the
pictures of Calvin Pete and Tiger Woods, he was reminded
of an experience he'd had some time ago.

Like so many others, Nagga had fallen in love with golf
around April of 1997, when Tiger shocked the world by

winning the Masters. Since that time, Nagga (and a few other thugs) had gone country club by purchasing memberships at golf courses. An avid and enthused hacker, Nagga could never score lower than one hundred, but he looked good trying. Fitted from crown to toe with the latest and most expensive golf apparel, he looked liked the best player on the course—until he swung a club.

Though he'd taken lessons and watched videos, Nagga simply lacked the skill and hand-eye coordination the sport demanded.

His low point had come several weeks earlier when, during one of his worst days on the course, he was reminded of how golf had, not long ago, been exclusionary. One of his tee shots had sailed over the hole parallel to the one he was supposed to be playing. Once he arrived at his ball, the group playing the proper hole drove their cart over and watched his awful, awkward swing. The ball jetted across the ground, never rising higher than a squirrel's tail, and ricocheted into a flock of trees. The pines cried out like a wooden pinball machine.

The group watching laughed. One of them commented, "See that, Tom, you can dress 'em up all you want, but if the hole is smaller than a basketball rim, they can't find it." Nagga, who would have ordinarily sent a crew to hurt the man, found himself wanting to beat him a different way. The issuer of the insult had completely disregarded all golf etiquette. He was having a bad round himself and felt the need to attack everything. The man had kicked the cart, thrown his clubs, run off some geese, and now it was on to Nagga.

"You say somethin' to me?" asked Nagga.

"What'd you say? I couldn't hear you from all the tree banging your ball did in the woods. Get the hell off our fairway! This ain't your sport anyhow."

"Tell that to Tiger," Nagga replied.

"Guess what? You sure as hell ain't Tiger and there's not another person around here with that kinda game."

"You must be outta yo' damn mind," Nagga lashed. It's plenty of brothas 'round here that'll clean yo' clock."

"Yeah, right. Find your best man and I'll get my average guy and he'll send you back to Africa," the man said, driving off in the golf cart and taking the last word with him.

Nagga wanted to stop him. Wanted to pull out a nine-millimeter and aim for a spot just above his neck. But this was a different place from where he conducted that kind of business. He had to use his universal weapon, the one that penetrated all boundaries and spoke all languages.

Nagga shouted as loud as he could, "Ten grand!" The sound echoed from the trees and bounced across the rolling hills for anyone within a reasonable distance to hear. The cart, once shrinking in size with each turn of the tires, began a U-turn and became larger as it headed back toward him. Soon the men were face to face again.

"You shouldn't write checks you can't cash. That is, if you have a checking account."

"And you shouldn't get up in my face when you don't even know me," rebutted Nagga.

The man smirked and turned away, mumbling, "Just like I thought, bluffin'. What a waste of space."

"Look here, fool. You want it or not? I called it. It's ten grand."

Still smirking, the man replied, "Tell you what, if and when you do find that kinda money, if and when you do find a 'brotha'," he said mockingly, "you call me. Here's my card." He placed the rectangular piece of paper in Nagga's hand. "Do you have a card? Or should I ask, do you have a job?" Nagga frantically reached in his wallet to prove the judgmental man wrong. He pulled out his own small rectangle. The offending man read the words

Up To The East Side Records.
Get yo' turn at bat.
Nagga, CEO.

Into the golf cart he jumped, laughing once more, making the electric vehicle smaller and smaller until it disappeared along the cart path. Nagga stood in the middle of the fairway, furious. He looked at the card, which read *Jones Outfitters, Billy Jones, President/Owner.* Thinking of his own chosen occupation, and his love for a game that did not love him back, Nagga spewed profanity, then grabbed his five iron at both ends and thrust it down over his thigh, snapping it in two.

After recounting the incident and pulling out the card he'd looked at every day since then, hoping for an opportunity, Nagga smiled at Jeff.

"Maybe there is somethin' we can do. How's yo' game?"

"It's a'ight. I get out as much as I can. Engineering won't let me play like I want to. We lookin' at some voluntary layoffs so you know what that means."

"Didn't you win the SWAC championship when you was at Grambling?"

"That was ten years ago, bruh."

"But still, you got some game I know. You wanna save yo' brother's life, you gon' play golf. I got this game I'm gon' line up for you."

"Against who?"

"Do it matter? They ain't no professional. You play in the match and we'll work things out wit' yo' brother...this time."

"For real?" Jeff's eyes lit up at the assumed good-natured offering of Nagga. "You promise? Can I get this in writin' or somethin'?"

"Fool, is you crazy? I look like a Equal Opportunity Lender to you? Hey yo, Deshawn!" Nagga yelled, summoning a witness from the next room.

A trusted pawn appeared. "Whassup, Nagga?"

"You know that mark that stole a stash and tried to set up shop?" he asked, never taking his eyes off Jeff.

"Yeah, you want me to put the contract out?"

"Naw, not yet. But this here is his brother. He gon' play in a money game and we gon' wipe the slate clean. You my witness to my word."

"I feel ya."

"Holla." And the pawn vanished. "That's better than any contract right there, bruh."

"A'ight," said Jeff. "What we doin'?"

"Ten large."

"What! Is that how much he owes?"

"Naw, bruh. Right about now he owes me his life. If you don't think his life is worth ten Gs, then don't play."

"Ten grand," Jeff said, rubbing his temples. "I thought we was talkin' about five hundred dollars or somethin'."

"What! Boy, you smoking crack? Who you think I'm gon' let wipe the slate for five notes? My mama owe me more than that. She gon' be gettin' a visit pretty soon too if she don't pay up. Look, I ain't got all day. I got runs to make and deals to do and contracts to put out. Question is, do I have one less contract this month?" Nagga asked. He walked around the room and allowed Jeff to brew in his predicament.

"Yeah," Jeff said.

"Yeah, what?"

"Yeah I'll play. But the slate'll be wiped completely clean, right?"

"You got it, dog. But if he do somethin' else stupid,

that's another issue."

Jeff avoided looking at Nagga, knowing his brother could regress to stupidity with every sunrise. Given his brother's trouble-prone life, they might be having this conversation again before too long. "And all I got to do is play in this money game, right?"

"Oh, no no no no. You got to do more than play. 'Cause if you lose, he don't live."

Chapter 2
Kevin Tanner

Four Handicap (If he practices before playing).
Strength: Hits irons like throwing darts.

Kevin Tanner had addictions. His first was gambling, but his worst was golf. If he could, he'd boil golf, draw it into a syringe, and rush it through his veins. Would take a sleeve of brand new golf balls, crush them into a fine powder, and vacuum them up his nose with a graphite shaft. Would take a chunk of grass from the nearest putting green, roll it up in a score card, and smoke it until his lips turned green. Yet it was here, in a doctor's office plastered with pieces of paper from institutions deeming the man in the white coat rich and smart, that his addictions would meet a head-on collision with life's necessities.

"So, are the tumors cancerous?" asked Kevin, concerned for his wife.

"They're fibroid tumors. Very common among women, but I don't think they're malignant," the doctor replied. "They're different sizes. Some are so small they're difficult to detect. Other times they can be as large as golf balls or larger."

Kevin's eyes lit up at the mention of his mistress's name—golf.

"Good Lord. Don't mention that word around him," said Kristen.

"Avid golfer, are you, Kevin?"

"Little bit. I play whenever I get a chance."

"He gets a chance whenever the sun is shining."

The doctor chuckled as Kristen continued. "That game has made me eat lots of dinners alone and made me miss some engagements because someone didn't leave the golf course when he promised to." Kevin's head lowered and the doctor's grin quickly disappeared behind a clearing throat.

"These fibroids, unfortunately, are a tad bit larger than normal," the doctor said. "They're six inches wide, some of them, and the ultrasound reveals more than one. It's the source of your extreme pain during your menstrual cycle. And there's a good chance it's the reason you're having trouble conceiving. I'd like for you both to see a fertility specialist, just to be sure. The specialist can also give you options for getting pregnant."

With each word, Kristen's head sank lower and the time between blinking eyes grew longer. She didn't want to see this moment or any moment that would follow. If she looked up, the future could be in front of her and it might be one without children. She wanted so badly to have them, to share the fruit of her womb and contribute to her family's lineage. For years they'd tried, afraid that the years of birth control had caused damage; then they thought their timing was off. After performing meticulous experiments of ovulation dates, perfect positions in bed, and timed moments afterwards of lying perfectly still allowing the swimmers to find their way, the result was always the same.

In the recent months, when the monthly reminder came, informing her that she was still amongst the flat-stomach tribe, excruciating pain accompanied her cycle. Some months it was so painful she would have to take days off from work. Her sick leave becoming increasingly sparse, it was finally time to come here to the doctor and receive whatever her maternal fate would be.

The doctor had more bad news. "Aside from the possible infertility, I'm more concerned about the size of the fibroids and the symptoms you're showing. The pain during sex, the aches in your abdomen and lower back, the fever, the nausea are all signs that your case may be severe. Depending on how long the large fibroid has been growing, there's a slight chance that it may be malignant. Just to be sure, I want to do a biopsy."

Kevin asked, "That means she might have cancer, doesn't it?"

"Yes, it does," the doctor answered with comforting sympathy. "But the good news is that it's very rare for that to be the case. Less than one percent of fibroids become cancerous." He turned back to Kristen. "But given the size of yours and the symptoms, I want you to consider a myomectomy after the biopsy results. The only other option we have after that is a hysterectomy."

Kristen threw a glance at the doctor as though he'd just pronounced her terminal fate. Her head fell into hands and tears jetted down cheeks. She was barely thirty years old, facing the possibility of an operation for a woman the age of her mother. An operation that would preclude any chance for her to become a mother.

Kevin had no words that would comfort, so he did the best he could. The husband who loved a game more than life itself held his wife and wiped her tears.

Some tears and sobs later, Kevin turned to the doctor and spoke, "Doc, we're gonna make it through this. What do we need to do and how soon do we need to do it?"

Kristen raised her head after hearing the willful statement. She sniffed and mashed the tears off her face. Daring them to return.

"That's the best attitude you all can have, Kevin. We'll get you set up for the biopsy as soon as possible. After that—"

"How much is the surgery, Doc?" Kevin asked. It was a strange question, asked at a strange time.

"I'm not sure. It can be rather expensive. Most insurance providers cover a good portion of it. You shouldn't have a problem. How's your insurance?"

"We've got great coverage," Kevin's wife asserted with confidence.

Kevin remained silent but looked in the doctor's eyes the way men do when they know one of them has done something terribly wrong. The doctor recognized Kevin's look—the look of forgetting to bring the wine home for the dinner party or leaving the office too late to make it to the children's recital.

But Kevin's screw-up was far worse than the occasional honey-do slip-ups. The doctor had a hunch as to what might have caused his look and decided now might be a good time to end the visit.

"Tell you two what. Talk about things on the way home and I'll have someone from the office call you tomorrow and set everything up. How's that?"

Kevin jumped from his seat, anxious to leave the topic of surgery costs.

The doctor escorted them to the door, patted Kevin on

the back, and said, "You two make sure and have some good dialogue on the way home." The doctor closed the door and exhaled a worried sigh. He knew exactly why Kevin had given him the look.

"What the hell do you mean our insurance is canceled!" Kristen exploded. They sat in the car, waiting for the light to switch hues and allow them to continue home.

"Honey, I've been meaning to tell you for quite a while. I had to cancel it because the bills weren't getting paid and we were gonna lose the car. We were two months behind on the mortgage."

"How? Where is all of our money going, Kevin? I haven't been spending any more than usual!"

"It's just one of those times, I guess. We needed something here and there. Something broke and had to be replaced. Car repair here, house repair there."

She looked out the window, watching buildings pass by, wondering about the people inside, thinking about what kind of financial problems they were having. After a few blocks, she turned to Kevin and said, "Well, I guess it's time to dip in the savings. If we get the insurance back this week, we might be able to do the biopsy by the end of the month—that's if they don't get us for a preexisting condition."

"The, uh, savings are what I used to pay the mortgage and get the house fixed."

"What? Kevin, what is going on? Tell me you haven't been gambling again. Where is our money? What have you done with it?"

The car was silent, but the anger grew deafening. Kevin knew he would have to reveal his losses—all of them. He'd been trying to work extra hours so he could make things right. He tried taking in some action at golf course where no one knew him, but he often found himself winning only five or ten dollars at a time. When there was a big money game, he usually found out at the last minute and arrived at the golf course just in time to tee off and start the round, which almost always ensured a terrible score for his match that day. In just six months, Kevin had dwindled their checking account down to $56.23 and depleted their savings to $239.12.

"I guess I should have told you, but I did have a relapse back into the action for a while."

His wife faced the window again. Her silent tears were louder than any scream she could have released.

"But the good thing is that it's only been golf. I haven't been doing the online casinos or the baseball games like I did last year. I think that's progress, don't you?"

She looked at him with sharp eyes, wishing her vision could prick his jugular and cause a slow, dripping bleed.

This was, however, progress. Much better than maxing out his credit cards on cashcasino.com just before they were to start a much-needed summer vacation. Then there was the time he'd spent all day at an electronics store, watching every baseball game he'd bet on and winning just enough to get their television out of the pawn shop he'd hocked to cover another bet. It was progress, albeit absurdly misplaced.

"I'm sorry. I'm still trying to get help and I was working to put all of the money back and get things back on track. But this thing just came out of nowhere. Who would have known you'd need surgery like this? If we could have just—"

"Fix it!" she yelled. His wife didn't want any more of his words. "You fix this thing. I don't care what you have to do. I'm gonna have children and I'm not gonna die because of some tumor. You get everything in order and don't even think about speaking a word to me until it's done."

"What can I—"

"Is everything in order yet?"

Kevin put the car in park as he pulled into their driveway and tried to camouflage the stupid sheepish look turning his face red.

"Then don't speak to me. The next thing I wanna hear from you is when you're taking me to the hospital for surgery and how you're paying for it. Or you can tell me when the divorce papers are arriving. I won't live like this anymore, Kevin."

Tears rolled again before she exited the car. Kevin fought back emotions of his own as he thought of the only solution he'd ever known. The number was already programmed in his cell phone.

"Billy. Hey, it's Kev. Your old Wake Forest classmate needs a favor, buddy."

"Hey, roomie. How's it goin'? I hope you're not asking for more money. The word's out, brother. You owe way too much."

"Yeah, I know, that's why I'm quittin'. No more action after this last game. I just need one more piece, a huge payday, then I'm done for life. Billy, I need the biggest money game you can put together. I can't tell you about it now, but it's for my wife." Kevin recalled the doctor's conversation and all the words that ended with -opy, -omy, and other terms he'd forgotten that meant nothing good. He thought of Kristen's warnings and ultimatums.

"Well, that's a whole 'nother proposition altogether. Brother, this might be your lucky day. Met some guy other day who thinks he's the Don King of golf. Says he can find somebody to beat any man. Serious money, too. I'll track him down. See if we can get somethin' done."

"Good. I'll take it. I don't care what it is or who it's

with. I'll put my house up if I have to. But seriously, it's gotta be huge. I'm thinking at least five large."

"Oh no, son. You're talking to the wrong man. Way this son of gun was talkin' smack, this'll be the match of your life. This old boy was talking about *ten* large."

Chapter 3
JoiMartina

Five Handicap
(From the men's tees...scratch from the ladies').
Strength: Unbelievable short game.

She'd made all the right moves but they always seemed to yield the wrong results. She was high school valedictorian—Harvard lost her application. Cruised through Bethune-Cookman college in three and a half years—entered the job market when no one was hiring business majors. Whizzed by graduate school in a year and half—learned MBAs are a dime a dozen. Unless, of course, they're from Harvard. Used her extensive networking connections to leap ahead of the job-hunting pack—wound up here in the worst of the worst scenarios she'd ever fallen into.

The company needed a token. Someone who would make them look good when prospective clients were curious about the diversity of the personnel. People had begun to take an interest in the number of Blacks, Hispanics, Asians, and disabled employees a corporation employed. Consumers were not only becoming wise, but very conscience-driven as well. This, however, had proven to be another of Joi's good decisions beset with terrible results. Her nice salary hardly seemed worth the politics she had to endure at the office: the smiles they gave her walking down the hallway, the knives they threw at her back when she turned the corner, and the lustful looks some gave her in the parking lot.

Life was wearing on her. The constant misfortunes despite her overachievement began to outweigh her motivation to strive for more. Her only solace, her only redeeming joy, was learning life's lessons while playing golf.

Joi's father had introduced her to the game with a new set of golf clubs on her ninth birthday and they had become her best friends since the candles were blown out that day. *Golf imitates life*, he would tell her when they played. If you play, there will be unlucky breaks and bad bounces. But if you keep playing the game and play long enough, the breaks will come your way and victory shall be certain.

Playing golf with her father was Joi's treasured birthright. She'd watched him go out on Saturday mornings for eight years. Saturday morning cartoons were of no importance when she watched him gather his things to go outside and play. Joi asked every time, *Can I come and play with you, Daddy?* Always the same answer. *Not now. It's not your time yet.* Finally, on one brisk October morning, she was given the answer. *Baby Girl, get your clubs if you wanna go play with Daddy.* Joi was so elated, she dashed from the couch where the cartoons went on without her, into the garage where her clubs awaited this day, and into the passenger seat of the car—all without washing up, brushing her teeth, or taking off her pajamas.

Joi's father had anticipated the reaction. With cool patience, he placed his own clubs in the trunk and sat in the driver's seat. Before starting the car he turned to her and said, *Baby Girl, I get excited too, but you might need these*, handing Joi a duffel bag with warm clothes and a toothbrush.

Joi developed into a talented golfer at the expense of her social skills. While others were hanging out after school and getting together on the weekends, Joi insisted on getting her studies out of the way and then heading to the driving range for practice. Her father saw this void during the critical development time in his daughter's life and suggested she do something other than study and play golf. She tried, but eventually she always came back to the game that allowed her time with Daddy.

Worried about his daughter's ability to get along with others and interact with her peers, he settled for instilling verbal lessons of dealing with people using analogies from their favorite game.

People are like putting greens—they feel a certain way one day and another way on another day. Gotta learn how to adapt to their changing conditions.

People you work for are like your clubs—if they don't feel right when you work with them you can't do your job.

People are like playing in rough weather—if you make adjustments to the conditions, you can achieve the desired results.

Meeting and networking with people is like hitting balls at the driving range—Each shot can do something different for you in a different situation, so don't forget a single one.

She never forgot those nuggets, nor the numerous others they shared eighteen holes at a time. The most enduring memory was a hellish one: She was standing over a putt at a college tournament and saw her father collapse in the high noon heat. What at first was believed to be dehydration actually turned out to be a large brain tumor. Joi's father was able to watch his daughter play golf for only six more months. Before his untimely death, he reminded her once again, *Baby Girl, golf imitates life.*

Joi felt that she'd always found the bad breaks because her father wasn't there to help her. Had he still been living, she might have been persuaded to do what she loved instead of looking for job security in corporate America. He would have told her to try and play professional golf and let the good breaks come her way. Instead, she entered the turbulent waters of working and dealing with people in the daily grind.

On the weekends, she'd visit her father. Every Saturday she made a tee time for two people but showed up alone— or so it appeared to others. For Joi, it was the usual round of golf with Daddy. Passers-by could see her in a golf cart, talking and laughing with herself. He was there with her for every shot, saying, *Nice ball, Baby Girl.*

She needed her father's guidance now more than ever because the company that had originally needed a token statistic now needed a token scapegoat. Joi's current work project was slowly becoming a debacle. Their largest client had changed the completion deadline and asked for an immediate audit of the entire project to date. After the audit, Joi was called into the president's office.

"Joi, come on in. Thanks for dropping by on short notice."

"What's this about?"

"Oh, it will only take a minute. How's your golf game? We hear you're quite a player. Why haven't you ever played in the company tournament?"

"Didn't want to. What's this about?"

The president sighed, looking at Joi, never having gotten used to her abrasive personality.

"Joi, the McMinville Group has run into some problems that were revealed in the audit."

"Okay."

"Some difficulties that we feel were a result of misallocation and oversights."

"Okay," Joi said again, still wondering why she was called in.

"Joi, I hate to say this, but it's a simple case of mismanagement."

"Okay." This time she raised her eyebrows and then shrugged her shoulders.

"Well, weren't you the only project manager for the McMinville Group?"

"Yeah, I was, but what does this have to do with me?"

"Are you serious?"

"Aren't I always?"

"You don't know about the audit results, do you?"

"Why should I? No one told me about the audit until it was almost complete anyway. My main focus has always been project completion and cutting costs."

The president's eyes widened at the mention of cutting costs. "Then that's why we have a problem, I assume."

"Why is that?"

"Your so-called cost cutting methods."

"What about them?"

"Joi, let me just put everything on the table. During the audit, a misallocation of funds was discovered. Over thirty-five thousand dollars."

"What!"

He looked away before saying, "I was as shocked as you are." The president removed a pen from his shirt pocket and scribbled on a pad.

"Why am I in your office?"

"Like I said, you're the project mana—"

"You should've had the comptroller and accountant in here. They have to sign off on everything, don't they?"

"I, er uh, we talked to the, uh, accountant and they already know what's going on." He hadn't expected the response and was thrown off course. This wasn't part of his planned speech.

"Seems like everybody knows what's going on except me."

Joi was standing now. Trying to decide whether she would run for the door or charge the president and give him a two-hand necklace snug around his throat.

"Joi, I want you to call this gentleman. He's a friend of mine and a great lawyer. Should be able to help you out."

"What?" Joi yelled, glancing at the paper. "Why do I need a lawyer?"

"We had to give the results of the audit to the McMinville group and they've notified us that they...uh...want to contact the authorities Tuesday morning if we don't have a resolution by Monday. We just feel it's in everyone's best interest if you're protected."

"Protected! Did you give this number to the accountant and the comptroller? Did you use the number yet? Are *you* protected? What do *I* need protection from?"

"Joi, just calm down. This is very serious. We're talking about embezzlement, fraud—federal offenses even. This is only a precautionary measure."

"Are you kidding me? You cannot possibly be serious."

"I'm afraid this is very serious. I mean, what other options do you have—besides, well, *recovering* the funds. Wherever they might be." The president gave her a coy look. It was a trap door or possibly an escape route. He waited.

Joi looked at the walls, wondering what her dad would've advised her to do. She saw plaques and degrees above the man's swirling executive gray hair. University of Georgia—Bachelor's Degree. Georgia Tech—Master's Degree. She began doubting herself all over again. Had she gone to the wrong school? Was this simply another pitfall in her failure-prone life? Then she initiated the mental chess match her father taught her on the golf course. Always think of your opponent making the best outcome and having to do one better. Never let your opponent see your reaction to their good shot.

Her reasoning left few choices. If this was indeed a setup to get rid of her, calling the lawyer would send a message that she was taking responsibility for the misallocation. By accepting responsibility, she was giving the company a reason to get rid of her on the spot—despite the flimsy façade that they were on her side. And if she offered to find the money, it would seem as though she had some knowledge of where it was, which would keep her under the eye of suspicion for the rest of her employment and brand her resume when or if she left. Not to mention that even if she wanted to, she simply didn't have thirty-five thousand dollars of her own money to somehow sneak into the company's bank account. Her only play was to somehow get the money and take it directly to the McMinville group and give it as some sort of under-budget, under-schedule customer refund—a cost savings passed along to the customer. And pray he'd take it quietly.

First she had to get the money. She remembered the outpouring of concern and love she'd received after her father's funeral, most of which came from a vast network of golfers her father had known for many years. There were several people she'd met playing golf who knew her father well. Wealthy people who said to call on them if she ever needed anything, anything at all. What she needed now was a low-interest loan. And she needed it before Monday morning.

Dad would agree with that plan, she thought. If he were here, he'd say, *Nice plan, Baby Girl*. Memories of her father slowed the seconds.

Before she realized it, the president was standing over

her saying, "Joi... Joi!"

"Huh?"

"You spaced out on me for a minute. So, what can we do to solve this problem?"

Joi looked once more at the degrees and the portrait-perfect hair.

"I'll see you Monday morning." As she rose to exit, the president's mouth froze open. This wasn't the answer he'd wanted or anticipated.

"Are you going to call my friend?"

"Who, me? No. I'm taking the rest of the day off." She reached the door, turned back to look at him, and said, "I'm going to play golf."

"What? Huh? But—"

"Talk to ya Monday."

Chapter 4
Bob Berry

Seven Handicap (Friendly rounds).
Two Handicap (When gambling).
Strength: Putts like a machine.

He was a political genius with the common sense of a snail in a salt mine. A people person, while at the same time a parasite's pleasure. Trouble was his inseparable Siamese twin. Take, for instance, the time he'd announced a remarkable idea for co-oping public school and private school teachers. The plan was met with widespread acceptance—until he met with a known criminal who just happened to give him a handshake full of hundred dollar bills. The criminal had stopped him in the parking lot and said, *Mr. Berry, here's a campaign contribution, would you mind posing for a photo op?*

Instead of telling the stranger to send a check to his campaign headquarters, the always-personable Bob Berry showed each of his thirty-two teeth when a photographer appeared, on cue, from behind a car. Just before the election, fliers were placed in mailboxes all over town with the photo, captioned: *Can you pick out the criminal in this picture?*

Bob lost the election by an overwhelming landslide. He'd held and lost just about every office the county had to offer. School board official, county commissioner, county solicitor. Bob's greatest embarrassment to date had to be the check-copying fiasco. After learning that cash contributions in the parking lot were ill-advised, he made certain that every cent he raised was in the form of a check. As motivation for why he wanted to be a civil servant and to remind him who he worked for, Bob took a personal check from one of his supporters and made color copies. One for his office, one for his home, and one for his campaign headquarters.

The check was given to him by an elderly retiree by the name of Fantha Lee who'd pledged a whopping five hundred dollars to Bob, specifically for his new proposal of taking social security benefits and paying dividends from younger family members' 401Ks if senior citizens needed extra health care. Even his opponents privately admitted that it made sense on paper.

Apparently, Fantha Lee's younger family members had no 401K, but what they did have was her checkbook. They too had been making color copies of the checks—not for motivation, but for mooching. As luck would have it (bad luck, that is), Bob left his copies of the checks at Kinko's, planning to pick them up and pay for them when his other campaigning material was ready. Copy centers, banks, and check cashing stores throughout the city had been given notice of the scam and were told to watch for anyone making color copies of checks.

Despite his public pleas and detailed explanations, despite the fact that the check he'd copied was already filled out and therefore impossible to kite, Bob Berry became known as the politician who'd forged Fantha Lee's fixed income.

Since that time, he couldn't find committed volunteers and didn't dare have a fundraiser to start a new campaign. And there was absolutely no working a nine-to-five job for him. His job was to work for and with people. It was a habit he'd picked up in college while playing golf at University of Georgia.

Bob quickly learned that his team played better when he shared tips on the golf swing, visualizing the golf course, and controlling emotions in the heat of battle. As team captain, Bob lead UGA to more victories than any other captain, but more importantly, he realized he could accomplish anything he wanted by helping others help themselves. A fearless and naturally gifted golfer, Bob practiced very little and coached whenever possible. His annual golf tournament had proven to be his best fundraiser ever. It was called the Beat Bob Tournament. He gave whoever was willing a one-shot advantage on whichever hole they picked. A person could buy as many shot advantages as they could afford. One shot cost a thousand dollars, two shots cost five thousand, and three shots or more— well, a person could fund his entire campaign for what a three-shot advantage cost. Along with the high-stakes challenge, Bob made donations to charity, passed out expensive imported cigars, and provided child care to those playing in the event. Each year, no more than two people even tied Bob on any given hole. Bob, ever the people person, gave them prizes anyway—a free full-year membership to his country club and a brand-new set of custom-fit golf clubs.

But now no one wanted to play in his tournaments, and people didn't want to be associated with him anymore. It was bad business to do business with Bob Berry. And unfortunately, Bob could only do two things well: golf and derive plans for the greater well-being of others.

What once worked for him now worked against him. The common sense that would have told an ordinary man to pack in the Bob Berry buttons and banners had fled this extraordinary man many years ago. Instead, all he knew was to keep prodding and things would work themselves out.

However, time was running out on his political clock. He was quickly approaching the dead end of his 30s. By this time, he'd planned to be on the way to Congress and implementing his Tri-Fold stimulus platform. Bob had been refining the model since his senior year in college. The three elements were education, economics, and equality. Each exploited the benefits of the other factors and flushed out their weaknesses.

Under his plan, Bob could get wealthy investors to fund, and profit from, healthcare organizations and public school enhancement business. Corporations would receive huge tax breaks for teaching business skills to the less fortunate and setting up learning centers in correctional facilities.

Everyone has to get an invitation to the party if you want have a good time, Bob would say. *If you bring more to the party, you can take more home. If you want to take more home, you'll need to learn how to bring more with you.*

The plan was useless without a selfless leader at the reins. There was no one he could trust with it. His opponents would take it and dissect it into pieces that fit their own personal agendas. His own party members had a limited vision of what it would truly take to make the plan successful. Even if they could implement it, they were sure to shy away from Bob's next plan—free healthcare and welfare depletion. Like all of his other political masterpieces, it worked on paper.

There was no other way. Bob had to be in office. In order to be in office, he had to run. In order to run, he had to have campaign funds.

"Tom, hey, it's Bob Berry. Time for that annual golf fundraiser. Got some great prizes. How many people can I put you down for?"

"Hey, uh, Bob," the man responded, wishing he'd checked the caller ID. "We really can't this year, buddy. But hey, good luck."

Once again, Bob was rushed off the phone. Same result for the last three days. The list was getting shorter and Bob didn't have one single player.

"Skip! Hey, buddy. It's Bob. How's the race organizing going?"

"Bob Berry, you old sly dog. What's goin' on? You still cashing old ladies' checks or you breakin' piggy banks now?" Skip boomed a long loud laugh through the phone and Bob did what any politician would do to avoid embarrassment—laughed louder.

Skip Breiser was one of Bob's oldest and most trusted friends. He'd racked up a small fortune organizing marathons all over the country. Like Bob, he loved the ladies. Unlike Bob, he had the common sense of Confucius and impermeable discretion. A straight shooter, Skip always told Bob how he felt, even when Bob didn't want to hear it

"Bob, I hope you're not callin' me to play in that charity money-launderin' golf tournament of yours."

"Well, Skip, in fact I am. Runnin' for state rep, you know?"

"Hell, ain't you been state rep once before? Buddy, you couldn't get elected septic tank sucker right now. Nobody wants to touch you."

"I know it's bad. Probably never been like this. I'm runnin' out of time here. I gotta put the Tri-Fold in place before the next presidential election."

"What? It's time already?" Skip knew how important

the plan was to the state and potentially the nation. He used to watch in amazement as Bob would work on the project, using diagrams and scenarios. Matching models to real-life situations. It was a symphony. Bob had once shown Skip the plan by standing in front of a large dry erase board, waving markers about like an insane conductor. He drew lines from the rich to the poor. He enclosed circles from middle class to upper class. He drew connecting dollar signs from corporations to schools. He filled in merging sections of Blacks and Whites. And, when verbalized, it sounded like music. Skip saw the plan and believed in it because he was one of those rich who could get richer by helping the poor. He was silent, then helpful.

"Bob, what do you need?" His tone was deadly serious.

"I gotta win the primary in August and it'll take…" Bob glanced down at his spreadsheet. "…$11,857.23 to do it."

"What's the twenty-three cents for?"

"Not sure. If I look at the projections for—"

"Bob."

"Huh?"

"I'm jokin'. I gotta tell ya, friend. Nobody's gonna play in that tournament this year or any other year until you get yourself cleaned off. You can—"

"Skip, this is all I got—all I ever wanted to do. Helping people. And, well, you know… play a little golf whenever I can."

"God, don't I know it. Bob, I'll help you, but it ain't gonna be how you might like. I'll help you help yourself. First off, you're gonna need more than eleven grand. More like twenty. You're gonna need money for a TV ad, a smear campaign, and a private investigator. The first—"

"Nope. That's never been my style, Skip. I won't start it now."

"You want the Tri-Fold put in place?"

"Yeah, but—"

"But nothin'. He'll bounce back. Everybody does. The private investigator is for you. First thing you gotta do is to get someone else to clear you of those checks. Nothing's gonna change before you do that."

"Okay, I agree with you there. So I guess we're talkin' about a loan. Don't kill me with the interest because I'm not sure how long it will take to pay you back."

"A loan! For you? Are you crazy?" Skip said with a coyote laugh. "Your career is the worst investment since the Yugo. There's only one thing I'll put my money up for you and that's your golf game."

"Yeah, but no one is gonna play in my tournament. You said it yourself."

"I got wind of a big game coming up. Guy I use for security at the marathons works at some outfitters place and his boss has a ringer playin' for ten grand. There's nobody around here that can touch you on a good day."

"I'll probably need a few weeks to get ready."

"Oh, you're ready." Skip replied. "You'd better stay ready so you won't have to get ready. It's for twenty grand and it's tomorrow morning."

Chapter 5
The Match
Mystery Valley Golf Course

Mystery Valley was a beautifully carpeted giant scorpion. It twisted and bent, then stung and pinched those trying to attack its holes in search of good scores. Nestled near the bottom of DeKalb County, it lurked off a main road and was guarded by iron gates that kept golfers out before dawn and pushed them out at day's end. There was no mystery about this valley: It was long and difficult.

Entry into the golf course was a tease, or an intimidator, depending on the golfer's attitude. Lush green fields manicured to prime conditions lined the asphalt-paved roller coaster that dipped and swerved alongside several holes. Today the road would be traveled by the players of a game unlike the course had ever hosted. Jeff was the first to arrive and begin practicing on the driving range as the clouds danced and swirled above, ready to unleash dripping soldiers whenever they felt the desire for battle. He'd spent the entire night flipping over in his bed, tossing from one end to the other. Recurring visions of a young man beaten to a pulp awakened him throughout the night. At 1:00 am he was up watching SportsCenter; at 3:15 am he was up again watching the Golf Channel. Finally, at 4:40 am, an action movie put him to sleep for a few hours. At 8:00 am sharp, he was at the gates of the golf course and the first customer to be seen that day. He rushed the gentleman working the pro shop, grabbed a bag of seventy-five practice balls, and began perfecting his swing for the day.

Fifteen minutes after Jeff got to the driving range, he noticed a man on the putting green with four rows of balls all lined up, pointing at different holes in different directions.

With smooth gliding strokes of the putter the man made each ball disappear. Jeff quickly did the math. Four balls, four holes. The guy had just dropped sixteen putts in a row. *That's sixteen possible birdies*, Jeff thought to himself. He thought about going up and complimenting the man on his stroke—maybe get a putting tip or two.

Instead, he thought of his brother and the torturous dreams. Jeff pulled out his driver and went back to work on his swing. He placed a ball on the tee, set up, and took the club back slowly, starting his back swing by wrapping the driver around his body on a perfect plane. He swung, cutting the air with a descending whip. It was a soft, quiet motion until he got within six inches of the ball, when he increased the speed of the club and made a turbulent rip just before ball impact. It was all grace and power—the winding of his body, the smashing of the ball, and the bouncing echoes shooting through the trees. Jeff's tee shots sounded like lethal collisions of small round objects and precisely manufactured metal.

The man on the putting green noticed the explosions. Jeff teed up another ball and commenced with the same poetic and powerful swing. They both watched as the ball jetted outward on a low trajectory, rising higher each millisecond until it began to turn ever so slowly to the left and finally disappeared into the woods at the back of the range.

"Oooh weee! That's a big stick. Friend, I once saw a man hit a ball like that. They called him Mr. Woods whenever he walked into a room and he had green jackets in his closet." Jeff grinned at the flattery. "Bob Berry's my name."

"Jeff King. Nice to meet you, Bob."

"Likewise."

The two gripped hands and Bob felt lightning strength shoot from Jeff's boulder shoulder, down his arm, and into Bob's hand with paralyzing force. Now he knew how Jeff hit the ball so far.

Jeff noticed the texture of Bob's hand. Not at all rough like the hands of golfers who beat balls day after day. He obviously spent more time on the putting green, massaging his golf balls over and around the undulations.

"You've got a great putting stroke," said Jeff. "You dropped, what, sixteen putts in a row?"

"Yeah, stroke's a little off today. Gotta work on it before I go out and play."

"What time are you playing?" Jeff asked, trying to find out if Bob was his competition.

"Not sure, supposed to be meeting an old friend out here, but he's not here yet."

"Your buddy's name isn't Nagga, is it?"

"Who?" Bob asked with raised eyebrows. He recognized the name only as something that sounded a lot like a career-ending racial slur.

"Nagga."

"No, I thought you said something else. Afraid I don't

know anyone by that name. But have a good round today."

"You too. Drop some big putts on whoever you're playing."

"And you crush some drives, my friend. You'll have 'em beat on the first tee if you hit one like you just did."

Bob walked back towards the putting green and Jeff smiled at the encouragement and the satisfaction that he wasn't playing Bob.

"Hey yo, Bobby!" Skip Breiser had just emerged from the parking lot, his hair still wet from a quick morning wash.

"Skip! Hey, you old sly dog."

Jeff saw the two men smile and shake. He assumed it was Bob's playing partner as they both entered the club house and were passed by another man in typical golf attire—polo shirt, walking shorts, saddle-oxford shoes, short ankle socks, and a hat with a popular golf brand stitched across the top.

It was a subtle wardrobe that spoke clearly to those in the know. Golfers could spot each other from clear across the store as they accompanied wives or children on shopping sprees and errands. One guy would see the trademark sign on a shirt or hat—Titleist, Strata, Calloway, Maxfli— and he would know that the guy was a fellow golfer. Or another player would recognize a golf emblem on the sleeve or breast of a shirt. It was a bragging right, as if to say *look where I've played—Pinehurst, Pebble Beach, East Lake.* These telltale signs caught the eye of every golfer and often began a conversation. *You play much?* one might ask. The conversation sometimes ended with an invite, an exchange of business cards, a phone number, a challenge, or simply a "nice meeting you" if one of them determined that the other's skill level was too high or too low.

Right now, Jeff simply wanted to find who he was playing—who stood between him, eighteen holes, and his brother's survival. This guy looked like a player and he seemed to be searching for someone. Jeff made up his mind that this had to be the guy. He put his game face on and teed up another ball. Just as he was about to boom another drive into the wooded oblivion, another type of noise disrupted the sanctity of the entire golf course.

Jeff looked up, as did the other guy. They both turned in the direction of the racket. Speeding down the snake-shaped road was a midnight black SUV spewing deep thumping bass sounds of hip-hop music into the air. The offensive vehicle disappeared into the parking lot, and Jeff saw the other man shake in his head in dismay at the rude entrance.

Jeff giggled just a bit, went back to hitting balls, and waited. He knew the next face he saw rising from the parking lot would be Nagga's. And up from the depths of whatever hell gave reprieves that day, whatever demon house had excommunicated one of their own, he came.

Adorned all in black, Nagga strolled near the clubhouse and looked over at the putting green. He finally saw Jeff. He also saw the other guy. Each gave the other a death look. For an instant, Jeff thought the two would draw their weapons for a gunslinger's battle. Instead, Nagga just smiled and walked down to the driving range.

Joi pulled in that morning along with the scores of other cars coming to get some practice before their Saturday round. Norbert Riley, one of her father's most trusted and longtime friends, had asked her to meet him there at 8:30 after learning of her predicament. Norbert was well-off and connected—more connected than well-off. He was also the president of the Mystery Valley Golf Association.

"Joi, I'm sorry. There's no way I can get my hands on that kinda money over the weekend. And I wouldn't feel right askin' people to chip in for a loan like that. It's nothing against you. I got your message Friday, but I had no idea you were in this kind of a pickle. When you called last night, it just stupefied me, I swear."

Joi's face seemed to droop further towards the ground with each word.

"No disrespect, Mr. Riley. I appreciate your help, but why'd you have me come out here this morning? Now I've gotta spend the rest of the day begging for money." Tears began to tickle the back of her eyes, trying to maneuver down her face. This wasn't at all the type of bad break she'd anticipated—in golf nor in life.

Norbert chuckled, trying not to appear cruel or insensitive.

"You're right about one thing. It's gonna take you all day. But honey, you won't be beggin'."

"What do you mean?

"I had you come out here because I got word of some bozos having a money game this morning."

"Norbert!" Joi blurted out with frustration. "Do you know how many money games I'll have to play to get that kinda money?"

Again Norbert gave the chuckle.

"Young lady, today all you gotta play is one good one. You go get warmed up and I'll make the introductions."

The first showdown was the at the starter's booth. Jeff and Nagga were conducting their own personal pow-wow.

Nagga reminded Jeff how much money was at stake; Jeff reminded Nagga that his brother's slate would be wiped clean upon his victory.

Bob and Skip were continuing their back-slapathon. Every time the other recounted one of many past shenanigans, he would throw a palm square across a shoulder blade and follow with spontaneous guffaws. Their laughing interrupted the pep talk Nagga was pounding into Jeff.

The well-dressed player Jeff saw earlier approached the starter's booth. Nagga switched from coach to cold-blooded.

"What's wrong, Billy? Yo' boy ain't showin' up today? This my dog Jeff, right here. All-Conference at Grambling and he 'bout take it to the house."

"Whatever, Neckbone," Billy mocked. "My man'll take this Division II hack any day. If not today, then tomorrow."

"Oh hell no! Somebody walkin' away with a win *today*. Yo' boy don't show up, that's fine with us. A forfeit is just as good as a win in my book and the payoff is just the same."

"Yeah, right. You try to get ten large off me without your boy teeing it up. I'd like to see that."

"You'll see it, if you can look up," Nagga said, lifting up his shirt just enough to show the butt of a nine-millimeter stuffed in his pants.

Jeff backed away. He looked around to see if anyone else saw the gesture. Billy didn't flinch or back down in the slightest.

"That don't scare me. Shoot me. I gotta two-million-dollar insurance policy, a private investigator, and a team of lawyers. You won't do nothin' but get a free trip to jail and make my family richer. If you want some, you can put that sissy pistol down and we can go for it man to man—I mean, man to *boy*." Billy touched his own chest when he said "man." Nagga started towards him, pulling his shirt out of his pants in preparation for the feud. He mumbled some profanity, and the commotion made the starter turn to look. The older gentleman guarding the booth reached for his radio to call the clubhouse just as they heard some shouting.

"Billy! Hey, Billy!" It was Kevin running from the parking lot, tucking in his shirt, squeezing his heel into a shoe by ramming it into towards the ground with every other step, all while trying not to lose his clubs, which were fleeing the confines of the golf bag that was sliding off his shoulder. He reached the starter's booth gasping for air and grinning.

"What's up, Billy? Sorry I'm late. Wife had me up late doin' this and that. I got time to run and hit some range balls?"

Billy clutched Kevin's arm and pulled him away from the small group.

"Hell no, you ain't got time to hit no damn range balls. You barely made the tee time. Do you know how much money I got on the line here? You out of your mind showin' up here late!" Billy continued the conversation with more curse words than breath. He would have filled a dictionary with ones he was inventing had it not been for Skip and Bob walking over.

"Gentlemen, everything all right?" Skip interrupted.

Billy unmussed his hair and composed himself after giving Kevin one more scornful look.

"Yeah, everything's fine here. You Skip?" he asked, nodding upward at the ever-smiling Bob.

"No, I'm Bob Berry. This is Skip."

They exchanged shakes as Kevin asked, "Aren't you the guy that's always runnin' for office?"

"I'm the one."

"I think I saw you on the news recently."

"So, let's things started," Skip quickly interjected. He

knew the only recent television appearances covered Bob's alleged scandals.

"Yeah, let's, since everybody's finally here," Billy said, eyeing Kevin.

"Looks like we got one more player. Hope you don't mind," Billy announced to Nagga. Jeff saw Bob standing with the rest of the men and felt his stomach jostle the way it did before he lost the division championship his junior year.

"What kinda hustle you got goin' on here? We ain't said nothin' about no two against one," Nagga replied.

"Hi. Skip Breiser," Skip said extending his hand. Nagga let it hang there. "Nice to meet you. We heard about the action and figured we'd increase the pot. Say five grand a man? That way everybody spends less money, but the winner still gets the whole pot. Fair enough?"

"Hell nawh! You want in, it's gon' cost you ten large just like Billy Boy. How I know you clowns ain't gon' try to beat my boy and split the money? Everybody gon' have the same thing to lose if they gon' play. Whatever goes in the pot is what the winner gets. You don't win, you ain't getting' nothin'. Y'all ain't gon walk up here at the last minute and pull this on a brothta."

Skip walked closer to Nagga. "Look, it's not like that at all. We just—"

"Fool, you bedda back up off me!"

The starter grabbed the radio again. A voice came through and he answered. "Yep, they're all down here. Better get here quick, though."

Suddenly the club house doors burst open and a man ran to the starter's booth.

"Guys, guys. How's everyone doing? Skip, Billy, Bob? Jeff, haven't seen you in a while," said Norbert. "Not sure we've met before," he said, shaking hands with Nagga. "I'm Norbert Riley, pleasure to meet you." Norbert whistled and waved someone over from the driving range who'd been hitting iron shots for the last twenty minutes. "Guess you've all met by now. I hear you've got a little game goin' on here today. You don't mind if we throw more action into the mix." He extended his arm just as Joi was approaching and it landed around her shoulder.

"What's up, Joi? Ain't seen you in a minute. Lookin' good," Jeff said, recognizing the familiar face.

"Hey, boy, good to see you," she flirted.

"Gentlemen, this here's Joi Martina. She's gonna be playing in your game today."

"Hold on, pahtna," Nagga began. "I don't know her or you and unless you got ten Gs, you need to get on away from 'round here."

"Son, like I said, this is Joi Martina and she *will* be playing in your game today. She's covered. And as for who I am, I'm the guy that can close those front gates and end this game before it even gets started. When you're ready, I'll call the safety and public administration director and tell him we got a problem that needs investigating immediately which requires evacuation. Now you try finding another tee time at the last minute on a Saturday morning."

Jeff pulled Nagga aside and whispered to him.

"I know this chick, bruh. I've played her at least a dozen times. She's good, but she can't beat me. Besides, if these other cats are trying to run somethin' me and Joi can flush out their hustle."

Nagga pulled his ear away from Jeff, looked at the chumps standing before him, thought about the possibility of forty grand in one day, remembered how many street hustles he'd won and said, "What the hell y'all waitin' for? Tee it up."

Chapter 6
Game On

The first hole at Mystery Valley—a par-five dogleg left—was a giant's arm reaching around a corner and choking the putting green, daring anyone to open the round with a birdie and making those in search of par think twice.

The order of play was determined and Jeff was to launch the first attack. He placed a shiny extra-distance ball upon a new tee. After three practice swings, the wind stopped, birds were still, and Jeff unleashed a circular ring around his body that seemed to create a small whirlwind. Upon impact, the echoing returned and trees amplified the sound of his club slamming against the dimples. The speeding bullet cut through the air as it appeared smaller and smaller, climbing towards the clouds and eventually curving ever so slightly to the left. Jeff's ball rode the giant's arm for 310 yards.

Nagga jumped up and down, yelling, "Oooh wee! Get in they tail, Jeff King! That's what I'm talkin' about right there! Get some! Get some, baby!"

Everyone else on the tee, after watching Jeff's tee shot with amazement—and fear—looked at Nagga with disapproving eyes. Kevin took the tee next as the one-man peanut gallery subsided.

Unlike Jeff, Kevin pulled a used ball out of his bag and searched on the ground for an old tee he might salvage. Billy shook his head, remembering these types of antics from their days at Wake Forest. Had it not been for Kevin's raw talent and skillful play during clutch tournament moments, he would have lost his scholarship. Even then, Billy was the only person to stick by his side—and here he was again, stuck at his side.

Without warming up, without even so much as taking a practice swing, Kevin stepped up to the tee as he'd done every day. It was as natural to him as breathing. He struck his drive toward the left side of the fairway and stooped down to salvage his old recycled tee before the ball even began curling back to middle of the fairway, albeit some fifty yards behind Jeff's ball.

"Good ball," murmured the group, with the exception of Nagga.

"Let's get it goin', Kev," Billy said, turning towards Nagga with a sly grin.

Bob was next and he smiled all the way to his tee position, saying, "Didn't know I was in the company of such accomplished golfers today. Skipper, why didn't you tell me I'd be auditioning for the PGA tour out here?"

No one laughed. Bob pulled out a driving iron and began a methodical and mechanical practice routine. The man who was so loose and free around people was a stiff, rusty robot while standing over a golf ball.

The practice routine took a full forty-three seconds. Everyone watched, waiting, hoping, begging for it to end. Finally, there was a pause in Bob's ricketing and a swing so quick that blinked eyes missed it. His ball traveled along a low flight pattern, straight down the fairway, never deviating more than two inches from its course. It came to rest ten yards ahead of Kevin's.

"Good ball," everyone said, offering the usual golf etiquette.

"The low ridin' rocket rides again," said Skip, following suit of the other money-backers turned cheerleaders.

Joi finally got her turn, sashaying down to the ladies' tees with all eyes glued to her backside. There was nothing more pleasing to the men than to see a finely sculpted woman play their game. Norbert watched the men and laughed. It was always the same. Opponents would watch Joi walk. She'd walk more than she had to just to let them watch. She'd take a practice swing with her back directly facing her male opponents. They would drool, not realizing it was part of her gamesmanship. *Use all of your assets* on the course, her father would say. Men watched, fantasizing, until they heard the crisp ping of her club and saw her ball sailing through the air and landing twenty yards ahead of Bob's ball. That's when they came to the realization that Joi was both pretty and pretty long.

"Nice ball," the men said once more.

"Still using your assets, Joi?" Norbert asked.

"Every single one of 'em," she replied with a wink.

Norbert, the self-appointed official, turned to the group, gave a blaring smile, and announced, "Gentlemen—and lady—the game is on!"

The course had been drenched the day before and the "cart path only" sign greeted everyone on the first tee. Norbert told the group they'd wind up walking more if they used golf carts. It was decided that the entire foursome would walk. No one seemed to mind—they'd all walked most of their collegiate golf careers. The backers, however, had no intention of trotting along in the heavyweight humidity that would undoubtedly affect play towards the end of the round.

Nagga was the first to retrieve a golf cart from the clubhouse, loaded down with beers, sandwiches, snacks, and premium cigars. He whizzed past the other four banks, not even thinking of offering them a ride. They all followed his example and commandeered their own carts for the day.

Each golfer walked towards his or her ball with golf bags hanging from shoulders. They walked in different directions at different paces, ensuring that there would be no immediate interaction or conversation. Kevin was the first to arrive at his ball and deliver the no-nonsense-get-it-over-and-done-with swing. His second shot drifted away from his target, then tailed back over to the middle of the fairway twenty yards from the hole. Joi came next, only this time without her first tee box routine. The audience was too sparse to bother with raising her curtain for a show. She also placed another good shot, just short of Kevin's.

When Bob reached his ball, he wound himself up again like an old mechanical toy, fidgeting, twitching, and in need of oil for his rusted parts. After he came to a halt and pulled the trigger on his super-speed swing, his ball stopped eighty feet short of the green.

It was time for the shot they dreaded. Jeff was less than 250 yards away from the green. If he hit his irons half as far as his driver, he would surely be on in two, putting for eagle and one stroke closer to the money.

Jeff gracefully walked over to his ball. As if summoning the perfect steps for the graceful performance of rhythm and power, he walked from behind his ball, stood over it, and released the hounds. Once again, gravity lost Jeff's ball, if only for an instant, then pulled it back down towards earth slowly and right on the green—landing thirty feet from the hole. Everyone gasped and gulped. Joi walked near Kevin and heard him mutter, "Gonna be a long day."

"Or a very short one," Bob said, joining them with a smile.

Kevin and Bob both hit their next shots on the green—Bob fifty feet from the hole and Kevin ten feet from the hole, sitting on a mound ready to roll all the way down a sloping hill if the wind so much as blinked. Joi hit her ball right at the flagstick, but with too much power and it landed in the back bunker of death.

She was furthest away from the hole, so it was her turn again. She took a few practice swings outside of the bunker, then walked gingerly into the sand trap, careful not to disturb her ball. After taking a look at the hole—her ball—the hole—her ball, and the hole one last time, she scooped a tiny portion of sand from underneath the ball. The white dot leapt out of the bunker and onto the green, running at a speed that seemed destined for the very bottom of the green and then back into the fairway. But as if the golf ball had brake pads inside, it came to an abrupt halt just inches in front of the hole. She walked up to the ball with her sand wedge, never even thinking about bothering with her putter, and made the ball disappear into hole. She immediately retrieved it. Norbert sat in his cart, smiling.

"Well done. Nice par. Great save," offered her opponents.

Now Jeff would make his first attempt at breaking everyone's hopes early in the match. He walked to his ball as though the blades of grass would be crushed beneath his feet like fragile colored glass. His putter was lined up towards the hole and he took one last look at his target, rocked his arm backwards with the motion of a pendulum—and hit the putting green three inches behind the ball and finished his stroke with lost momentum. The ball stopped fifteen feet from the hole. The eagle had landed and suddenly escaped.

The putting politician stood over his ball and, surprisingly, didn't fidget one time. With a slow takeaway and a faster follow-through, his ball was off and running. It took a hard left turn, following the shape of the green. When it seemed the velocity was done and the ball was about to stop, the ridge sucked it down. The ball picked up more speed and neatly disappeared into the hole for a birdie.

"Thataway, Bobby!" Skip yelled, perched in his cart.

"Good bird," Kevin said out of obligation. The others were silent, presumably cursing under their breath and hoping the putt was more luck than skill.

It was Jeff's turn to try and match Bob's birdie. He overcompensated for the last mishap and hit the putt much too hard, jacking it five feet past the hole. He refused to look at Nagga. Instead, he assumed the racket of an aluminum can being crumpled and tossed on the ground was none other than his bank-turned-coach-turned-upset-fan.

Kevin popped up to his ball as fast as he had done with the other shots. Rolling in a perfectly straight line towards the hole, the ball suddenly hit a small imperfection on the green left from the spike of another player's shoe. Hardly visible to humans, the mark was a mountain to ants and a speed bump to golf balls—just high enough to make Kevin's ball stop right at the hole, hang on to the edge, and not move one millimeter more. He tapped the ball in, and Jeff thought a while before he made his five-foot putt for par.

Silent and swift, the foursome marched on to the next hole. They walked right by their own personal gallery, never raising a head or looking in the direction of anything other than the tee box and their individual fates.

There was nothing glamorous or intimidating about the par-three number two hole, except that the back of the green was a severe slope, the middle was a downhill slalom, and the front part of the green was nothing less than an avalanche.

Each player scored three with no drama or breathtaking mistakes. The boredom of good play was looming and nothing ruined a match more than par after par after par. Fairway after fairway and green and after green. But they'd yet to play hole number three, where the golf course abducted fifty balls per hour.

Leaderboard	
Jeff	-
Kevin	-
Bob	-1
Joi	-

Chapter 7
Friendly Game of War

When recreational weekend golfers and downright hackers played Mystery Valley's third hole, they reached in their bags for the oldest, rattiest, most worn out, run-over, chewed up, gone-but-not-forgotten ball they could find. They knew it would soon join the other dearly departed golf balls in either the woods or the ponds suffocating the fairway on both sides.

Two hundred twenty yards from the blue tees, the hole completely lost its mind and took a horrendous ninety-degree left turn on an upslope. It was an insane crack-smoking hole to those with a fear of hazards, but to the foursome, it was merely beauty waiting to be saddled. The tee shot had to be long and accurate. The approach shot had to be crisp and calculated. And finally, putts had to be smooth yet strong.

Bob had the honors. He began his jerky Michael-

Jackson-dancing-machine routine while the others tried not to watch. His ball landed in the center of the fairway on the upslope, which became a downslope if a ball was hit in the wrong spot.

Jeff was next and he smashed an iron that ballooned high above the trees and began fading towards the pond on the right side. He leaned and contorted his body in the opposite direction of where the ball was heading, as if body-English could will it to a safe landing spot.

"Anybody see it come down?" Jeff asked.

"Nope, sure didn't. That's wet," Billy replied from his cart.

"It's fine. Should be just on the other side of the pond," Joi said.

Kevin teed his ball and hit it, seemingly all in the same breath. Everyone watched as it headed down the middle and landed two feet from Bob's shot.

Joi strolled down to the ladies' tee. The men's eyes strolled right along with her. She took out an iron and also faded a ball towards the right side pond. Once again they were off, bouncing down the fairway.

"So, who's the gangsta?" Joi asked Jeff as they headed for the slimy frog haven and golf ball cemetery.

"Oh, Nagga. Somebody I've known for a long time. Grew up on the same side of town," Jeff replied.

"Nagga? That clown's name is *Nagga*? I know his mama didn't name him that."

"No, that's what everybody calls him. It's a combination of nasty and...you can guess the other part."

"I'm not sure I wanna know the nasty part. You been playin' much?"

"As much as I can. Work won't let me and it's too crowded out here on the weekends. What about you?" he asked.

"I try to get out three times a week and hit balls at least

twice a week."

"What? That's half of my college practice schedule. Your game should be tight then, huh?"

"It's all right. There's your ball right there," she said, pointing to a white spot resting on a small twig. "Should have a shot at the green,"

"Where's yours?" Jeff asked.

"Right where it always is. On that side hill just over there. I swear, if I ever hit this fairway I'm gonna birdie this hole all day long."

Jeff emerged from the shaded area to get a better look at his landing area. He walked back to his ball and produced a high, hard slice towards the left-side pond that kept turning to the right, falling safely on the green.

His opponents' compliments were drowned by the shouts of "Yeah! Yeah! Good shot, dawg! That boy ain't no joke! Y'all might need to stop by the teller machine to get yo' money. Stop by the teller, I say."

Joi looked at Jeff and said, "I don't know where the nasty party comes from, but I definitely see the other part."

They both laughed as Joi set up to punch out into the fairway. Her ball landed just ten feet from the green.

Bob and Kevin were both playing the hole as it was intended, by hitting two approach shots on the green. But Bob's was forty feet from the hole and Kevin's was at least twenty-five feet.

Again, Joi pulled off a marvelous chip shot to eight inches from the cup and tapped in for par. Bob pulled off a near-miracle putt that missed by two inches and gave him another routine par. Kevin and Jeff followed suit and what could have been score suicide turned into more boring pars.

The next two holes were not as adventurous as their predecessors. The fourth was a par three and hole five a par four. The group handled them with no problem and the match was still close with Bob leading the group by only one stroke going into hole number six. The clouds boiled and brewed heavier as they played on. Jeff and Joi hit their tee shots to the right, missing the fairway, while Bob and Kevin were neck and neck for distance and only five feet apart.

"Who's *your* guy?" Jeff asked Joi as they walked towards their shots.

"Mr. Riley? Friend of my dad's. Good man to know around here, too. He runs the golf association and most everything else this side of town."

"What's his interest?" Jeff asked, crossing the boundary of gambling justification.

"Why does he have to have an interest? Why can't he just be out here watching me play?" Joi replied, offended.

"Hey, I'm sorry. I was just asking. No harm meant."

Joi looked away. "What if I asked what's nasty man's interest in you?"

This time Jeff turned away, prepping his lie.

"Like I told you, I knew him from way back when. He likes golf and wanted to see me play."

"Yeah, right. You bring a thug out here and he's not backing you a with pocket full of cash? I ain't stupid."

"Whateva. Believe what you want. He's just here, that's all I know."

As if the lies had offended the heavens, the skies boomed. Pounding bullets of rain came from above. Joi and Jeff ran for cover under a pavilion up ahead. Kevin and Bob sprinted back to the tee box to a covered bench. The banks stayed in their golf carts—eating, hoping, cellphoning, and worrying.

"Whew! Seems like the bottom dropped out of the sky, didn't it?" Bob said to Kevin. Weather was always the best segue. Bob remembered that back in college, the career center's class on job interviews instructed them to talk about the weather if there was an uncomfortable silence. Never politics and never, ever religion. Bob, being a career politician, used the weather to bring up politics.

"I checked the weather on the net last night," replied Kevin, looking out at the rain and staying focused on what he had come to do. "Didn't think we'd even tee off before it came down."

"Guess we got lucky, huh?"

"Luck ain't got nothin' to do with it. This is destiny."

"Maybe a little destiny, maybe a little desperation too. I guess you've got a nice wager on today's match."

Kevin whipped his head towards Bob.

"And so do you." Kevin snapped. "Don't see why you'd be out here with your house money if you didn't."

"I suppose you're right. We do have a lot riding on this game."

"Mister, you couldn't possibly have more riding on this than me."

"How so?" asked Bob.

"You got health insurance?"

"Well—yes."

"You get sick, need surgery tomorrow, you can go in there, drop down that little plastic card and say 'I'll take one operation to go, please.' Right?"

Bob chuckled. "I suppose so, but—"

"Ain't that easy for everybody else. See, while you're out here thinking about teein' off in the rain, I'm thinking about my wife who needs to go to the doctor for some-thing...er...uh something private and we don't have the in-surance or extra cash to pay for it. While you're thinking about beatin' the rain, I'm thinking about beatin' your brains out on the course and anybody else that's got a bag of clubs out here today. So you'll excuse me if I don't seem too cordial."

Kevin had unwittingly just given Bob the perfect lead-in. Bob hit his press-here-for-political-rhetoric button. Showing just the right number of teeth before the camera flashed, holding babies ever so gingerly, gripping a hand with just the right touch, looking people squarely in the eyes when they talked, and calling everyone friend.

"Friend, and I mean that sincerely, you're right to be hostile and frustrated. Quality affordable health care is one of the many concerns that I have for this state and the country as well. This may be hard to believe, but I have a plan ready to launch that will help people in your situation who may have fallen on hard times and who may not have been afforded the same opportunity as others. It's not your fault that you've gotten yourself in a tight spot."

Kevin thought to himself, *its absolutely my fault, but you keep talking. It sounds awful good.* Bob was so polished an orator, Kevin thought he heard the faint sound of Glory Hallelujah in the background.

"We cannot heal the sick if we are not healthy ourselves," Bob preached on. "It is our duty to help one another. A sick citizen means one less productive person at work—more duties for someone else to worry about, possibly making themselves sick as well. One less person to work and give to the needy through their abundant wages. And when the needy get greedy, they start stealing, increasing our crime. My friend, *you* are why I'm here today. Because you need my help today and I need yours."

"That's a great speech. But how in the hell is this gonna help my wife?"

"Friend—and you know I mean that sincerely—if you help me win this match, I'll get your wife the doggoned Surgeon General."

Leaderboard	
Jeff	-
Kevin	-
Bob	-1
Joi	-

Chapter 8
Us vs. Them

Rain beat rhythms atop the shed where Jeff and Joi were held up. It was a 2/4 beat splashing a tune that seemed to go on forever.

"Did you ever win a tournament because they cut it short on account of rain?" Joi asked.

"No, I won because I had the lowest score and *then* the rain stopped the tournament," Jeff answered with a sly smile.

"You know what I meant, silly."

"Yeah, I did. But this match won't be won that way, trust me. I got a feeling this thing will go into the night if it has to."

"It better," Joi replied.

Jeff looked to see if her face showed the same desperation he'd heard in her voice.

"Got a lot riding on this?"

"Obviously not as much as you if you have to bring a dope dealer out here to back you. What's he got on you?"

"Nothin'," Jeff said, walking over to a drink machine tucked in a corner of the shed. It buzzed and vibrated, waiting for currency in exchange for refreshing coolness. Jeff saw the illuminated sign that read one dollar. *Every piece of relief has a price and this isn't my relief so why am I paying for it,* he thought to himself.

"Come on, Jeff. No one's in here. Tell me. I'm not gonna say one word. Promise."

He looked from the Sprite button to her trusting face, hoping he could confide in her.

He relented. "Like I told you, Nagga ain't got nothin' on me." Jeff paused. "He's got my little brother by the nuts. After my dad left, he lost his mind. Stopped studying, stopped going to school, started smoking weed, started selling weed. Got caught up in the game. I thought I had him straightened out a few times, but he always went back to his old ways—which I found out were Dad's old ways. I kept pulling him out of trouble. Maybe we spoiled him too much. It might be our fault that he's how he is. I'm startin' to think I oughta just let him fly on his own. If he falls, then that's on him."

Finally, Jeff was revealing to someone the suppressed emotions that were slowly killing him, eating away at his flesh and gaining ground on his soul.

"I remember one time, I had to go pick him up from a golf course because he'd broken into the pro shop and was stealing clubs. I got him a job there washing carts and this fool was selling the stolen clubs to the members. Tried to sell a whole set back to a guy and turns out the set was his. Stole them from the storage area. Luckily, the guy was cool with me and Dad 'cause he'd won a big bet from Dad on the course. So he had sympathy for me and didn't press charges. I mean, *stupid* stuff like that. And it's been going on for years. Now he's so deep in with Nagga, this fool has a contract on him. How can you be seventeen and have a contract out on your life?"

"Are you serious?" Joi was astonished at the entire story. She was waiting for Jeff to add, just kidding, we're just to trying to pull a big hustle on these guys and you just happened to jump in. The announcement never came.

"I went to Nagga and asked him what I could do. That's when he set up this match. If I win, my brother's off the hook."

"And if you don't?"

"That's not an option. No offense, but nobody's got more to lose here than I do. Although I'm beginning to think that…nothing."

"What?"

"Nothing. I'm just wondering how many times I can save him and how much more of myself I have to give before somebody has to save me. Do you know that when I went to get that fool for stealing those clubs, the first thing he asked me was, 'When you gon' find me another job?' I could have killed him myself. I should have shoved golf balls in his mouth until he couldn't breathe anymore and said, 'Here's your new job—you're an official golf ball washer. Just sit, spit, and rinse.'"

The two laughed, Jeff harder than Joi. Finally, he'd given himself some much-needed relief. Just as he lifted, so too did the clouds. The rhythm on the roof slowed to a halt as beams of light shot down over the course.

The two walked from the shed to play their shots. Bob and Kevin were already standing near their balls and for the first time talking to each other as if they were planning strategies or giving advice.

Joi and Jeff both recovered well, landing their approach shots near the hole for two sure pars. Bob and Kevin did the same. Despite the temporary torrential rain, they all continued the par party.

Norbert announced on the next tee, "We should probably institute lift-clean-and-place as a result of the wet fairways. That seem fair to everyone?"

They all nodded in agreement, a few murmuring yes. Jeff turned to Joi and said, "If my brother was here, we could use his mouth to spit-clean-and-place."

The two burst out laughing with the camaraderie of teammates. Some giggled as courtesy, pretending they knew the source of humor, while others were slightly offended, none more than Nagga. He jumped out of his golf cart and marched towards Jeff. Never one for subtleties, he grabbed Jeff by the arm and stood so close to him they were inhaling each other's breath.

"What the hell is this? You bedda remember why you out here, fool! Ain't no time for laughin' and gigglin'. That trick is the enemy, so you need to act like you wanna kill her. Make somethin' happen fast, boy. Y'all almost halfway through and somebody need to make a move!"

"Chill, bruh! I got this!" Jeff said, usurping any authority Nagga held over him. He was flirting with throwing it all away. Letting his brother fend for himself. Saving his own life. Growing up. Facing reality.

The group watched the event play out. Billy was waiting for Nagga to pull out his nine-millimeter and drop Jeff in front of everybody. He believed the thug was stupid enough to do it.

Instead, Nagga backed away from Jeff. They were all surprised, especially Jeff. Nagga looked around and saw that his respect was being threatened. He gave a deceptive smile, walked backwards down the tee box, pursed his lips, nodded his head to himself, jumped in his golf cart, and disappeared down the cart path back to the clubhouse.

Leaderboard	
Jeff	-
Kevin	-
Bob	-1
Joi	-

Chapter Nine
Get the Gallery

"**A**re we gonna tee off today, or are we gonna just sit steamin' in this sauna?"

There was a growing crowd of golfers becoming antsy at the starter's booth. Rain had delayed everyone's tee times, and Norbert had arranged for a thirty-minute gap in order to give the big-money foursome space from other golfers.

"We gon' get chu out there 'rectly," replied the starter. He was tugging at his wide black suspenders, which held up a pair of saggy shorts that just barely covered his wrinkled knees, which led down to a long pair of black dress socks hiked up over his calves. His feet and socks were caged by a pair of wing-tipped brown dress shoes. His job was to be relentless, not fashionable. "Had a big group go out this mornin'. Quick as we get 'em on the back we'll let loose."

"Why didn't you guys just do a shotgun start and let everybody tee off at the same time?" an anxious golfer asked. Unrest brewed from the back of the crowd. He was seemingly speaking on behalf of everyone else waiting to play.

"Reckon we coulda done that, but it's only four peoples in that there group."

"What? We're waiting on a group of four people? It had better be the president up there or somebody's gonna have hell to pay."

The group overheard the conversation and mumbled back to other golfers that they were being held up by a group of four. Slowly, men in shorts and spikes converged on the starter's booth.

"Now, hold yer britches down to a slow simmer there, fella. No use in boiling over out here in this heat. Ain't my fault they's got most the course to themselves. Seems they've got a money game goin' out there."

"And what do you think we're playing for in my group, a hug and a handshake? We've got a twenty-dollar pot over here." There was more grumbling and more disgruntled golfers were converging.

"Young fella, that little pot of your'n won't even pay the price of admission in this game. They're playing for forty grand out there."

The crowd hushed with awe.

"Get outta here. I don't believe that for one minute."

"Do you actually think we would hold up half the course if there wasn't a serious match like that? What do ya think, we're morons from the moon?"

The crowd passed the word around that a forty-thousand-dollar match was going on.

"Who's playing? Is it a pro? The agitators' tone had gone from furious to curious. Most golfers had only heard of big money matches where big players would show up with nerves of steel and big bank rolls. But to actually be on the same course with one was an anomaly. And to see one would be a once-in-a-lifetime deal.

"No, 'fraid not. If Tiger was out here, we'd shut the whole place down. Seems it's just some local folks that know the right kind of people."

"Are you kiddin' me? You sure a sprinkler hasn't broken or somethin' and you're holdin' us up until it's fixed?"

"Honest-to-God truth. I swear on my dead mother's headstone buried in my great uncle's cemetery, built on my great-great-grandfather's Indian burial ground," the starter said, removing his hat in memory of his mother, then wiping his nose with a wrinkled handkerchief. He'd talked up a small tear.

"What are we doin' sittin' here? I wanna see some action!" The golfer jumped in his cart and slammed the accelerator, speeding down the cart path.

"Wait a minute, dadblasted! You can't tee off yet!"

"I ain't goin' to play," the golfer yelled back flying away from the booth. "I'm going to watch the match! I'll get a rain check when it's over!"

A convoy of golfers followed suit by rushing back to their carts and jumping in line one by one. They formed a caravan of eleven golf carts, zooming up and over the cart paths in search of the big money match.

"Hold your Clydesdales, buddy," the starter yelled to the last cart. The two remaining golfers were confused, thinking the starter was not going to allow them to join the others. Giving his suspenders a tug and locking the booth door, he said, "No use in me stayin' here when the party's on the course. Scoot over. Make some room in this contraption. I comin' along."

Nagga was darting along the course himself when he saw the train of carts coming his way. He had no regard for golf cart traffic laws. Instead of yielding to the group or moving to the right side of the path, he plowed straight down the middle. There were shouts, gestures, and profane phrases thrown toward Nagga. He ignored them all because they had no bearing on his mission. His player needed some motivation for winning.

After he'd mowed through the oncoming crowd, Nagga reached for his cell phone and spoke the name for a voice recognition dial.

"Jackjaw."

The phone rang once. Those in Nagga's crew were trained to answer the phone quickly once they saw his number in the caller ID.

"Yo, whatup?"

"I'm on my way. Gotta do that," Nagga said.

"I feel ya. We ready."

The par-five seventh hole was a beautiful portrait. It required a long tee shot through a chute and over a hill. To the left were ball-snatching trees marked by out of bounds markers. To the right were tall pines that looked like jail bars. And straight ahead over the hill crest was the valley of death—an undulating fairway with downhill and sidehill lies.

Bob fidgeted his way to the tee and landed his ball over the hill in the middle of the fairway. Jeff ripped a tee shot down the right side of the fairway—a shortcut for distance. His ball hit the cart path and skipped left, advancing down the fairway another seventy-five yards.

Kevin was a strange bird on the course. He'd play on autopilot for a few holes, then realize that he hadn't practiced and didn't have a swing thought for the day. Standing over the ball, he could visualize his tee shot shooting to the left—*hard* left. His brain had already told his body what it was going to do even before he'd swung the club. Kevin tried to psych himself up, saying under his breath, *Do what you've been doing, do what you've been doing.* He made his usual Quick-Draw-McGraw back swing and smacked the ball as he'd been doing, but looked up just in time to see the ball balloon unusually high, curving to the right and landing in tree jail just right of the fairway. His first slice of the day.

No true golfer laughed at another's misfortune. The good ones all lived by the same creed and the same set of rules. They knew the golf gods kept close watch and an even closer score, and that cruel turnabout was never more than one shot away. When Kevin's head drooped after his slice, no one said a word, no one rejoiced. Nagga might have, but he'd already sped off in his mad fury, bowling for golf carts. The others in the foursome stood and watched as Kevin slammed the head of his driver on the ground. Everyone was quiet and careful not to smile or snicker because they knew the golf gods were listening.

Joi pranced to the ladies' tees, which were much closer to the hill's crest, giving her a great chance at getting the best tee shot. She waggled her club, they watched her butt. She took her back swing, they watched her butt. She crushed the ball, they watched her butt. She made a picture-perfect follow-through, they watched her butt. She had out-driven them all, except Jeff. And they realized they'd been too busy watching her butt.

Off they walked to hit approach shots, sloshing through the rain residue. The road adjacent to the hole was beginning to steam. The steam rose from the black asphalt as though lurking ghosts of golfers once forgotten were rising from graves, wafting, turning, dancing inside the steam.

Thick, lush grass padded the ground leading up to the

valley. Joi was the first to approach the crest and she stopped immediately once at the top. Norbert knew the feeling. The sight of a white ball sitting perfectly still amidst the sculpted bending green field. The architecture of this hole dipped swiftly, as though the earth were drawing the landscape downward to its center core. At the bottom of the valley the fairway rose again like a sweet reward for surviving the tumultuous ride. It ascended and met the large green that seemed to ebb even in its stillness. The beautiful green fairway was immaculately contrasted by skyscraping brown pines on both sides and two golden sandbunkers sculpted ever so slightly to the right. What God hath created, man hath visualized and perfected into 526 yards of golf glory. But that's not what had stopped Joi.

Bob and Jeff caught up with her at the hillcrest and they also saw the sight.

"Norbert, what's going on?" Joi asked.

"Well, I'll be," said Norbert. "Hope none of you folks don't get nervous playing in front of an audience."

Leaderboard	
Jeff	-
Kevin	-
Bob	-1
Joi	-

Chapter 10
Action on the Action

Surrounding the green were over forty golfers who'd all foregone their Saturday round to watch what was transpiring on the course. They'd exited the carts and were standing around the putting surface, electing not to sit on the wet grass. While the spectators waited for the foursome to approach the green, they speculated about who might be playing. A few of the regulars joked about how bad they might have played today and how some of them had been spared losing their wife's lunch money by watching this match instead of playing their own. Then they all wondered why the foursome was standing at the top of the hill, no one moving, no one playing golf.

"What is this?" Billy asked. Kevin was in the woods

facing a dangerously high score if this hole turned out disastrous. "I thought we were gonna have space out here today."

"Look behind you," Norbert said. "There hasn't been anyone behind or ahead of us all day."

"What do you call that down there, a bowling team?"

"Billy, it looks to me like they just want to watch some golf."

"Well, they need to go watch the damn Golf Channel. I don't want 'em out here. So get 'em off the course." Billy was irate as Kevin searched for his ball.

"Afraid I can't do that."

"Why not? You got her in the foursome at the last minute," Billy said, pointing at Joi, then stealing a glance at her butt. "You run this place, don't you?"

"This is a public course. People can do whatever they want as long as they abide by golf course and county law."

"Oh, that's a bunch of crap and you know it!"

"What's the big deal? Anybody else got a problem with it?" Norbert asked, looking around.

"What if we get down there and they start heckling my guy?" asked Billy.

"We can wait 'til Nagga gets back and he'll shoot 'em," Jeff teased. He was feeling carefree now that his bank had left.

"For some reason, I could see that happening," said Norbert. "If there's any heckling, I'll have 'em thrown out of here before the ball stops rolling."

"Whose ball? Joi's ball or anybody's ball?" Billy asked.

Norbert chuckled, as always. "Look, guys, this has been a fair match so far and it's gonna stay that way. But I can't just make those paying customers leave the course. You three gotta problem with it?" he asked, looking at Jeff, Joi, and Bob.

"No, I played in front of crowds all during college,"

answered Jeff.

"Me too," said Joi.

Bob was looking at the crowd, counting heads, determining age and race demographics, gathering votes. He forced himself to suppress his urge to walk over and start shaking hands.

"Friends, those are citizens of this county and maybe visitors. It is our obligation to ensure their comfort and entertainment while we—"

"Hush it, Bob," Skip interjected. "Win the match first, *then* start campaigning."

Norbert faced the woods where Kevin had disappeared. "Kevin, you got a problem with the crowd watching for the—"

SCHPACK!

The trees slammed echoes of impact just as Kevin blistered an iron against twigs, dirt, pebbles, and his ball. The remnants of the shot splashed out of the woods. Tiny pebbles were hurled in the air landing, dancing on the cartpath, while dirt floated on gentle wind kicked up just as Kevin swung his club. He'd created a small explosion. The group looked down the fairway awaiting the result. Almost out of nowhere, a tiny object speared through the air with a guided-missile trajectory. Kevin's ball glided along its path, finally hitting the fairway and rolling with unbelievable momentum until it ended its adventure in the middle of the fairway, ten yards in front of the 150-yard marker.

Once lost and almost forgotten, Kevin broke free from the wooded jail and said, "Somebody say somethin'?"

Billy turned to Norbert and the others with a sinister smile. "He ain't got no problem with it at all. Let's play."

Bob waited for Kevin to walk towards him in the fairway to give him a *nice shot teammate* wink and nod. They both trotted over to Bob's tee shot and everyone waited for machine-man to crank out the fleeing ball. It was beginning to seem like a factory. A large, awkward contraption shaking, grumbling, bumbling, making odd sounds, then spitting out a product. Kerplunk, eeeezle, wahbadawop, sherbooooing—flying golf ball. Off it flew, as accurate as his others, landing 130 yards from the green—in the right side bunker. Bob turned to Kevin and said, "I'm on the beach. Guess I'm gonna need your help on this one, friend."

"Just how do you suppose we help each other? This isn't a two-man scramble," Kevin asked.

"Well, I guess the way I envisioned it is that we each play to birdie the hole until the other gets into trouble. Then we play for par. Our strategy has to be that we never lose a hole to either of those two. So now that you're out of trouble, you can play for birdie. When you were up in the woods, I was going for par, but you're in good shape now."

Joi was going through her practice routine and the two stopped talking. She pulled out her driver and crushed the ball off the fairway. It came to rest one hundred yards from the green.

Jeff had again positioned himself to get on in two and make eagle, his ball sitting only 170 yards from the green. He took an unusually long time trying to decide which club to use. Finally the one-man club-selection jury reconvened with a five iron. Jeff smoked the ball over the green and into the onlookers. The ball parachuted down towards them and the crowd split open.

Laughs and *whoas* rang down the fairway from the gallery. Jeff's swearing spewed from the opposite direction.

As Bob and Kevin walked closer to Kevin's ball, Norbert took notice of the two conversing.

"You shoot for the pin, I'll aim for the middle of the green, and we'll be fine on this hole," Bob said, heading for the sand bunker.

"I ain't agreed on anything yet," Kevin replied, louder than he should have. The other players and their banks heard the remark.

"Trying to get every vote I can," Bob said to the group.

Kevin stood over his ball. Before anyone had time to think, he pulled the trigger and sent an approach shot into the left greenside bunker. Two bad shots and one lucky escape shot.

Bob saw the results and held up his hand to Kevin. A gesture letting him know that everything was okay. Again, Norbert took notice. Bob wizzy-wiggled over his shot in the sand trap and landed the ball towards the back of the green thirty feet from the hole. The crowd, uncertain about the rules of the match, did what came natural and gave a polite clap. The players and banks alike threw looks at the crowd, wondering if this was the beginning of a heckle or genuine courtesy.

Skip looked at Norbert, who glanced at Billy, who was of course shaking his pessimistic head. Skip shrugged his shoulders because—naturally—the crowd was clapping for his guy. Bob did what he always did in front of an applauding audience: smiled and waved.

Joi reached her ball and quickly pulled out a trusty pitching wedge. She took numerous practice swings, trying to barely graze the grass with her club. Backing away from the ball and then walking towards it again, getting the perfect line towards the flagstick, her face was rigid and serious. Seconds later, she clipped the grass as she had in the practice swings. The ball rocketed high in the air and fell with feather softness five feet from the hole. The crowd shouted and clapped. A few whistled. Joi gave a hint of a smile but refused to break her game face.

Once the players were within earshot of the crowd, the starter who'd abandoned his post jumped from the crowd and threw both hands in the air, a gesture that overworked his already stressed-out suspenders.

"Stand please, all quiet!" He'd wanted to shout those

words ever since he'd watched the decorated marshals on televised golf tournaments throw their authority around. The crowd, surprised by the gesture, could offer no reaction except to do as they were told.

Kevin felt his pulse quickening while he stood in the bunker, waiting for the crowd to quiet and sit still. The trigger was quickly pulled again and he hit the ball instead of the sand. The ball took off with its own intentions and landed in the other bunker on the opposite side of the green.

Billy let loose his favorite barrage of four-letter explicits while Jeff prepared to chip his ball. The crowd gave him room but stood close enough to watch his technique. His shot landed softly on the green and rolled two feet from the cup. Once more, the crowd clapped and mumbled.

"Hell, this is like being at a PGA event," one of the onlookers said.

"What did he say? What did that guy just say?" Billy exclaimed, rushing into the crowd. He pointed at the man as though he were taking names in a teacher's absence.

"He said it's like the PGA," Bob replied. "No harm. He's just paying a compliment."

"Mm-hmm. The hell he is. Norbert, I ain't gon' take much more of this. I'll pull my guy out right now!"

"Okay. Have a nice day." Norbert said, calling the bluff. "The pot is plenty big the way I see it. You pull him out and that betters my player's chance at winning. Don't you tell me what to do at my course, son. This is my house. You're in my valley of death." Norbert was flexing his influential muscle. Perhaps it was the presence of the other regulars or Billy's insinuations of unfair play, or possibly the private conferences Bob and Kevin were having.

"Hell with it. Just play. Just play the damn game!" Billy relented.

The crowd began to talk amongst themselves, realizing the tension in the event.

Kevin, the only player not yet on the putting surface, twisted and swished his feet, dancing further down into the sand. With a whipping swing, he slid his club underneath the ball, sprinkling sandy brown specks onto the green. The ball landed and was on line to the hole, until it seemed to hit an invisible wall and stop fifteen feet from the cup. The crowd consoled him with quick and quiet applause.

Bob stepped over his putt and lagged the ball across the green and down a steep ridge. It began swinging fast to the right—an impossible putt by all measures. Twenty-nine feet and eleven inches later, the ball was hanging on the edge of the hole—held up only by a spike mark left by another golfer's shoe.

"Ooooooh!" the crowd crooned together and then gave more claps. Bob tapped the ball in for par.

Kevin was practically pulling his putter back before Bob even tapped his ball. As his fifteen-foot putt turned into another six-foot putt from the opposite side of the hole, and then a two-foot putt and eventually a double bogey, Bob walked towards him, placed a hand on his shoulder, and whispered words of encouragement.

Joi sank her putt, as did Jeff. The two received the best applause the crowd had to offer. With birdies in tow, Jeff and Joi smiled, laughed, and strategized their way to the next green. Bob and Kevin followed behind, continuing the verbal and very noticeable interaction they'd begun on the sixth hole. Norbert looked at Billy, ready to raise an inquiry about the camaraderie of Kevin and Bob. Billy turned his head, ignoring Norbert, thinking of the money he was losing.

"Hey, I know that guy," a wide and round spectator said as they walked to the next tee. "That's that son of a gun who stole them checks from that old lady. He's a doggone dirty politician."

"No he ain't," another man said, sweeping the mid-life

strands of hair across the top of his balding dome.

"I swear he is. I seen him on TV. I didn't know he had a game, though."

"That there gal's name is Joi," an onlooker shaded by a wrinkled bucket hat said. "She'll clean anybody's clock that steps on the tee. Plays out here all the time—and from the men's tees."

"Oh yeah, right," said the round man. "You see how that poly-tick lagged that thirty-foot putt? *He's* walkin' away with some money today."

"Not with Joi here," the bucket-hatted hombre replied. "I'll take whatever odds you give me on her."

The balding gent chimed in, "Whoa, whoa, whoa. Let me in on some of that too. I just wanna know who these other fellas are. I'll add to the pot, but only after I find out what the others are about."

"Let's lay the action after we watch 'em tee off and find out the score," the wide man announced.

Bucket Hat remarked, "Yeah, sure. And why don't I give you a blank check before the match is over. Are you crazy? We'll watch 'em tee off, but we'll find out the score *after* we make the bets. That fair enough with everybody wantin' some action?"

Everyone responded favorably and began reaching in pockets, wallets, socks, and hats. They rushed for the next tee, only to be cut short by the suspender-stretching starter exclaiming, "Stand please, all quiet!"

Leaderboard	
Jeff	-1
Kevin	+ 2
Bob	-1
Joi	-1

Chapter 11
Extractions

The traffic lights were useless. Green meant drive recklessly, yellow meant drive dangerously, and red meant what the hell, keep driving anyway. A grim-reaping SUV had just zoomed through the last light on Flat Shoals Road. Amazingly, the heavily patrolled strip was vacant of police cars. The gas-sucking, parking-space-smuggling ship was in pursuit of an old restored Caprice Classic. Once Chevrolet's assembly-line pride, it was now relegated to ghetto makeovers funded by young men having their say at implementing cultural icons.

The chased car was glossed over with a hologram-rainbow paint job. It was purple ten feet away, green fifteen feet away, and blue when too far away to measure. Windows were tinted two shades darker than the black hole.

The shiny black Armor-All-drenched tires held sparkling twenty-inch rims with ball bearings inside. Once the car came to a halt the tires stopped spinning, but the ball-bearing rims kept turning. "Spin rims" they called them, the latest design from a West Coast street-runner turned-artistic-entrepreneur. But the car had no intentions of stopping. The Caprice's driver thought he could out-maneuver the Ford Death Star, or the Dodge Space Shuttle, or the Chevy Enterprise, or the Toyota Space Station, or whatever name the marketing team had given it. He swerved around corners, hoping he could make the SUV tip over.

The Caprice turned onto Brown's Mill Road and knew the best escape was back towards the winding course of Flat Shoals leading to Henry County. A driveway provided a quick turnaround but nearly ended the chase. Out of the SUV sprang a band of hooligans brandishing sidearms and sticks.

They rushed the chameleon-colored car, only to retreat when the driver sped in their direction trying to run them all over. The crew saddled up again inside the rolling brick, while the Caprice gained the valuable seconds needed to head back out towards the main road.

Back on Flat Shoals, it sped around turns and twists. The chased driver's heart was racing faster than the pistons pushing the old faithful machine. It zoomed by a chapel named Life AME church.

In the sideview mirror he noticed the image of his predator growing larger. It gained distance as they neared the border of DeKalb county. The two lanes stretched and became four lanes as the SUV came alongside the Caprice. Neither of the drivers thought about ramming the other. Life and death took no precedence over a premium paint job.

A passenger window of the SUV disappeared down into the door panel, exposing a thug pointing a gun at the shining front tire of the Caprice. He hung out the window as wind ran through his black doo-rag. The shooter looked like a bootleg superhero with a homemade cape suffocating his brain. Head-hero took dead aim and steadied his weapon, but he was suddenly thrown back into the truck as the four lanes became two, making the SUV swerve back behind the Caprice once again.

They passed another church. There was a portable sign out front, the kind that at other locations displayed messages like *Now Open, All You Can Eat, No Down Payment.* Here there were only two words: *Jesus Saves.* The Caprice driver was waiting for Jesus to part the road, turn the SUV's gasoline into wine, or some other miracle that would save him.

They screamed around another corner and the Caprice tried to flip the top-heavy truck once more by making a sharp left at a sign pointing towards Little Mountain Golf Course. Tires peeled and burned around the corner. The SUV slowed to a safe turning speed, then the engine yelled as the accelerator was gunned trying to catch up with the Caprice once more. Both cars blazed onto a dirt road when the Caprice's driver fell victim to his own frugal practices.

He'd always done it despite the constant warnings from others. It was senseless to him. Why overspend when money could be used for other luxuries. Alas, he'd finally learned why it was important to put more than three dollars worth of gas in the tank. His engine stopped, his wheels halted, and he imagined his heart would also soon stop.

This time the gang rushed the car and extracted the driver through the window without bothering to roll it down.

Though traffic frequented the street near the golf course, they'd turned onto a dirt road that was seemingly deserted. An old rusted tractor sat several yards away in a field that had already been harvested by a faster, younger tractor. There was no one close enough to hear him scream, call for help, or watch the first blow smash against his head. They began to punish the driver. The thug who'd almost been run over after their first attempt approached him slowly, carefully. He thrust a powerful kick into the victim's ribs. He kicked once more with his steel-toed workboots. Others joined him with bombing fists across his head and against his jaw. A kicking gangster clasped both hands together, raised them high above his head, and chopped through the air, landing on the beaten man's back. Thuds of flesh smashing against muscle and bones sounded like a machine pounding away at some object that would soon be destroyed.

In desperation, the man rose to his feet, hoping for a small opening between his aggressors. His attempted escape met another boulder fist exploding against his nose, filling his eyes with water and painting his face with warm red blood. He was on the ground, praying that death would arrive soon because life at this moment was nothing more than torture. Still, the beating went on. He felt relief for a moment as the first wave of kicking, hitting, and pulling stopped.

Seconds later it continued—this time at the hand of only one person, but much worse than before. The lone attacker had taken a long thick leather strap and was flogging the man all over his body. At first, quick stinging lashes across the back. Then slow, skin-ripping lashes over the legs. Then deliberate, calculated lashes burning whelps across his chest. The strap finally rested in its user's hand—worn, wrinkled, adorned with streaks of blood.

The man lay motionless, except for the desperate attempts of his lungs to maintain life. Allowing the strap to fall to his side, the lasher rushed the victim with a drop kick directly to his mouth.

"Pick him up. Let's go," he ordered.

As his crew picked up what was still alive, the drop kicker picked up his leather strap and the broken teeth lying beside it.

Leaderboard	
Jeff	-1
Kevin	+2
Bob	-1
Joi	-1

Chapter 12
Markers

"Let everybody come on through," Norbert said to the starter. "They're fine. We'll let 'em watch from right here on the cart path."

The crowd marched up quickly, most of them clutching bills and ready to lay down bets.

Bob walked to the tee smiling, polished. He thought of making such an impressive tee shot that it would spark a conversation with someone in the gallery who would, in turn, spread the word about his platform. Little did he know they'd already begun spreading a word about him. His platform was far from the topic of discussion.

Bob fidgeted and fidgeted, then fidgeted some more. He

finally released his swing through the ball. Spectators' heads whipped by in unison, trying to follow the ball's flight. They watched as it sailed off to the right, landing in the woods next to the fairway. Bob's first miscue off the tee. He looked at Kevin, who was still bogged down by thoughts of his previous double bogey. Bob widened his eyes, grinned, and nodded at Kevin with a wink.

It wasn't one of the more difficult holes on the course, but gorgeously deceptive. From the tee box, the hole dipped and rose, then dipped once more, leading to a large green. A magnificent roller coaster of brilliant green painted its voluptuous curves. And, like most adventurous rides, it was challenging, visually and emotionally. A nice shot to the top of the hill provided a good look at the green, yet with a sideways/downhill lie and an increased pulse. Shots to the right gave a flat lie, but a poor view of the green and extra stress. Shots far to the right, like Bob's, risked flying into the woods, with no chance of seeing the green, and producing only a splitting headache.

Those who could manage such a feat drove their ball over the hill, allowing it to roll to the second dip and leaving a short iron to the green. Such a task would most likely be accomplished by Jeff, who was now approaching the tee. Jeff disregarded the audience, seeing no need to impress them. In the absence of Nagga, he was enjoying the round. With a relaxed attitude, Jeff whirled the club around his head and blistered the ball with John Henry power. The steel-driving shot fled over the hill, heading for the second dip in the fairway as though his tee shot had been given a map with an X marking the birdie spot.

"Good God awmighty!" yelled the balding spectator. Other members of the gallery chimed in with *Wow, Holy Smoke*, and any other exclamations they could think of to describe the longest tee shot they'd ever seen or heard about on this hole. The ball had been hit so far, they had no clue as to its final destination.

"Nice shot," Joi said, smiling.

Kevin hurried to the tee box, feeling his confidence head for vacation as it had many times before when he realized things were slipping away from him. Everyone was surprised to see him pull an iron from his golf bag.

Bob nodded in agreement, thinking Kevin was finally playing along with his strategy by hitting a safe iron shot since Bob was in serious trouble. Before the crowd had a chance to finish admiring Jeff's shot, Kevin yanked his club back and smacked the ball in the sweetest spot of the club. It charted a straight line hard and fast to the middle of the fairway. The iron would never have been enough club for Kevin, not even if wind hurled ferocious gusts at his back carrying the ball as far as physics would allow. The ball that looked as though it would go on forever rested some 210 yards away from the green. No one clapped or kowtowed for his shot. In fact, the crowd did nothing but turn to Kevin with a puzzled look.

Joi headed for the ladies' tees. This time, so many heads watched her walk, the short distance had been transformed into a fashion show runway. Mouths dropped open, eyes blinked rapidly, and the men were hypnotized by the side-to-side swaying of the round object in front of them—and the ball hadn't been placed on the tee yet. A spectator whistled and offered a "Do you wiggle when you waggle, honey?" He laughed, hoping to be joined by the others. Instead, he was given looks of disdain by the foursome and their banks. Norbert turned in the direction of the comment.

Billy smiled at the outburst, hoping it would upset her. But of course, it did not. Joi pounded her drive and paused in her perfect follow-through, watching the ball descend a few feet in front of the 150-yard marker.

"Whoa! Y'all see that?" said Bucket Hat. "She hit farther than the other two guys."

"Yeah, but she hit from the red tees," said balding man.

"Don't matter. Look where she's sittin' and look where they are. Plus, she almost dropped it in the jar from a hundred out on the last hole. Give me twenty on the skirt—who wants some of that action?"

"I'll take some against that big field hand. Ain't nobody ever hit the ball that far before on this hole, have they?" said Round Man. "That boy's gon' have a wedge in for birdie I bet."

"Hell, I'll give ya twenty for the guy that hit iron off the tee," said Bucket Hat. "He's the smart player. Anybody that's got 210 left for an approach has gotta be a player."

"Nope. As usual, you're full of it," said another spectator. "Drive for show and putt for dough. The fella that almost dropped a thirty-footer on the last hole is the guy. Give me twenty on him."

Everyone else laid down their action choosing a player based on what they'd seen and gut instincts. Someone chose Jeff because he liked his practice routine. Another person chose Joi because she hit from the red tees. A guy bet on Bob because he was wearing the same brand hat, shirt, shoes, and golf glove as his golf bag. The person thought if he looked like a pro, then he must play like a pro. Then there was the older gentleman who placed his money on Kevin based solely on the Wake Forest mascot covering his driver. After the money had been collected and dividends calculated, the walking odds-makers trotted off down the fairway behind their hopeful thoroughbreds.

Bob searched for his ball in the woods to no avail. Skip pulled his cart over and helped his friend. The other golfers followed suit, offering the traditional help and courtesy one golfer gave to another.

Ball searching was a peculiar event. Basketball players stopped play to argue over fouls, baseball players yelled for several minutes about an out, football players all but pulled out rulers to dispute a first down. But golfers took five minutes to help an opponent find his ball. Even though they were attempting to beat the other's brains out, players would enter bushes, fight weeds, and wade in water to help with the reconnaissance, all the while acting as though they were genuinely concerned about finding the ball. Oftentimes, the help was given to make sure someone didn't pull a ball from his pocket, drop it on the ground, and exclaim, *I got it! Right over here. Must have hit something and bounced out.*

Skip was turning over branches and kicking pine needles, hoping to get a glimpse of a white spot hiding amongst nature's blankets. Three minutes passed and all of the spectators who'd placed money on Bob rushed the wooded area and walked with heads bowed trying to find his ball. They looked like a group of curious ostriches searching for ground to hide their ugly existence. Two minutes later, the starter tugged at his suspenders and slapped the face of his watch, yelling, "Five minutes, y'all. The search is over."

Everyone turned in his direction. They looked at each other, wondering who'd dubbed him rules official. Norbert, smiling, confirmed the man's self-appointed position by saying, "I guess you're right. You all heard the man. Anybody else keepin' a watch on the search? If not, we gotta move on."

Bob looked at Skip, wondering how generous the group would be in rendering a decision for a lost ball.

"What do you guys think?" Skip asked, worried about his player. "It's clearly over here somewhere. We just can't find it. Any chance of a free drop?" Those with money riding on Bob looked at Norbert thinking he had the final decision. The players all looked at each other, except Kevin, who was still licking his wounds from his double bogey.

Groans came from the camp of spectators who'd bet against Bob. "Noooo, unh-uhhhhh," they rebuked.

"Hell no!" yelled Billy, who hadn't budged to search for the ball. "You'd better get that boy back to the tee and hit another shot. You know the damn rules! Free drop my a—"

"Okay, okay," Norbert said, cutting short a profane explanation of the rules.

"No problem. No problem at all," Bob said, smiling and walking back to the tee box. "We want to keep this match fair and honest. There's no other way to treat people," he added, ever the campaigner.

While Bob made the lonely walk back to the tee, Jeff and Joi resumed their conference.

"Jeff, I think we should strengthen our chances," Joi announced.

"Huh?"

"We need to give ourselves better odds. It's obvious that we're right there in the middle of competition. Bob will kill us if he gets hot and Kevin is having a nervous breakdown."

"Yeah, maybe."

"If we teamed up, it might help us beat 'em."

"You crazy? This is stroke play. How is that gonna' help us?"

"If we knock them out, then we only have to compete with each other. Would you rather try to beat me or try to beat me *and* those two clowns?"

Jeff stared at Joi, realizing the logic and the probability of beating her. He then looked over the hill at his tee shot, which had left him one hundred yards to the hole.

"Has potential, but how do you suppose we do it?"

"It's easy. Gamesmanship."

"You mean cheatin'?"

"No, sirrr. Gamesmanship is *not* cheating. If a guy can't

keep his head straight while things go on around him, then he doesn't need to win anyway. It was one of the first lessons my dad taught me."

"Okay, explain it."

"Just play golf and pay attention to what they're doing. Kevin plays way too fast, so you make conversation with him and it delays him gettin' to the tee. Bob stands over his ball and has those spasms before he tees off. Before *you* hit, fidget like he does, step away from the ball, make extra waggles, whatever it takes to throw him off. Just mess with their heads. As long as you don't touch their ball or their swing, it's fine."

"This how you won tournaments down in Florida?" Jeff asked, giving a sly smile then a quick laugh. Joi was not amused.

"No, I won tournaments by shooting below par and going lower than the rest of field," she said with a frown. "I'm just tryin' to help you out. You so worried about your brother, seems like you'd be doing whatever you can to keep him alive."

With that, Joi walked away from him and to her ball as Bob launched his second tee shot into the middle of the fairway, 150 yards from the green.

Jeff began doing the math, as always. If Bob put his next shot near the hole and made the putt, he'd bogey and still have the lead unless Jeff himself made birdie. The math was favoring Bob's putting instead of Jeff's irons. He looked at his long drive, then back at happy, confident Bob—the automatic putter—then at Joi, who was brewing less than twenty feet away from him. He gave a glance over the entire hole to find out where his opponents were standing, careful not to be heard by everyone and said, "So how soon you wanna start?"

Leaderboard	
Jeff	-1
Kevin	+2
Bob	-1
Joi	-1

Chapter 13
Alliances

Kevin's ball looked as though it were two time zones away from the green. He was the first to play his approach shot and, as usual, he hit his ball before people had a chance to watch him perform what could have been mistaken for a practice routine—two quick breaths and uncoiling the club. His ball had been resting, waiting on the upslope of a sidehill lie. Kevin deliberately exaggerated his aim to the left—too far left. A heavy sweeping right shoulder followed the club at ball impact, pushing the ball 209 yards and into the trees left of the green. Kevin was frozen as the ball brushed branches and cracked limbs, finally disappearing.

For an instant Kevin began thinking where he could go when the match was over. He could move in with his parents, but that'd be the first place his wife would call. Maybe Billy would let him stay at his house for a while. Perhaps he could drive down to Florida, get a job at one of the golf courses that practically outnumbered churches. Start a new life there, play a few games to get himself ahead and play on a miniature golf tour. Not an option. Good hustlers were a small fraternity and soon enough word would get back to Georgia that Kevin was playing for money just below the border. If the worst was bound to happen despite all that he could do, running from it would never save him. He had to see it through.

Joi was a few yards behind Bob's ball and it was her turn. She looked at Jeff and tried to get his attention. She wanted him to witness gamesmanship. Joi stood over the ball and twitched her shoulders. Then she rocked back and forth from her left foot to her right. Her feet dug deep into the turf, then lifted in a dancing fashion. For a few more seconds, she jingled and waggled, then struck a crisp iron that landed fifteen feet from the pin.

"Nice shot," Bob remarked, wondering if there was something that made her move the way she'd done before hitting. It was odd, strangely odd.

Bob approached his ball and without thinking imitated Joi's movements and shakes. They weren't his own; they were moves that had subconsciously been ingrained in his mind. He couldn't get comfortable over the ball. It didn't feel right. Finally, he felt no other option than to hit. With an odd back swing and unbalanced follow-through, Bob shanked his shot with a sweeping curve, rolling to the right-side bunker just off the green.

"Whoa," Skip said. "I haven't see you do that since junior golf." Bob tried his best to turn on a plastered smile but couldn't seem to find the switch. He laughed nervously. "You don't have any more of those in your bag, do ya, buddy?" Skip asked.

"I hope not," Bob replied.

"Neither do we," one of his gamblers remarked. They chortled, hoping he wasn't a misplaced bet.

Jeff was still looking at the bunker where Bob's ball landed, amazed that Joi's theory had apparently worked. He began thinking of the times he'd been rattled by opponents during college tournaments. *Were they applying gamesmanship or had he fallen apart on his own?* he wondered. Jeff was exactly one hundred yards from the flag—a nice lob wedge for him. Most players would have needed a pitching wedge or sand wedge from there, but not John Henry.

A close stare at the flagstick and two practice swings later, Jeff's ball was five inches from the hole. The spectators cheered and clapped, even the ones who'd bet against him. A smile gleamed from his face and he walked swiftly to his ball.

Kevin walked towards the jungle where his ball had headed and was joined by another cordial search party. This time the starter dove into the woods before anyone else. It was familiar territory for him. He and the other marshals of the course knew where the treasure chests of lost balls were. During their hourly patrols, they would scurry off into heavily populated golf ball refugee camps—areas where the dimple defectors hooked or sliced away from their hacking slave drivers. On any given day, a marshal might find ten balls with a face value of three dollars each. Premium golf balls were everywhere. Recreational players believed the clever advertisements. The golf equipment manufacturers should have sold their products with asterisks and fine print:

Ball go far* in the water hazard
The number one ball in golf* lost in the woods
Play a better ball* but first get a better swing
True* you should be a bowler

Smart Core* dumb golfer

No matter the technology nor the promise, they would all inevitably retire to a watery grave or a wooded oblivion.

The group arrived at the area where the ball had entered, only to be met by the scouring starter.

"Hold where ya are! Stop where ya walk! Ball found! Ball found! Ball found here in the rough!" The energetic man was hovering over the ball with stretched arms and shuffling feet. He moved in a circular motion, protecting the ball from predators—invading feet, stray branches, wayward pine cones, or whatever other enemy he'd declared war on. The man had set up a golf ball quarantine. "Fella, please identify your ball!" the starter yelled to Kevin, who hoped that it might actually be his. "This is a Titleist, Pro V1, three black dots over the 'T', brown scuff mark three-eighths of an inch in diameter on the upper left hemisphere, right below one solid green line, I reckon...let's see..." He paused, tilting his head and contorting his body to get a better look. "Looks like a green line about five-sixteenths of an inch long. Can you deem this as your ball?"

The crowd was amused, although eerily frightened by the starter's attention to detail. One of them cried out, "How much does it weigh?"

Others began laughing until the starter replied back, "Don't be no imbecile. Everybody with a half a gnat brain knows that according to the USGA rules of golf, appendix three, line item one, the golf ball shall weigh no more than 1.620 ounces or 45.93 grams...stupid."

Abashed, each one mumbled to the next, "You know that? How'd he know that?"

"That's my ball!" Kevin yelled with new life. He could chip it close to the green and perhaps walk away with par. Everyone moved away. They hadn't even settled still before he grabbed a club from the bag and chipped the ball to within six feet of the hole.

"There we go, Kev!" Billy exclaimed from his cart. "Thattaway to stay alive! Come on, let's turn it on now!"

Bob was standing in the bunker. With no one to out-fidget him this time, he went through his extended routine. He jumped up to get a better idea of where the ball needed to land and to see how the green sloped. Despite his leaps, he still couldn't get a good picture. Bob walked out of the bunker and analyzed the contour. He decided to try and make the ball rise high out of the bunker and land softly close to the hole. Walking back into the bunker and taking one last look, Bob tripped over the rake and fell toward the sand trap. Just before toppling over, he jumped into the sand, landing on both feet. He recovered by stretching his arms. The left was held out towards the green and the right arm leaned on the club, which was touching the sand inside the bunker. Bob gritted his teeth and whispered, "Goshdar-nit." Skip was also watching and made a remark of disbe-lief. Bob looked at the rake and laughed, miffed at the bad luck. Always ready to give a concession speech or spin a bad event, Bob said, "I grounded my club in the hazard. That's a penalty stroke."

"Hey, wait a minute," a gambler protested. "He fell in the bunker. Don't you have to be over the ball and ready to hit to get a penalty like that?"

Those with money on Bob chimed in, but Bob cut them off. He saw it as an opportunity to show his integrity.

"Friends, the rules of golf are clear and I cannot ma-nipulate them to suit my own benefit."

Billy was quiet. This would put his man back in good position.

Bob regained his composure, careful not to wiggle his club into the sand before playing his shot. He accurately swept the club underneath the ball, sending it out of the bunker on a perfect arch. It dropped gently and easily into the hole.

"Yeah! Wooohoooo!" The crowd rejoiced.

"You old sly dog, you! Nice shot," beamed Skip.

The other golfers joined in congratulating Bob. Joi gave Jeff a shaking head with raised eyebrows.

She'd already had her putter ready before Bob's minor miracle. Joi lined up the shot and stroked the ball aggressively with a slight misalignment. It missed the hole on the left side by an inch and rolled past another two feet.

"Agh," she grunted. Without waiting for anyone, she tapped the ball again. It skirted the far outside edge of the hole and circled the entire perimeter, trying to decide whether to fall or stay above ground. Finally, it relented to gravity and dropped, slowing Joi's pulse back to normal. Next time she wouldn't be so cavalier with the short putts.

Kevin was next and had begun aligning his shot before Joi could even retrieve her ball from the cup. Back and through came his putter and away went his ball into the hole for a remarkable par. He received a hero's applause and got Bob's approval with a wink and several nods.

All that remained was Jeff's short putt for a birdie. There was no need for extended deliberation over which way the ball would roll or what the contour would be. His ball was so close he could wish it in. Jeff stepped to the ball as a car came driving down the long swerving road next to the green. It was a common sound; the curve was so close to the course that golfers had become accustomed to it. Most cars slowed at the area out of respect, knowing someone would either be teeing off or putting as they drove by.

Jeff took his putter back while the vehicle sped by. Just before he tapped the ball, drum-crushing waves of bass music slammed the tranquility resting in this quiet corner of the course. The hip-hop harassment returned, as did Nagga, blazing the saddle of his SUV. Jeff looked away when the music blared and away went his birdie putt. He missed it by one inch. Disgusted, he tapped in a disappointing par and shook his head, joining his own cheering section, who were also shaking their heads. One of them waved a carefully chosen finger in the direction of the fleeing SUV.

Norbert had motioned over to Suspender Starter, who radioed to the clubhouse and instructed someone to meet the driver in the parking lot and demand that he turn his music off.

Joi walked up alongside Jeff and tried to console him with a joke.

"Well, that proves it."

"Proves what?" Jeff barked at her.

"You can take the Nagga out of the ghetto...as long as you don't take him out in public."

The game's momentum had swung like a deceptive tropical storm at the beginning of seasonal transitions. What at first seemed like a Bob Berry eighteen-hole campaign donation had now become a full-fledged golf war. Each side had formed allies in order to conquer its enemies. Weaknesses were identified in an attempt to exploit areas of vulnerability. Strategies were carefully devised in hopes that victory would be ensured. And, like all wars, there would be casualties.

"You're hitting first," Joi said to Jeff as they arrived at the next tee box. "Don't forget to fidget for Bob. If you want, take a little extra time before you hit. It might throw Kevin off, too." Jeff remembered the errant shot Bob had made after Joi all but imitated his every move on the last hole. He would try it here this one time.

The crowd was settled, as were the banks and players. Jeff stood over his ball, shaking, moving, gyrating. Then he stopped. He backed away from the ball and looked into the trees as though he were searching for the wind to make up its mind. Another long look down the fairway. Another look into the trees. Three practice swings. A deep breath. A deeper breath. The crowd turned curious heads toward each other.

After finally ending his show, Jeff struck a mighty blow that landed over the hill and bounced to the red one-hundred-yard marker. Another blistered three-hundred-yard drive.

The ninth hole was a running escape of rolling magnificence. Elevated high above the fairway, the tee box acted as a perch for what was yet to come. Two hundred yards down the fairway, the topography seemed to vanish into one of the course's miniature valleys only to reappear, elevating towards a severe uphill climb leading to the green. To the right were the snatching pines and the left side was held hostage by more trees, brush, and fallen leaves that would provide a hideaway for stray golf balls—such as Bob's. After watching Jeff shake his shimmy, Bob couldn't figure out why he couldn't concentrate, couldn't get comfortable while addressing the ball. Bob smashed his tee shot hard left this time, hooking it into the woods. It disappeared from everyone's view as they heard the all-too-familiar colliding sound of golf ball and tree bark. He wasn't smiling anymore. Couldn't find the campaign contrite that helped him elude the reality of fragile emotions. His previous tee shot had sailed right and now he'd curved this one far left. Something was going terribly wrong. Bob stood on the tee box, looking, hoping his ball would suddenly appear rolling into the fairway.

"I didn't see it kick out," said one of Bob's supporters.

"Should be down by the trees," Skip said, trying to offer encouragement. "Wanna hit a provisional?"

Bob shook his head, a bit flustered now. Kevin stepped

to the tee, trying to maneuver around Bob, who was slowly taking his time to get his broken tee out of the ground. All of this delayed Kevin's eagerness to tee off.

A few too many moments had passed and Kevin swung faster than he had all day. Before he'd even made contact with the ball, Kevin's head rose to see where the dimpled sphere would travel this time. His entire body pulled up and the bottom of his club struck the top of the ball, causing it to skitter along the ground. It rose just a few feet above the ground and traveled less than two hundred feet.

Kevin dropped the club on the ground and screamed as loud as he could without making a sound—the golf scream. Pressure of lungs constrained by ribs and captured by skin, made blood rush through arteries, flowing and pushing beyond normal rates. His head began to throb. His throat felt constricted and he wanted so badly to pass out, or better still, drop dead right here on the tee box. He felt as though it were the only way out.

Joi walked down to the red tees, feeling very confident now. Her strategy was more effective than she'd hoped. She'd been the master at gamesmanship in college, but it had never worked as well as it was working now. Perhaps it was the male psyche, or the arrogance of testosterone. Reveling in her march towards victory, Joi placed another perfect tee shot just at the top of the hill, 160 yards from the green.

After watching Kevin and Bob suffer, and Jeff and Joi struggle, the crowd was unusually quiet. Even they had begun to feel the weight of the large payoff. The entourage headed to get in position for the next shots and they could see another group had formed around the ninth green.

After realizing that he was nowhere near death, Kevin trotted out to his ball, snuggled in the rough grass. The distance from the ball to the green may as well have been galaxies away. Chances were slim that he'd land on the green from here. Nevertheless, ever impulsive, Kevin grabbed his driver, much to the crowd's astonishment, and swiped through the ball. He knew it would curve right so he'd aimed slightly to the left, praying it would not grow into a horrid slice. Whizzing through the air, his shot flew over the valley and landed on the upslope five feet away from the green.

"Great recovery!" Bob shouted, as did the crowd. Kevin's heart returned to normal and it was easier to breathe now. There was hope—albeit slim to none, but there was hope.

Bob headed off into the woods looking at the ground and kicking pine needles. Kevin quickly joined and exclaimed with excitement, "It's right here, Bob!" He was pointing to a ball barely sitting in the fairway. "You got a good kick there partner—er, uh, I mean Bob." They exchanged glances, warning each other to be more careful.

"Well I'll be," Bob said. "Guess the golf gods don't hate me after all. Looks like I'm what, 165 out from the green?"

"It seems to…oops, I'm sorry." Kevin stopped himself, realizing he had come dangerously close to giving Bob advice. He didn't want a two-stroke penalty. Instead, Kevin began a lonely trek to his ball.

Bob examined his distance and selected the appropriate club. After his pre-shot moving subsided, Bob chopped the ball out of the rough, but he never got the proper compression between ball and club. He'd hit a flier that was soaring much farther than he'd intended. It landed hard near the back of the green and skipped off into an even thicker cut of rough twenty feet from the hole.

Joi, as smooth and controlled as ever, hit an accurate approach shot to within twelve feet of the hole. The crowd in the fairway cheered along with the newly gathered group around the green.

Jeff was only one hundred yards away from the hole. He could see the flagstick, but not the putting surface itself. He pulled out a wedge once more and watched as his shot blasted upwards and descended very near the flagstick. When the ball came to rest five feet away from the hole, the crowd at the green yelled and clapped, signaling that Jeff was in birdie range.

The players made their way to the green. Kevin arrived at his ball and appeared to hit his chip shot without even breaking stride. It rolled to nine feet from the cup. Joi reached in her pocket and pulled out her ball marker, placed it on the green and cleaned her ball.

Jeff reached in his pocket, searching for a ball marker. Thinking he must have dropped it somewhere before the last hole, he asked the group, "Anybody got a coin? I dropped my ball marker somewhere."

"Hey yo! I gotcha," Nagga yelled. He'd returned to watch the match and had already commandeered another golf cart. Nagga slammed on the parking brake and jogged closer to Jeff. He hurled a small object through the air with an underhand toss. Jeff reached out, caught it and cupped it in his hand. He turned to Joi, shrugging his shoulders as if to say *maybe he's not so bad after all.*

Jeff placed the object just behind his ball, then bent down for a better look. His face was overcome by a frightening stare of cold death. His bottom lip quivered. He looked at Nagga, who was already walking back to his cart. Jeff looked down at the object once more to confirm. It was a bloody gold-capped tooth—with his brother's initials.

Leaderboard	
Jeff	-1
Kevin	+2
Bob	+1
Joi	-1

Chapter 14
Motivation

Jeff couldn't move. He didn't know if his brain could function. Wasn't sure if his eyes were really seeing what was on the ground. Jeff stared down at the putting green, now contaminated with the symbol of violence. It reminded him of the time his brother had stolen an older boy's bike and the victim knocked a tooth from the little brother's mouth. Then, as now, the bloody tooth had gripped his gut. This time it was much different. After the bicycle incident, Jeff had unleashed a cadence of fists into the older boy's stomach, followed by an uppercut to the nose.

But now, years later, Jeff was simply terrified. Afraid that the tooth was extracted from a lifeless being. The incisor obviously meant that they had found his brother and hurt him—bad. If he moved, if he walked away, he might see Nagga's smiling face, which meant the deed had been done and there was no reason to finish the match. If he so much as glanced around, he was afraid that he might see a finger in the hole or a toe in the bunker. There was no telling what Nagga would do.

"Heads up! Hey, Jeff!" Joi shouted. Bob was over in the rough, wiggling, getting ready to play his chip shot. Joi walked over and nudged Jeff. "Step back. You all right?" She saw his eyes wide, filled with water waiting to spill over. "What's wrong, Jeff?"

"Nothing. I gotta go. I need to...Where is my..." He rambled, not knowing which way to go or what to say.

They moved off the green and watched Bob's shot roll close to the hole. He walked up and tapped in the eight-inch putt for par. The crowd clapped. Joi and Kevin both dropped their putts with no problem, leaving Jeff to finish the hole. Everyone began walking away, thinking that Jeff would easily make the putt.

He looked down at the bloody tooth he'd used to mark his ball and then picked it up and threw it into the bunker, hoping never to see it again. He stood over the putt—and stayed there. Jeff couldn't make himself move the putter back and strike the ball. Fifteen seconds passed, then twenty-five seconds. Kevin and Bob exchanged looks. The crowd mumbled, wondering about the delay. Each bank watched, knowing that there was a problem. A minute had elapsed and everyone was getting concerned. Jeff stood there, hands shaking, mind wondering, eyes now dripping onto the green, his tears just barely missing the ball. The sight of his drops falling to gravity broke the static monotony. After a minute and a half of standing over the putt, Jeff hit the ball and missed his birdie. His gamblers moaned in unison. Joi gritted her teeth. Jeff quickly pulled himself together and made the short putt for par. He joined the other golfers as they headed for the back nine.

"Yo, Jeff!" Nagga yelled from his golf cart. "Jump in the cart, bruh. I need to holla at chu for a second."

Jeff's feet stopped the instant Nagga spoke. He looked at the man, refusing to do anything he asked. If he jumped in the cart, he was afraid emotions might take over and Nagga might get the same pounding he'd given to the boy who'd knocked loose his brother's tooth. If he didn't get in, he was afraid there might be another tooth on the next green or a larger extraction from his brother's body.

"What chu need?" Jeff said, slowly walking to the cart.

"Put yo' clubs on the back and jump in. I think you left somethin' in my truck."

Everyone heard. Joi was perhaps the only one who would make the connection with Jeff's disturbance over his birdie putt and Nagga's appearance. Once in the cart, Jeff stared ahead, knowing a terrible fate was awaiting him. He had the eyes of a man walking to his own execution...or someone else's.

"I see you missed that easy birdie putt back there," Nagga said, swerving through the parking lot headed for the last parking space on the bottom row. "You been missing putts like that since I left?" He paused. "Huh?"

"I guess my ball marker messed me up," Jeff said, fighting the urge to fight Nagga.

"Let me tell you somethin', homeboy. Yo' ball markers gon' get a whole lot worse if you don't do somethin' out there. I ain't come all way cross town to give some cracka white boy ten large. You hear me? And I damn sho' ain't come out here for you to talk to me like *you* runnin' this show. What the hell was that back there on the sixth hole? Fool, you don't disrespect me like that...*ever!*" Nagga moved closer to Jeff. "You give me a reason why I shouldn't do you and yo' brother and walk out with that white boy's money right now. One reason!"

Jeff was quiet as they approached Nagga's black earth shuttle. His wrecking crew got out. Then Jeff remembered a reason why.

"You gave me yo' word."

Nagga stopped the cart and applied the parking brake. He got out of the cart and walked to Jeff's side. "And that's the only reason," Nagga said. "I knew you was smart, Jeff. Question is, why you do dumb stuff?"

"Look Nagga, just because—"

"I'm through talkin' about how you played on the front nine," he said, pulling a keyless remote from his pocket, pointing it at the back door, and pressing the open button. "What matters to me is what chu gon' do from here on out."

Slowly, the back door opened. It was as though a curtain was rising, exposing the drama of a show's second act. There was only one character in this scene—his brother lying inside beaten, bloodied, and bruised. He was barely breathing and the few breaths he could make were painful. Rising lungs pushed against broken bones, sending signals of pain to his brain. The boy was shaking. His face was distorted and covered with blood. He lay curled in the last position he found that gave him the best defense against feet, fists, and leather straps. Two purple lumps had risen on his forehead and his nose was broken. His clothes were ripped, exposing the cuts on his legs and arms. Life was fleeing.

"Muthafu—!" Jeff yelled, lunging towards Nagga only to be restrained by a head lock, a twisted arm, and a bear hug. The crew had him wrapped from head to spikes. "Let me go! Get the hell off of me!" Jeff yelled, squirming and wiggling, thinking he could somehow escape and grab his brother, make a dash for the hospital. "Let my little brother go!" he screamed. Tears burst from his eyes. Tears of the painful realization that he had failed to protect his sibling.

All these years he'd been there, never missed an opportunity to play hero. He'd never missed a chance to save him from whatever boogey man scared him in the night's darkness.

Jeff had once caught his brother before he would have fallen from a tree on the playground. Placed his hand on the seat of his bike just before he would have lost balance and fallen on the sidewalk. Stopped him from putting a piece of candy in his pocket without paying for it. Yelled at him before he threw a rock through an elderly woman's window. Stopped him the first time he'd tried to smoke a joint. Sent him money from college when he'd gotten a girl pregnant so he could do whatever he thought was best. But this was the worst. When he was really needed, when he could have softened the blows, Jeff thought to himself, he was playing golf.

"Let him gooooo! Help!" Jeff screamed, trying to draw attention.

Nagga reached in his pants and retrieved his nine-millimeter. The action stopped the squirming.

"Jeff, keep yellin' if you want to," Nagga said, reaching in his pocket and pulling out a silencer.

"Hey! Help!" Jeff yelled again, but not as loud as before. Nagga screwed the silencer on and lowered the gun to Jeff's brother's temple.

"You wanna say somethin' else? Scream again. Go ahead. Jackjaw, how far is the nearest carwash?" Nagga asked.

"It's one off Rockbridge Road," the man replied, gripping Jeff's head.

"They got a vacuum machine? I need to get all this brain matter out before I go to dinner tonight."

"Yeah they got all that stuff over there."

"Jeff. Do I need to stop by the carwash?"

Jeff was frozen. He'd stopped resisting the crew and

didn't even think of yelling. Instead, he felt strength leave him. His legs buckled and he fell to the ground, sobbing.

"Don't hurt him no more." He sniffed and wiped, trying to clear his face of humiliation. With a quiet, humble voice he turned to Nagga. "You gotta get him to the hospital, Nagga. You gave me yo' word. He won't make it if you don't get him to the hospital."

The monster removed the gun from the boy's head. "Get up off the ground, Jeff. Stop actin' like a lil' trick."

Jeff rose, keeping an eye on the crew and walking closer to his brother. He placed a comforting hand on him, but his brother flinched. Everything was painful to him. Every touch. Every movement.

"Nagga! Come on, man, he gon' die!"

"Jeff, he gon' die anyway if you don't do somethin' on the last nine holes."

"But at least get him to the hospital."

"Yeah, that's no problem. We can make sure he get dropped off, but we ain't gon' take him. You think we stupid? He'll get there just fine. But you need to do somethin' first or we might just drop him off in a ditch."

"What is it? What chu need?"

"I don't need nothin'. Stand back for a minute. I don't want this door to close on ya. Then we'll all be out of luck," Nagga said, unscrewing the silencer and tucking the gun back in his pants. He pressed the button on the keyless remote again. Slowly, the back door lowered, closing the curtain on what Jeff hoped would not be a Shakespearean tragedy.

"If you want yo' brother to make it to the hospital...you need to go birdie the next two holes."

Leaderboard	
Jeff	-1
Kevin	+2
Bob	+1
Joi	-1

Chapter 15
The Turn

At Mystery Valley, there were golf holes, and then there were adventures in searching for par. The tenth hole was a hybrid of climbing Mt. Everest and kayaking Niagara Falls. It was a par-five dogleg left which first required a tee shot over a ball-sucking pond. Some believed the pond had risen over the years because so many balls had been kerplunked into it. The teebox was elevated and those who lied to themselves—saying, "There's no water, there's no water, there's no water"—found themselves eventually professing, "Look at all that damn water."

Unbeknownst to many, the tees were aimed at the cloud-nudging pines, which is where most golfers pointed when setting up to the ball. On rare occasions, a ball flying towards the trees was spit back out into the fairway, but most times it was another inevitable sentence in tree jail. If players were too greedy and tried to turn their shots left and ride the dogleg, they might find themselves scratching heads looking into a wall of tress, brush, weeds, thicket, and anything else green that only horticulturists could name.

If one did find the fairway, the second shot was no problem, but the approach to the green was just as stressful as the tee shot. The humongous putting surface was guarded by a bunker so large it could have been classified as a small shore. The green sloped, dipped, undulated, rolled, and elevated—on good days. On bad days it simply punished.

By now, Suspender Starter had learned the names of each player and could report the results *properly* from hole to hole. As Jeff made his way to the tee box, he found himself wading through an ever-growing crowd of spectators. The group had grown to over fifty people. Cart boys and snack bar workers from the first shift heard about the match—and, more importantly, the money—and decided to watch the action despite their early morning shifts and need for sleep. Those onlookers in golf carts left them at the club house and placed their clubs in vehicles, but brought umbrellas for the threatening skies overhead.

Jeff was sniffing and blinking away the remainder of his emotions. The banks saw that he was solemn, while Joi noticed that something had upset him.

"Ladies and Gentlemen," announced the starter. "As the match stands now, Jeff King is at minus one, Joi Martina is at minus one, Bob Berry is at plus one, and Kevin Tanner is at plus two. On the tee, Jeff King!"

Cheers were thrown from those happy gamblers whose player was in the lead. Jeff disregarded them all; he'd been given the only motivation he needed.

"Jeff, you all right?" Joi asked. She worried that he

might not be able to carry out the strategy. Then she found herself genuinely concerned. "Jeff," she said again, trying not to seem too obvious that she was making a small fuss over him. He walked right past her the same way he'd brushed through the crowd ignoring everyone. Jeff unstraddled the golf bag from his shoulder and yanked the driver from its position. He removed the headcover and carelessly tossed it aside. His face was a portrait of chiseled stone, with eyes cold and focused. After his ball was teed, he sucked in a swirl of air and exhaled, allowing his body to deflate some of the fear and anger.

The starter held up both hands and Jeff could feel a breeze racing through his shirt heading towards the direction of the fairway. He took his club head behind him, over his head, and around his back until it practically pointed toward the ground. Tension and torque from his body fought the movement as he uncoiled like a powerful spring. Hips rotated, shoulders turned, hands swept, knees shifted, legs pushed, arms dropped, wrists whipped, teeth gritted, lips pressed, eyes widened, and Jeff roared like an unleashed beast as the momentum carried him forward. He was thrown off balance and lost sight of the ball.

"God almighty!" a man from the crowd yelled.

"Oooo weee!" someone chimed in.

Jeff was breathing hard from the sudden storing and releasing of energy in such a short span. The crowd watched with mouths open, the players watched with disbelief, and the banks watched with disgust. They all watched...and watched...and watched as the ball tracked the exact path of the dogleg. It rode the wind, flying away, seemingly headed for orbit. It finally tailed off to the left and eventually hit the fairway. Then it rolled and kept rolling, still following the fairway's shape, until it came to rest out of their sight.

"Where'd it go?" the starter asked.

"That ball is on the other side of the hill," a spectator answered.

"Can't be! That's 320 yards to the other side!" said the starter.

The spectator eyed the starter and replied, "I don't care what the yardage is, but it's on the other side of the hill."

Everyone was deterred from gawking in wonderment by a slow rhythmic applaud coming from behind the tee box. Nagga was clapping his hands, grinning.

"Well, well, well. That's a tee shot by a man who playin' for somethin'."

They saw the grin and the stark contrast on Jeff's face. People could smell the tension between the two and a soft murmur came over the onlookers. Jeff didn't look at Nagga, didn't even glance in his direction. He simply snatched the headcover from the ground, placed it back on the driver, and gave the club a shove back in the bag. Jeff folded his arms and waited for the others to tee off.

"What's goin' on?" Joi asked. Jeff was silent. "Jeff, come on. Talk to me." Still, nothing but a piercing stare into a world he didn't want to reveal.

The starter separated himself from the mumbling crowd and threw his newly authoritative hands up again. "Quiet, please."

Bob waited for motionless people and the sound of birds calling out. When he was satisfied with the conditions, he too ripped a drive that caught a boosting ride in the breeze. Before the claps and compliments ended for Bob's shot, Kevin had taken his back swing and watched his ball sail into the middle of the fairway next to Bob's.

Joi cut a path for the red tees, which were only a short distance away from the pond. Joi could have thumped her ball over the water. She smacked a drive that landed in nearly the same spot as Kevin's and Bob's.

Jeff was possessed. With demon eyes, he speed-walked

down the cart path alongside the pond, his teeth grinding. Each breath was a gust of air trading rhythms with his quickened pulse. As if Jeff's rushing and pounding feet were an offering to a spirit world, the clouds began running above him. They were turning and churning, brewing the atmosphere for trouble. Thunder whispered from a distance, hinting that it would soon begin rolling louder claps of sonic booms.

"Look like the skies are about ready to open up again," said a spectator standing near Suspender Starter.

"Play will continue unless there is lightning in the area, at which time we will evacuate the players first and the spectators later." Having volunteered for fifteen years at the BellSouth Classic PGA tournament, the starter knew the procedures of protecting players from threats of lightning. Each year he served as hole captain, supervising marshals and scorekeepers. He demanded that everyone hold their "quiet" signs with a fully extended arm. Anyone not completely extending their arms was demoted to rope holder. Being relegated to only holding a rope as the pros walked to the tee box was the ultimate golf volunteer downgrade—complete with confiscation of quiet sign and volunteer pin.

Jeff could hear no thunder. He didn't see the pot boiling above his head. Each stride was one step closer to helping his brother. Instead of blades of grass beneath his feet, Jeff saw the contrasting colors covering his little brother's body. He was calculating in his mind the amount of time it would take to get him to the hospital. Jeff wanted to hear an ambulance screaming its way onto the golf course, saving his brother. There were screams, but not life-saving vehicles. People were screaming at him.

"Jeff! Hey! Heads up!" He'd almost reached his ball and was in a direct line with the other players' shots. Jeff had momentarily lost all sense of golf etiquette. Having hit his tee shot the farthest, he was supposed to stay behind his opponents and allow them to hit first. But at this moment there was no one of significance on the course except him and Nagga.

The shouts in his direction broke him from his trance as he stepped to the side and allowed the other players to hit. Jeff watched as the three balls landed and he could tell who'd just hit.

First there was a low-flying ball that skirted along the fairway and ran twenty more yards. He'd determined that the first shot was Joi's, because she'd teed off from the closest distance to the pond. There was a long wait between the next ball landing, which meant it could have only been Bob—and his fidgets. Only a few short seconds passed before the last ball flew overhead. Quick-hitting Kevin, Jeff thought to himself.

When it was all clear, Jeff walked to his ball. He seemed to disappear from the golf mob as he walked down the hill's crest to his tee shot that had settled 150 yards from the green.

A spectator finally saw where Jeff was standing and wailed, "Jesus, Mary and Joseph!"

"And the donkey they rode in on too," Suspender Starter added. "That's gotta be the longest drive on this hole ever."

Barks, shouts, and comments floated through the crowd until the starter threw his hands up to summon silence once more. Jeff took a few practice swings and then struck a nine iron. During the entire swing, his feet hardly twitched, his head never flinched, his body barely moved. With perfect balance in his follow-through, Jeff eyed the ball through its flight and watched it land in the middle of the green. He was on in two.

People with money on Jeff jumped and shouted. They slapped hands and hugged. Even those betting on the other three golfers chimed in and clapped in appreciation of the feat. Nagga stared with a sinister smile. He walked past Billy, his original challenger, and said, "Ain't no boys out here now, is it? You say somethin' about this ain't our sport?"

"Get outta my face," Billy replied.

"Get my money ready."

As the other golfers played perfect approach shots to the middle of the green, Jeff was weaning himself from the crowd. Eventually they all walked on the green and saw the hellish deed of the golf course superintendent. The hole was in the back of the green on top of a small slope leading off the green and down a hill. Sucker pin suicide.

From the middle of the green, the hole was at least thirty feet away. Joi, Bob, and Kevin all lagged their puts to within ten feet of the hole and marked their positions. It seemed as if they were all imitating one another. Jeff saw how short the other putts had been and was determined not to leave himself with such a long birdie putt. He was more concerned with making the eagle, which would give him a cushion on the next hole. He took careful aim towards his target—a spot two feet to the right of the hole. If he hit it hard enough it would start a breaking curve to the left and drop in.

Jeff took the putter back away from the ball, made a crisp stroke, and kept his head still then looked up hoping to see the white pill scurry off into the hole. He saw the ball heading exactly where he'd aimed it, magnetized for the cup. The putt was approaching the other ball markers and whizzing by just as he had intended. It had plenty of speed to reach the hole as it kept rolling along on target. Jeff could already see himself slashing his fists through the air in celebration for the eagle. He could already hear the spectators cheering

What he heard instead was more rumbling above the clouds. What he saw was his ball rolling farther away. It neared the hole and just barely missed the outside edge of the cup. The crowd released a huge collective *Ohhhhhh* as the ball ran by its target and kept going. The putt reached the slope and climbed over, as if in search of something. It picked up speed on the other side of the slope and then accelerated towards doom. Before the journey ended, the ball had run off the green and down the hill leading to the cart path. Suicide. Jeff's heart stopped. A lump in his throat flexed with a strange swallow. He coughed and his heart kick-started again. The instantaneous death and rebirth brought a quick spell of vertigo. Jeff could feel his bladder and bowels trying to release. This was the death of his brother and he had no idea what to do. Nagga was too far away for Jeff to rush and vise-grip his neck, choking him to death. Even if he could get close enough, there was still the nine-millimeter and crew of thugs to contend with.

He wanted to revert back to boyhood ways when playground rules granted do-overs whenever a kickball had been rolled improperly, or when a free throw met with some made-up interference. But he was too far past that equator of life separating boys from men.

The crowd ran to a spot where they could see Jeff play the impossible shot. His gamblers were praying he'd get the ball close and save par. Jeff grabbed a lob wedge and scurried down the hill where the ball had stopped. He was twenty feet away from the hole, standing on an upslope. The ball was buried in rough grass three inches high. Triple suicide.

"You can get it up and down from there for par," one of his gamblers shouted.

Jeff wanted to shout back, *Par means death*. He looked down at the ball and waited for it do something because he was clueless.

"That must've hurt. We need to call the paramedics?" Billy yelled. The crowd and other players all threw him re-pulsive looks for poor sportsmanship.

Jeff wanted to say yes. Call the paramedics, send them to the parking lot and take my brother away. That was another impossibility like the one staring up at him hiding in the rough.

"Sir, I'm gonna ask you to play your next shot or take a warning for slow play," the starter yelled. He had become more aggressive with his one-man rules committee.

The crowd murmured, "Can he do that? Does he have the authority to do that?" At once they all seemed to turn and face Norbert. He returned the stares with a shrug.

The starter flexed his authority a bit more and stated, "Rule six-dash-seven of the USGA rules, roughly paraphrased, states that a player must play without undue delay and in accordance with any pace of play guidelines which may be laid down by the Committee. Mr. Riley has bequeathed this authority to me."

More shrugged shoulders and puzzled stares circulated the crowd as Jeff took his stance over the ball and prepared to throw a futile chop into the tall blades of green obstruction. With a swift, descending blow, he tangled the club inside the grass an inch behind the ball, which squirted out and up towards the greens. Jeff saw the face of his club covered with extracted grass. He flicked off the hairy green follicles scalped from the earth and walked up the hill, unconcerned about the ball's destiny. The birdie putt was what he needed and wanted. He'd almost reached the top of the hill when his already shaken nerves were disintegrated by a piercing wave of cheers.

Jeff walked a few steps closer and saw heads bobbing, arms flapping, and fists pumping. As his eyes approached the green, only three balls were visible. His was in the cup.

Leaderboard	
Jeff	-2
Kevin	+2
Bob	+1
Joi	-1

Chapter 16
Brotherly Tough-Love

The other three had made their pars without thinking. The crowd cheered Jeff's heroic shot as the players left the green. Nagga caught up with Jeff before he reached the next tee box.

"Now that's what I need to see right there. That's why I brought you out here in the first damn place. One down, one to go. Let's hit it. Yo' little brother's waitin' on you."

Jeff heard him, ignored him, and walked away. There was nothing on his mind but a strong iron shot and a good putt. He reached in his pocket and pulled out a tee, but stopped abruptly. There were trees and houses all around. No roads or exits. Suddenly Jeff realized there was no way of seeing his brother taken away for medical attention, at least not for the next five holes, when the golf course would meet the parking lot again. He walked back to Nagga's cart.

"I want him on the phone."

"Who? What chu talkin' about?"

"I want my brother on the phone tellin' me that he's leavin' the parking lot and somebody gettin' him some help."

"Bruh, I gave you my—"

"You gave me yo' word that you wasn't gon' kill 'im if I won. You ain't said nothin' about gettin' him to the hospital. I make this next birdie and you put him on the phone and let me hear him say they leavin' the parkin' lot. Let him keep the phone and he calls me from the emergency room."

Jeff dropped the ultimatum and waited. Nagga sucked his teeth and replied, "Or what? What chu gon' do, big man?"

"Or else he gon' die anyway and I leave you out here and you can finish the round yo'self. See if you can win yo' own damn money. After that, we'll see what happens."

"You think you wanna go down that road? You think you ready for a move like that?"

"Way I see it, you the one wit' choices. I ain't got no options. If—"

"Come on, birdie man!" Bob yelled, ending the showdown. "There's no way I'm gonna tee off before a beauty like that last shot. You've got the honors, buddy."

They were standing on the tee box of the next hole, a 216-yard par-three nightmare. The green was a straight shot, but most golfers didn't have a 216-yard straight shot. Many players opted to curve the ball in with a fade swooshing high in the air from left to right. Others elected a strong curving draw flying in right to left. Both shots were risky. The left side was plagued with branches stretching out like giant kleptomaniac hands shoplifting for golf balls. The right side, though free of the thieving branches, was besieged with thick rough, making it impossible to make a decent shot to the green—a large green guarded on both sides by sand bunkers.

On any given day, those who could sweep a magical fade or maneuver an elusive draw missed the green. This hole was rarely birdied. Bogey was expected, par was a celebration.

Jeff drilled his tee into the ground and brushed an iron on the ground before making practice swings. He stood four feet behind the ball, looked straight ahead at the flag, and took his address position. A man in the crowd looked at a buddy and held up five fingers on one hand and a thumb on the other hand. He mouthed the words. *Six iron.* Eyes that saw the number were wide open over dropped jaws.

Jeff slapped the ball and held another pose of perfect balance.

"That was a six iron?" the wide-eyed man asked, seeking confirmation.

"Six iron," his buddy replied.

Heads were pointed at the green as they awaited the arrival flight of his ball. Seconds later it turned left, descending to the right side of the green. It landed near the middle of the green, kerplunked, then rolled back to the back left quadrant of the putting surface—five feet from the hole.

"That boy can play!" one of the ladies from the restaurant staff yelled. Others all broke out in laughter. They were running out of superlatives for Jeff's performance.

The other players and their banks weren't laughing. They were growing tired of hearing the same thing on each tee box after Jeff's shots. *Wow! Look at that! Ooo Wee!*

Joi was still worried about Jeff. She'd forgotten that they were opponents and wondered what had transpired in that parking lot to bring about his Frankenstein level of warmth. Bob was trying his best to control the perspiration beginning to creep through his iron-clad political coolness. Kevin was simply a wreck.

Each of the three placed equally average tee shots on or near the green. With putts and chips they all placed second shots less than ten feet from the cup. Kevin walked up and dropped his putt from seven feet. Joi sank an eight-footer. Bob, who could sink putts with his eyes closed, made a six-footer without even thinking about it. It was Jeff's turn. The other putts hadn't been made from the same area of the green where Jeff's ball was sitting, so he couldn't gauge his own shot by the way the other putts danced, swayed, and rolled through dips and flattened blades of buzzcut grass.

He walked around the hole and around his ball, crouching, trying to read the green and learn what it wanted the dimpled treasure to do. Jeff stepped away from the ball and rocked his putter a few times, making hard strokes and then softer ones. He tried to find the perfect tap, hoping the ball would stay on its intended line. The starter walked over and was about to give a warning. Jeff stretched his palm to the authority stopping his charge.

"No need. I'm playing my shot now," Jeff said with confidence. He stood over the ball and held his breath, not wanting to move anything except his shoulders and arms. He wanted to be a grandfather clock—stout and static, a pendulum swinging with perfect rhythm in a room where no one would notice until the hour struck, reminding people that it was time. Just as it was time now to save a life.

Shoulders pulled back perfectly fixed arms and soft cradling hands. Then the shoulders pushed through with delicate precision, like the clock. His eyes and head never moved. He wouldn't look, only listen. He listened for the satisfying sound of the cup's bottom capturing the elusive spherical creature. The sound of the mouse being captured, the dragon being slain. The sound that meant his brother was going to be safe. Jeff waited. The sound never came.

"Aggggh!" the crowd yelled.

Jeff finally looked up and in disbelief saw his ball resting on the very edge of the hole. His stomach sank and thunder pushed louder through the clouds. He grabbed the end of his putter and squeezed it as punishment for not being heavier or lighter, whichever would have made the difference. He knew what had to happen, he had to tap in the putt and beg Nagga for one more hole. He placed the putter on the ground and prepared to tap the ball. But before he could take one step, it fell in the hole. The crowd's cheering momentum spilled over once more and they let loose for what was an ever-growing spectacle of golf.

Jeff put the putter in its slot, shouldered his bag, and headed for Nagga, who already had a phone in his hand. He extended it to Jeff.

"Baby brother. Where you at?"

"In the truck. I think we leavin'. Where you at?"

"I'm on the golf course. They gon' take you to get some help, all right."

"Yeah, I know," the boy said, his voice raspy and winded. "They bedda hurry up too. I got packages to deliver and some collections to make."

"You *what*?"

"These fools think they gon' stop me. This just gon' make me stronger. I'm real about mine. Tell dat punk Nagga he can't crush me."

"What the hell you say?" Jeff asked.

"I'm takin' over. This just the beginnin' right here. When I get out the—"

"Yo, put Nagga back on," a deep bass demanded.

Shocked, Jeff handed the phone to Nagga. More shocked than he'd been after the missed putt and the gold tooth. More shocked than he'd been when the ball ran off the back of the green.

"He did, huh?" Nagga said into the phone, snickering.

"I ain't surprised...Nope. Gave this fool my word, but hey—if it ain't me it's gon' be somebody else," he said and closed the flip.

"Jeff. You talked to your brother, right?"

"Yeah," he replied with a spinning head and angered heart.

"He in the truck and he's gone, right?"

Jeff adjusted the golf bag on his shoulder. His facial expression transformed and he stood taller, as though a weight had been lifted. He replied, "Yep. He's gone all right."

Leaderboard	
Jeff	-3
Kevin	+2
Bob	+1
Joi	-1

Chapter 17
Confessions of a Troubled Golfer

They were waiting for Jeff again. Norbert Riley was talking to the starter, pointing at his watch, then at Jeff, then at Nagga.

"I'm sorry, everybody. Won't happen again. Didn't mean to hold you up," Jeff said, giving a smile and wink to Joi. "I'm sorry," he whispered to her personally.

"Don't be sorry. Be teeing off. You still got honors," Joi replied, smiling back.

Jeff ran up to the box, teed up the ball, quickly hit the shot, and watched it glide to the right with an uncharacteristic slice. Carefree and relieved, he moved aside for the next person to play. The crowd was puzzled about what had caused such a bad shot and why Jeff didn't seem concerned about it.

The twelfth hole was a broken dogleg left with the last 180 yards of the layout falling on a downhill slope and the large green rising slightly uphill. Skilled golfers tried to swing the ball from right to left, hoping it would land on the slope and gain a few more yards. Recreational golfers often tried to squeeze their shot through a narrow strip bordered by pines and what was left of the fairway. Those shots rarely found the short grass and almost always landed in the pine prison on the left.

The trees on this particular hole were one of the many mysteries of Mystery Valley. The earthly floor in which the trees were rooted was vast and open. One could see the entire area by standing in one spot and turning 360 degrees. But no matter how many ways a person turned, their wayward shots always seemed to disappear. It was like looking for an ink spot on a Dalmatian.

Kevin and Bob both played safe shots straight ahead that landed at the bend on the dogleg, 160 yards away from the green. Joi was at the red tees swinging, just before the skies opened up and unleashed more showers. The crowd transformed from a group of mumbling heads into a potpourri of parasols. The foursome whipped out their umbrellas as well. Bob and Kevin walked down the fairway to their balls while Joi and Jeff headed into the woods to search for the slice.

"What was all that about?" Joi asked.

"What?"

"All that drama over the last three holes."

"Nothing."

"Sure was a whole lotta nothin'."

"Nothin' to worry about. Let's just make sure we win this thing for you."

"Huh?"

"You know, strategy. Like you said earlier."

"I know what I said earlier, but I didn't say nothin'

about winning for me. I said let's make both our chances better."

"Well, I'm sayin' it. Let's make sure you win and you can get outta whatever trouble you in."

"What makes you think I'm in trouble?" Joi asked.

"Everybody's in trouble. You think people come out here, shut down a golf course, play for thousands of dollars 'cause they ain't got nothin' better to do?"

"So what kinda trouble you in with Nagga?"

"I ain't in trouble."

"Is that why you get shaken up every time he comes around and why you've been havin' meetings between the last few holes?"

"I'm not in trouble and now I don't give a damn what Nagga does," Jeff said, lowering his head and squishing the dirt with his feet.

"Why not? Something happen?"

Jeff was quiet. He kicked rocks and twigs, thinking of the games he and his brother once played. He remembered how even then his little brother broke the rules and never had regard for consequences.

"Something *didn't* happen," said Jeff.

"What do you mean?"

"Somebody didn't raise their kid right and the kid hasn't learned that life isn't a TV show or a video game when you get to start over whenever you want."

"Huh?"

"Like I said earlier, my brother's in debt to Nagga and I'm playing to get his marks paid off."

"How much is he in for?"

"Don't matter."

"Why not?"

"If I get him out of this he'll be back in something else tomorrow."

"You don't know that."

"I *didn't* know that. Now I do. I mean, I realize it now."

"So what happens if you don't win?"

"I'm not worried about it anymore," Jeff said, staring into Joi's concerned face.

"Why not?"

"Because he's who he is. He's probably just like our father—whatever *he* was like."

"But I mean, what's Nagga gonna do if you don't get him the money?"

Jeff's head lowered again and he was still. Without speaking, he conveyed the message of doom.

"Jeff, you can't let anything happen to your brother. All we gotta do is make sure—"

"I'm done, Joi. I can't help him if he doesn't want to do right. You think I sliced my tee shot by accident? I haven't sliced a ball since I was in high school. You think I'm gonna let Nagga keep his foot on my neck for the rest of the day for something that's gonna come out bad anyway? Why should I give him that much power? This ain't even about me!"

"But it's your *brother*, Jeff. What if Nagga—"

"I've done the best I can. He's playing in a grown-up game and he's gotta have some grown-up consequences. I'm done, Joi. Stop talkin' about it!" Jeff was drawing the attention of others. Norbert and Nagga kept watching the two.

Jeff tried to recant his fury. "Look, my bad. I'm sorry. It's not your fault. I'm just through with it. Been tryin' to please people and hold stuff together for too long. Today's my last day. I may as well try to help somebody that wants help. Like you. My brother's gone so why not help you?"

"Well...I'm gonna be all right." Joi looked at the ground and avoided telling lies in Jeff's face.

"Not if you lose, you won't."

"I hadn't planned on losing."

"But you wanted *me* to win? That doesn't make sense."

"What I meant was—"

"What did you do?"

"Huh?" Joi asked.

"What kinda trouble you in?"

"That's not important. What you need to do is—"

"Wait a minute, I can spill my guts and go along with your strategy, but you can't tell me what brought you out here?"

"Well it's not really—"

"Fair?" Jeff interrupted.

"No. I was gonna say it's not what I did, but what got done to me. But I really think you should focus on—"

"Somebody hurt you? Physically, I mean?" Jeff found himself with an instinct to protect Joi. It was more than general concern for another person or the habit he had developed for his brother. It was an desire to make her feel secure.

"No, nothing like that," Joi said, noticing his protective tone. "Just got into something at work."

"Something that made you come out here and play golf for stakes you couldn't afford to put up yourself? What— you steal something?" he asked, joking.

"I didn't steal anything!" Joi shouted, once again bringing attention from others. "Just forget about it," she said in frustration. "Let's find your ball. Rain's lettin' up."

"It's right over there," Jeff said pointing to a ball taking refuge. "I saw it as soon as we got over here. Now, what did you *allegedly* steal?"

Joi answered with a contemptuous look. "I told you I didn't—"

"Play will now resume!" shouted the starter. Norbert, remaining close to the one-man rules committee, had looked up at the clouds and given a nod to the man just before he'd shouted for all to hear.

"Well, why are you out here playing like your life depends on it?" Jeff asked Joi's back as she walked away from him and headed towards her own ball.

Jeff had to punch out into the fairway. His ball had been trapped by an exposed tree root that wouldn't allow for a good swing. The rest of the foursome played shots that all hit the green and they made three pars. Jeff was forced to settle for a bogey. Grunts came from his gamblers as he strolled to the next tee box, carefree, as though he'd made another birdie.

The thirteenth hole proved to be another routine par for the entire group. It was a straightaway 355-yard layout with no frills except for the breathtaking view of Stone Mountain. From a distance, it looked like emerald tears were running down its slope.

Bob was the first to tee off at the fourteenth hole—the longest par five on the course. A wide fairway narrowed, then dropped off to the right and rose again to another massive green. And, of course, the security pines guarded all sides.

The wiggle-master eventually settled down and launched a drive that came to rest 280 yards from the green. Kevin had managed to find some method to keep his ball in play and he, too, was a little under three hundred yards from the green. Jeff pulled out an iron and whacked his ball straight ahead like he was throwing darts. His ball nestled 320 yards from the green. Joi finally drove her shot to the middle of the fairway and in the vicinity of the other players.

"Are you gonna tell me?" Jeff asked. He'd rushed to meet Joi in the fairway.

"Tell you what?" Joi asked, buying time. She hoped that they would reach their next shots before the conversation ended. "Jeff, in case you haven't noticed, we're in the middle of a very important match with only five holes left to play."

"I know that. What I don't know is why is it so important to you? Tell me what you—I mean, tell me what you're being accused of taking."

Joi stopped walking and looked into the woods, then above her head at the clouds rumbling. After a long sigh, she replied, "Thirty-five thousand dollars."

"*What?*"

"Shut up," Joi whispered as loud as she could. The crowd turned in the twosome's direction once more. The crowd was getting suspicious.

"How'd you get accused of stealing thirty-five large?"

"I'm being set up. When somebody wants you out, they'll do whatever it takes."

"What did you do? Who wants you out?" Jeff asked as they resumed walking.

"I didn't do anything except not play their games. I went against the grain and now I'm paying the price."

"What does the money have to do with it?"

"I need it to make everything right."

"And what if you don't get it? I mean, not askin' for my sake 'cause I ain't tryin' to play no more."

"I don't believe that for one second, Jeff."

"Whatever," he said, losing eye contact for a moment. "But what if you don't beat those other two?"

"I don't know. Nobody's gonna die, that's all I know," she said, arriving at her ball. She pulled a fairway metal from her bag and took a few swings before crushing a perfect fade that gently descended to the 150-yard marker.

Jeff walked over to his ball and whipped out the same iron he'd teed off with. Another darted laser peeled through the air layered with a misty drizzle. Kevin and Bob were waiting at their shots and each struck two shots close to the green. The two were slowly becoming skilled surgeons, cutting away at Jeff's lead.

The crowd's enthusiasm had lulled. The sporadic rain combined with the boredom of routine had taken its toll. And those who had bet against Jeff and Joi didn't approve of the between-shot meetings.

Joi landed her approach within fifteen feet of the hole and was rewarded by whatever cheers the crowd could muster. Jeff reached into his bag and grabbed a club with a line underneath the number. He imitated Kevin by swinging the club before even thinking about the shot. The ball sprang from the club on a rifled trajectory headed straight for the flag stick.

"Ooo, that looks right on it!" a gambler said, coming alive again with the hopes of more excitement. The ball continued to sail for its target, never fading or drawing to the left or right. As it approached the flag, the ball didn't descend toward the green. It kept flying by the flag, past the green, and finally into the woods some twenty feet behind the putting surface.

Everyone looked on with disbelief. They wondered if Jeff's adrenaline had driven him beyond his capabilities. Jeff himself wondered who could hit a nine-iron more than 160 yards. He placed his club on the ground to prop himself up while he recovered from the shock. As he leaned on the club, Jeff noticed how tall the club stood. Quickly, he twirled the club around and looked at the number on the bottom. It was a six iron. In his extreme haste, Jeff had played the wrong club.

Kevin and Bob prepared to make their short shots to the green. Kevin's ball landed on the green and kept rolling down another camouflaged slope each green seemed to have. It came to rest twenty feet from the hole. Bob played a brilliant shot that hit the green and slammed on brakes just three feet from the hole—a near-guaranteed birdie.

Jeff entered the woods and met other spectators searching for the ball. After five minutes of scavenging, six balls were found and not one of them belonged to Jeff. He was forced to go back and play the shot again. Jeff made sure he selected the right club this time and settled down before swinging. It was identical to the previous play, only this time it dropped when it should have and ended its journey very close to the hole. But the damage had already been done.

The foursome walked off the green. Joi and Kevin each had a par, Bob a birdie, and Jeff skipped off with the second bogey in three holes.

Nagga took notice of Jeff's attitude since he'd learned his little brother was on his way to safety. Billy, who had been silent, was waiting for Kevin to come around and make his move. But with four holes left to play, he was losing confidence in his man. Billy approached Skip Breiser, who was thrilled with Bob's charge.

"Skip," Billy said quietly as the crowd passed by onto the next hole.

"Hey Billy. Gettin' good out there ain't it? I know your guy is just waitin' to turn it on any minute, you old sly dog."

"I'm not worried about that right now. I've got some concerns about those two lovebirds always talking to each other between shots. It's time to do something about it."

"I noticed that too. What are you thinking about?"

Billy shot Skip a baneful look and said, "I'm about to get 'em both disqualified."

Leaderboard	
Jeff	-1
Kevin	+2
Bob	-
Joi	-1

Chapter 18
Crowd Control

The sky had yet to release its hold on all things beneath it. Curls of clouds continued to race by, trying to decipher where and when they would pour down again. The geese that contributed to the course's fertilizing efforts had taken refuge under shelter or some other course with drier accommodations. The slightly soaked crowd trudged on, hoping the rain would hold off long enough to finish without delay. Most of the spectators were trapped on the course because of their gambling obligations. Each wanted to know the outcome so they could cash out, pay up, or defer their payments until they paid up for wagers previously lost and owed. Those along for sheer entertainment were too far away from the clubhouse to leave. The crowd of over fifty people enclosed the tee box of the fifteenth hole. Death on earth.

It was a sick joke, the hardest hole on the entire course. A bird's-eye view deceptively invited players to pull out their driver and hit the ball as far as they could imagine. But the descending fairway had a severe drop-off to the left. It was more like an infant cliff. To the right was a landing area from which the green was barely visible. At the white 150-yard marker, the fairway became a forty-foot-wide dead-man's alley guarded by a swamp on the left and a pond on the right. The only way to reach the white marker from the tee was with a long accurate bomb. If tee shots landed short of the 150-yard mark, approach shots had to be played from sidehill downhill lies. From there, the green was elevated and huge. It was barely golf. A first time visitor to the course had once labeled it the Devil's Wish List.

Bucket Hat, Round Man, and Balding Guy were never far from the front of the crowd. Having initiated the stakes, they had the most interest in what was transpiring. They were also holding the money for the other gamblers.

The golfers were on the tee box with their clubs of choice in hand. Bob started the shakes as Billy made his way over to the starter. His footsteps crushed twigs and kicked small pebbles—an obnoxious concert on a golf course. The starter snapped around and held his hands up to the approaching Billy.

"Stand where you are, please. All quiet."

Billy gave the man a crooked grin. Bob eventually finished and ripped an iron shot down the middle.

"You do that for everybody, or just the guy you have money on?" Billy asked the starter. The aged man wasn't sure of the comment's purpose. He'd been primed only for technical rules and golf questions. Accusations of preferential treatment were foreign to his ears. He was confused and didn't respond. Billy spoke again. "Guess *my* guy's not on the right team to get any type of leniency, huh?"

"Stand please, quiet," the starter yelled just before Kevin smashed his ball down the fairway.

"See that?" said Billy. "My guy gets ready to hit and you wait till the last minute to make everybody shut up. We're on the wrong team, I guess."

Again, the starter quieted the man as Jeff teed off. Norbert made his way over to help his starter while Joi teed off. The golfers walked away as the situation started to grow on the tee box.

"Everything all right here?" asked Norbert.

"Depends on whose team you're on," Billy replied. Gamblers stayed back and the casual observers headed off with the golfers.

"This match is individual stroke play competition. Team consultations and advice from any outside source are not allowed," the starter rattled away.

"Yeah, right. Then why're you lettin' some people get away with it?"

Nagga heard Billy's ranting and pulled his cart up to the group.

Said Norbert, "Nobody's getting away with anything. Why don't you just—"

"The hell they ain't. Those two lovebirds been having secret meetings damn near between every shot. Nobody's said a word to them. You don't think they're helping each other out? I'm tellin' ya, I ain't gonna stand for this."

Skip pulled up to the group and the gambling crowd eased over.

Norbert replied, "Look, just because they're talking to—"

"Didn't you warn that boy about slow play three holes ago?"

"Ain't no boys out here," said Nagga.

"Oh...will you...just...go sell some crack, will ya?" Billy said

"Hey!" yelled Norbert, sensing the kettle about to spill over.

"I got yo' crack...cracka."

"Hey!" Norbert yelled again. This time silence followed. "I don't need to remind you that everyone here is a guest and this course has been very accommodating to this match."

"Don't give me that," said Billy. "A player was given a warning and he continued to play slow. He should have been given a one-stroke penalty. He wasn't and now I want him disqualified."

"What?" a man from the crowd yelled.

"No way!" cried another person. The Jeff followers were crying out while the others were silent.

"You must be out yo' damn mind," said Nagga.

"Billy, let's not mention that your guy has been awfully chummy with another player," said Norbert.

"What are you talking about?" asked Billy.

"Kevin and Bob have been just as close as Jeff and Joi. So if we're talking about disqualification, then maybe we need to look at Kevin," Norbert said, nodding to the starter as though he were the executioner.

"Hell no!" came a voice from the crowd.

"Nu unh. I don't think so!" Kevin's crowd began to rally this time. They were a bit more vocal, having witnessed Kevin fight off whatever golf demons had haunted him. Boisterous voices rang out from both sides and were joined by more people in the crowd, regardless of where the money had been wagered.

The golfers, who'd just hit their approach shots, turned back to look at the commotion. Focused, they ignored the uproar and walked to the green where all four balls lay waiting.

"If you want to be fair, then be fair. But don't give me this under-the-table-home-course crap. You disqualify that man right now!" Billy shouted. Skip looked on in amazement, surprised that Billy had taken such an extreme stand.

"No!"

"You can't do that," came more cries from the crowd.

"Look, Billy. Nobody's getting disqualified for slow play. Just drop it, okay?" said Norbert.

"Okay, that's fine. Tell ya what. You won't disqualify anybody, I'm withdrawin' my guy."

"Whoa. Wait a minute," Balding Guy shouted. He had been noticing the momentum swing in Kevin's play and felt as though he had a good chance at winning.

"If that's what you wanna do, then fine," Norbert said.

"I know it's fine," Billy said.

"Just make sure you meet your financial obligations before you leave," Norbert said.

"What the hell are you talking about? I don't have any obligations. I'm taking my guy out."

"We're well over halfway through this round. Therefore, you need to compensate the other members of this foursome for your investment in this venture."

"Go to hell," Billy said, dismissing the comment. "Go screw yourself. All of you. I'm taking my guy and my money."

"Nawh, bruh. I'm taking your money," Nagga added. "You can write me out a check if you want. But I ain't come out here to retire nobody's jersey. Ain't gon' be no quittin' on my juice."

"What...who..you thug. Get outta my way." Billy jumped in his cart. He tried to pull off but Nagga stood in the way, thumbs hooked over the waistband of his pants. "What are you gonna do, shoot me?" Billy asked.

"No, no, no. Of course not. Why would you think I'd do something like that?" Nagga said facetiously. "What a terrible thing to say," he added, his diction clear and articulate.

"Then get the hell out of my way."

Nagga stood his ground. Instead of drawing his gun, he pulled out a phone and one-touched his crew.

"Ray-shaun, how are you?" Nagga's voice transformed as though he were reading Hallmark cards for a commercial. "How far are you from finishing our charity health care issue? You've already returned, great! Hey, I've got a chicken I want to put on the grill later. It's gonna be delivered over to you in just a few minutes. Do me a favor, take it into the kitchen and tenderize it for me, will ya? Really pound it out, okay? No, don't go that far—I'll grill it myself. Just pound it out and that'll be great...It's on it's way now... White meat, about two and half pounds," he said, sizing up Billy's weight. "Got it? Great! Love to the kids and the missus." The SUV had pulled into the parking lot as the driver barked to the passengers who were playing video games using flat screen panels embedded into the headrests of the vehicle. "Yo, Nagga want us to jump some 250-pound white guy when he pull into the parking lot."

"Damn, we workin' overtime today, ain't we?" a pawn replied as the video game ended.

Nagga pressed the end button and moved, stretching his arm grandly in the direction of the cart path for Billy to drive by. "Take care of yourself," Nagga announced.

Billy gripped the steering wheel on his cart and tried to rip it off. Hues of pink then red ran up his back and covered his face. "You people make me sick," he whispered to Nagga. "Wish y'all would fall off a cliff somewhere."

"Huh? What did you say?" Nagga asked. "Mr. Riley, Mr. Breiser? I think Billy here just changed his mind. The game is on. Let's load up and head out." Nagga was behaving much too jovially to be questioned. Faces in the crowd sensed that souls were being auctioned off.

"What was that all about?" Round Man asked.

"I gotta feeling we don't want to know. Just keep telling yourself it's a gentleman's game," replied Bucket Hat.

There was a mad dash for the green. Banks jumped in carts while others held onto the back steps. Those that missed the carts sprinted to the action. It looked like an avalanche of people, a spectator stampede.

"What's goin' on up there?" asked Bob.

"Your boy is probably up there showin' out," replied Joi.

"Y'all mind? I'm tryin' to putt," Kevin said. "I'm playin' for something here. I don't know about you all, but this game means somethin' to me."

"It means something to me, too," Joi replied.

"If it did, you'd shut the hell up," Kevin said.

"What? Who you think you talkin' to?" Joi asked. Kevin's tone was offensive, just like her boss had sounded when he'd given her the ultimatum. As the course neared its finale of challenging holes, tempers were rising.

"Just shut up, will ya? I'm sick of this!" Kevin yelled.

"Don't you tell me to—"

"Whoa! Hey, hey, hey!" Bob said, walking between the two. Jeff moved in closer to help. "Let's just settle down, everyone. We're having a great match so far. Let's not spoil it. Nothing wrong with a little competitive banter, long as it doesn't get out of control."

"Tell that to her. And tell it to him too," Kevin said, pointing at Jeff.

"What did I do?" Jeff asked.

"You and your damn thug buddy been holding up the match ever since we started the back nine. If you wanna make drug transactions then you shoulda stayed—"

"You mutha—" Jeff blasted.

"Whoa! Hey!" Bob yelled. The foursome had merged into a clump of anger. Fingers were pointed and putters were raised when suddenly they heard, "STAND PLEASE ALL QUIET! HALT ALL ACTIONS! HOLD ALL COMMENTS!" the starter was holding on for dear life to Norbert's cart as it zoomed down the cart path. He waved his free hand in the air and shouted his commands. His face was pale and Norbert grabbed the starter's pants just before driving over a bump in the cart path so the old man wouldn't fly from the cart. As they neared the green, the starter leaped from the cart and rushed for the players.

"For the remainder of the match, slow play will not be tolerated!" The starter was gasping for air. "Penalty strokes will be issued upon the next occurrence of slow play. There will be no giving or accepting of advice from any outside agencies. Anyone found accepting advice will be penalized." His chest was pounding as his old lungs forced wind behind his warning while trying to supply the rest of his body with oxygen as they had for so many years.

Other carts were approaching the green and the sprinters were finally catching up. The players were captivated by the starter's rambunctious demands. They paid careful attention, wondering if he would pass out before he finished the sermon. He took a moment to catch his breath while the sprinters did the same as they reached the green

"May I remind you all that the United States Golf Association does not object to informal wagering among individual golfers or teams of golfers when the players in general know each other, participation in the wagering is optional, wagers are limited to the players, the sole source of all money won by the players is advanced by the players on themselves or their own teams, and the amount of money involved is such that the primary purpose is the playing of the game for enjoyment. Having said that—and having thrown it all out the window—lady and gentlemen, the game is *still* on."

"Let's do it!" Balding Guy shouted.

"Come on Jeff!" someone yelled.

"Kevin, let's get it goin', buddy!" a gambler said.

"Bob, you're right there, son!" Bucket Hat exclaimed.

"Joy-eh, you go gurl!" a man said with a thick southern drawl. His attempt at the urban idiom drew lighthearted laughs and much-needed relief. The laughs and murmuring met once again with, "Stand please, all quiet!"

The foursome finished the hole with pars all around. It was a testament to their skill when they needed it most. Despite the golf course's greatest challenge, they had all stared problems in the face and proclaimed that it was not their day to die.

Leaderboard	
Jeff	-1
Kevin	+2
Bob	-
Joi	+1

Chapter 19
Gut Check

Threatening clouds had taken interest in the last few holes, hovering above the players and the group. The par-three seventeen was a 158-yard gift. Not too much drama, not too many things seeking golf ball hostages.

Bob, still in control, teed off and landed safely on the putting surface. The crowd stood along the cart path and couldn't see exactly where the balls were landing. Kevin whacked away next. His ball traveled an exact trajectory with the flagstick and seemed to have been a good shot. Jeff slammed a nine iron to the middle of the green and Joi marched once again to her lonely perch at the red tees.

She was still upset from the verbal spats on the previous hole. Joi was again feeling oppressed at the hands of her white male counterparts. Her father had once tried to explain the difficulties she would encounter being intelligent, ambitious, female and Black. But he had held the discussion too soon.

Joi was in high school at the time and more concerned about controlling the spin of her wedge shots than learning life's stumbling blocks. She'd just played in an open tournament in which country club brats took her for the sister of one of their opponents. Surely she could not have been there to *compete* with them, they'd assumed. The boys teased her about the golf shoes she wore and suggested she trade them in for pom-poms if she was going to make a name for herself watching her brother play golf. When she explained to the boys that she was entered in the tournament, the boys broke out in slide-splitting laughter.

In hopes of taking home a trophy, she'd practiced on the course for days before the tournament, increased the number of range balls she hit, and made fifty putts every night on the living room carpet. Joi was prepared for that match and was ready to beat anyone who stepped on a tee box.

But the laughter and demeaning cheerleader comments slowly crept into her mind and circulated through her body, infecting her thoughts and coordination. The tempo and rhythm of her swing were ruined from her first tee shot. Joi needed her mental game more than anything else on that day, and it failed her. The boys had beaten her so badly, they didn't have the nerve to rub the defeat in her face. Despite her preparation and will, the disrespect of her adversaries had cost her the match. It was then that Joi's father tried to impress upon her more wisdom for the world. Joi, however, thought the answer was hitting more balls.

Kevin's comments were still swimming in her mind when she pulled the trigger on her club and watched the ball shoot high in the air and plummet down into the deep bunker just in front of the green. Joi stared at the sand trap, cursing its existence. Then she cursed herself for not using the proper club, not keeping her wrists cocked long enough, and hitting too much grass and not enough ball. Whatever might have caused the bad shot, she cursed it.

The crowd and carts rushed by. Joi's frozen disbelief was broken by shouts from the spectators. They'd reached the green and seen where the shots landed.

Jeff was in the middle of the green, as expected. Bob was twenty feet from the hole, but the yelling was for neither of the two. Kevin's ball was sitting one inch from the hole. Had he lined up his tee shot a shoelace to the left, it surely would have been a hole-in-one. Joi threw her bag across her shoulder and walked briskly to the green, trying to determine if the sounds were birdie cheers or ace cheers.

Relieved to see three balls on the green, Joi jumped in the abysmal bunker, and spent little time assessing what to do. With a quick sweep of the club, small sand grains made of tidal wave of brown speckles arcing up out of the bunker and splashing the green. Her ball sprang out ahead of the sand and rolled by the hole, until it eventually stopped thirteen feet away. The crowd exhaled with conciliatory moans.

While Bob and Jeff finished out the hole with pars and Kevin made his birdie by practically blowing his ball into the hole, Joi—her mind still laced with Kevin's attack—walked away with her first double bogey of the day. She'd suddenly fallen behind at the worst possible time. Two holes to play and two of the toughest to make birdie.

The last two adventures on the course were excavations across long green chasms. Seventeen, a par four, kept with the Mystery Valley theme of rising and falling landscapes. The green sat atop a hill protected by a hellish bunker in the front, a demonic bunker to the left, and a small bunker in the back just in case anyone had escaped the other two evil traps. To land on the green in two shots was indeed heaven.

Eighteen was a par-four trek over and down slopes that merged with dips and rises. If ever there was a roller

coaster on grass, it was here. The green was not dangerously surrounded like seventeen. In fact, it was very easy to
reach in two shots—if a player managed to hit a tee shot far
enough to make it over the hill, avoid the looming pines on
the right, keep the drive from going left and being swept
down the contour of a downhill-sidehill descent running
into the woods—all while praying that the ball would
somehow land in the middle of the fairway.

There was no talking now. Each player was within
range to lose or win the match. It was at this moment that
they remembered it was more than a round of golf. In between the downpours and the adventures in crowd control,
there had been moments when each of the golfers had en-
joyed themselves. As if this round counted no more than
one played for a hot dog at the clubhouse or dinner at a nice
restaurant. Golfers often played for nourishment, but this
round was feeding more than hunger. It was feeding life's
necessities. There could only be one winner and the rest
would not merely lose—they would face personal devasta-
tion.

Kevin, having birdied the last hole, claimed the honors
on the tee box, hurried to the tee, and crushed a drive down
the middle

Bob took his time fidgeting more than he had the entire
match. He needed the perfect drive to allow him the perfect
approach shot. He needed to help others. It was all he knew
and all he ever wanted. After a full minute of mind-
numbing shakes, Bob cut through his ball with a wind-
ripping swing. The grabbing pine trees pulled his ball toward their branches and eventually hijacked what could
have been a perfectly smooth flight. The crowd was quiet.
Jeff lazily drove his tee shot in the short grass and Joi
somehow placed a ball in the middle of the fairway without
thinking about what she was doing. Her mind had begun to
wander to thoughts of Monday morning. What would hap-

pen if her plan didn't work? Where could she spend all day Sunday begging for money?

The group moved to the next shots as quiet, concerned gamblers helped Bob find his ball. He found it and punched out into the fairway, sixty yards from the green. The other three all avoided the traps and, with nerves of steel, put three balls on the green. Jeff and Joi had played safe shots to the middle of the green while Kevin—who'd considered himself dead if he didn't win—was going for pin placement suicide. Although the flagstick had been stashed away to the right side of the green, sitting on the edge of a slope, Kevin fired right at it and almost landed another bull's-eye. The crowd burst through its solemn state. Billy filled the air with pumping fists and recognized the strong finish he'd seen his roommate make so many times at Wake Forest. It was often desperation because Kevin rarely got off to a good start, due to his inability to arrive early and warm up properly. Billy told his friend many years ago, *If you ever start thinking with common sense and get to the course on time, you'll drop birdies on the course like geese drop shit.* Just like the birdie he was about to drop here.

Bob chipped up to fifteen feet from the hole—gimmie range for him. He and Joi stood aside after making gut-checking pars, and watched Kevin tap in his second birdie in a row. Jeff missed his par putt and took another twirl on the bogey boogie. There was only one hole left to play and there could be only one winner.

Leaderboard	
Jeff	-
Kevin	-
Bob	-
Joi	+1

Chapter 20
Raindrops Keep Falling on my Fate

L adies and gentlemen," the starter yelled. "As it stands, Mr. Bob, Mr. Jeff, and Mr. Kevin are at even par. Ms. Joi is one over. This is the final hole. Stand please. All quiet."

The gamblers had no concept as to what was transpiring. They had no idea that lives and livelihoods were resting on this game, on the outcome of this one hole. Their concern was focused on excuses to give wives for not having money to eat a nice dinner that night, or trying to hide the new equipment they would buy with the winnings. The tee box was empty as eyes turned to Kevin, who hadn't yet taken his spot.

"Kev," Billy whispered.

"Huh?"

"You're up, buddy. Let's knock it down, get it close, and take it to the house," Billy said, bringing his hands together for applause but making no sound. No one dared make a noise. Nagga wanted to jump, shout, hold up a sign that read "John 3:16." Whatever fans did to make athletes miss field goals or brick free throws, Nagga thought about it. But even he felt the serious tension and decided no risk would be worth helping his player. Not a sneeze, not even a blink of an eye that might shift the wind to the slightest degree. Nagga, like many of the other people watching, held his breath.

Kevin finally claimed his rightful position and stuck his tee in the ground. The circular top of the wooden peg had a small triangular chip missing, ruining its stable diameter. No matter, the ball rested on the tee tilted slightly to the right Billy knew there would be trouble when Kevin had been on the tee box for fifteen seconds and had still not hit the ball.

Kevin did everything right away. Wake Forest was the first school to offer him a scholarship and he'd taken it without even opening mail from other schools. Kristen asked him about marriage the day after they'd graduated. Kevin proposed the next day and they were married the following spring. Had Kristen not insisted on a large wedding, Kevin would have sped down to the courthouse that same day.

Had he been comfortable over the ball, he would have teed off several seconds ago. Billy closed his eyes because he knew what was coming. Kevin drew his club back faster than he had all day, perhaps trying to compensate for the time he'd taken standing over the ball. The club curved around his body, splitting the air and whipping by the ball as it shot off the club screaming to the right. It flew dangerously close to the crowd as it curled over into the next fairway only a hundred yards from the green—the dreaded shank.

Kevin choked the grip of his club, heaved it behind his head, and slammed it into the ground. It made a thud, awakening and killing all unsuspecting creatures below the grass. He yanked the club back again, thudding the ground once more. The thuds continued as he slammed the ground, hammering the tee box like a jackhammer.

"Hey, hey, hey!" Norbert yelled. "This ain't that kinda course, son."

Kevin was disrupted from the tirade and saw the indentations he'd made in the earth. He placed his hands on separate ends of the club and broke it across his knee. With a hurl of strength, Kevin slung one half of the driver into the woods and stabbed the other end into his man-made craters.

"What the hell was that?" a gambler asked.

"Damned if I know. That boy looked like he was making a ceremonial surrender to the golf gods."

"Kevin, whoa! Hey! Calm down, buddy," Billy said as he rushed over to him.

"Careful, sir," the starter said as he shook a disapproving finger in the air. "Advice is not allowed during the match."

"I'm not givin' 'im advice. I'm tryin' to make sure he don't kill hisself," said Billy, walking with Kevin and waving off the watchdog.

"Don't you dare. Kevin, don't even think about quittin' on me. You get your head right and play out this damn hole. You're three shots from making par and I've seen your sorry tail make birdie outta worse spots than this. I swear you quit on me now, I'll kill you. I been there for you and by God you better be here for me."

"Stand please. Quiet," came another bark. Billy and Kevin stopped as Bob smoked his tee shot over the hill. It gained more distance by drawing from right to left. His ball bypassed the hill and kept going left—heading for the slope towards the trees.

"Stand please!" the starter yelled before anyone had a chance to react.

Jeff took his turn and pulled out an iron.

"What the fu—" Nagga began.

The starter snapped his neck at Nagga, demanding total silence.

"You bedda—" Nagga tried again.

"Sir, I'm gonna ask you to stand please and be quiet before I deduct one stroke from your man."

"Huh?" asked one of the gamblers with more money wagered than anyone else. "What the hell rule is that?"

"Sir, I'm gonna ask you to do the same," the starter answered, avoiding a question that had no valid rebuttal. He thought of making up some local rule, but considered the mayhem that might ensue. He simply held his hands high and hoped Jeff would tee off before the next disturbance. Jeff blistered his ball with a tight fade that beautifully turned from left to right until it began tracking for the top of the hill, where it dropped into a sand trap on the right side of the fairway.

Joi was already at the red tees before Jeff's ball landed. She waited for the announcement. The starter gave his order again and Joi wasted no time pumping her tee shot to the top of the hill in the middle of fairway as though she had placed it there by hand.

Kevin, Bob, Joi, and Jeff—crazed, worried, and hopeful—all raced to their resulting shots with the weight of shouldered golf bags burdening the load. The sky was holding its rain, keeping its clouds zipped until it was time for another release. A thundering POW frightened the group. Everyone stooped down as though the bottom were falling from the heavens.

Kevin was first to arrive at his shank. He looked up to the sky, hoping lightning would strike him and end it all. Then he yanked a three wood from his bag like a matador unsheathing a sword. He thought about the slices, the hooks, the mis-hits, the shots too far, the shots too short, the putts he'd missed. He thought about the times he'd choked in college tournaments. Every negative thought, every bad vision he could recall had resurfaced. The gray clouds turned black above him as his head swirled. He seemed consumed by his own personal golf poltergeist. He tried to block out the visions but was only able to replace them with thoughts of his wife. Her demands, her illness, her fate. The world was ending. Kevin was on a bad trip like the ones he'd had at school when youthful stupidity justified chasing No-Doz with 90-proof vodka during final exams. The clouds dropped another roar, this time heavier than the last. Kevin snapped from his illusions. He stood over the ball and aimed where he thought the hole might be. Kevin swung the club as hard as he had pounded the ground after the shank. His body fell forward with the momentum of his swing. The ball was off on some unknown trajectory that no one could see.

Faint rain brushed across the faces of the group. Something was coming. Something bad.

"We need to get off the course!" yelled Skip Breiser.

"Like hell we do!" Billy shouted. "There's no lightning and we're damn near done! Tell your boy to hit the ball and let's finish this thing!"

Everyone had finally reached the top of the hill where Joi stood proudly in the middle of the fairway and Jeff stood in the bunker, not really caring what happened. A few people headed for the woods to help Bob just as he shouted, "I got it!"

"Crap!" Billy said.

"Nope, this isn't mine!" Bob yelled as the loudest roar of thunder slapped the skies and made mice of men. Some ran for trees, while others covered their heads and the rest tried to hold bladders and bowels. "Here it...No, that's not mine either. Jesus, where are all of these balls coming...No wonder," Bob said, giving his everything-is-okay-smile.

"The driving range is adjacent to this hole. What a hoot!" he said. "I thought I'd gotten lucky and...oh willickers," he said, wanting to replace the wholesome phrase with a four-letter burst.

"You got it?" one of his gamblers asked.

"Yeeup. I'm afraid so," he replied as they looked down at his ball hiding behind a tree.

He had only one option with the storm tapping them on the shoulder. Bob punched out a low skidding missile shot that found its way to the fifty-yard marker. The faint drops had become tiny pricks of wet darts on the back of necks and exposed forearms. There was crackling in the skies now and they knew the lightning would be the next performer.

Everyone was in the fairway, standing, panicking, looking at the golfers and the green.

"Hey! Somebody left a ball on the green," said Norbert.

The starter announced, "No they didn't. That is the approach shot of Mr. Kevin."

"Are you kiddin' me?" Billy shouted with jubilation.

"Stand please, all quiet!"

Billy jumped from his cart and pumped a tight fist in the direction of Kevin, who was still under the influence of his poltergeist.

Jeff whacked his iron shot into the darkening air and watched it bounce onto the green and scurry off the back, fifty feet from the hole.

The boom and cackle chorus was almost deafening and the day had been transformed into a sheet of a rain soaking everything and everyone. Joi stepped to the ball, not concerned about the elements. She only concerned herself with perseverance, vindication, and a father's most adamant teaching—finish strong. Joi ballooned her shot into the sky and watched with squinted eyes, blinking every second to keep her vision clear. In between blinks they saw the ball land on the very front of the putting surface and stop. Joi had intended for the ball to release and roll to the middle of the green. Instead she had a twenty-foot putt for birdie.

The population of crazed troopers rushed for the green and finally saw the sky's stop sign. A stream of lightning with electric branches reached down and split the golf course's backdrop of falling darkness.

"Play is suspended. Golfers into the club house," the starter yelled. He was smiling because he'd finally get to execute his evacuation plan. The enthused official had spent many nights devising the plan in between infomercials about revolutionary golf clubs and space-age knives.

"No!" said Kevin. "That lightning has gotta be five miles away. We'll be done before it even gets here."

"The hell it will!" Bucket Hat hollered. "You nutcases stay here if you want to. I'm goin' in the clubhouse." The man's common sense won the crowd over. They all opted for safety over excitement and ran into the building as the golfers and their banks finished out the hole that would change each of their lives.

Chapter 21
The Decision

"What? You lyin' son of a gun! There is *no* way—"
yelled one of the gamblers.

"Norbert, are you tryin' to tell me—"

"If I hadn'tna been there I wouldn'tna believed it either," Norbert replied.

"What on Earth am I supposed to do now?" asked Balding Guy.

"I don't know. I honestly don't know what to tell ya. It could have been worse. You could have lost a thousand dollars or more. I don't know how much you bet. I'll talk to the starter, maybe he can help. You guys are old friends, right?" said Norbert.

"Yeah, but I don't know how friendship is gonna get me out of this one."

Everyone in the clubhouse was complaining or laughing. Some celebrated while others expressed frustration at the outcome. Over four hours of fighting the elements and anxiety had come to this. As the banks made their way into the clubhouse, the gamblers kept asking how could this have happened.

Billy entered after he'd taken his golf cart to the corral. The short walk from the corral to the door soaked him. He shook water from his clothes and wiped it from his face.

"Billy, what happened?" asked a person with money on Kevin.

"Get outta my face," was all he offered.

Nagga came through the door next, his clothes drenched like everyone else's. The water was sucking the excess from his clothes and exposed the outline of his gun. He reached in his pocket and dialed the number of his crew. No one had approached him during the entire match, but people were desperate for details.

"Excuse me," said a Jeff gambler. "How did this happen? I thought Jeff was in a good position."

"Do I know you?" Nagga snapped. "Better yet, do you know who I am? Get the hell away from me!"

Finally the golfers began to emerge and their faces told only of confusion, bitter anguish, regret, and relief.

Kevin came in with his head lowered, his eyes searching the ground for answers. How has this happened? How had his life come to this? How could he remain married to his wife? He sat in a chair and was approached by his supporters.

"Kevin, what happened out there? You were on the green in two."

He looked into their faces and simply shrugged his shoulders. He couldn't answer their questions before he answered his own.

Jeff entered, just as soaked and baffled as everyone

else. His eyes were wide open, stunned with the headlights of reality. He realized that his passive demeanor had cost him the few strokes he'd needed.

"Jeff, is this true? You didn't win?" asked a man with a large wager.

"I guess..." Jeff started. "I guess it was really back on number thirteen. I could have won it back there, but I just couldn't think straight."

Joi walked through the doors, her inverted smile more noticeable than anything else. She removed her hat and revealed the tangled mess of hair the rain had made. Norbert looked at her with raised eyebrows and she responded with a shaking head. Monday morning had never been as close as it was now. She wanted to call her father and ask him what to do. He, just like the money she needed, was gone.

Finally, Skip Breiser and Bob burst through the doors wearing smiles and arms wrapped around the other's shoulder. Bob thought it best to handle the situation with humility and perhaps a bit of humor.

"Well, folks," he said with a gleaming manufactured smile of early morning election results. "I guess you've heard. How about that? A four-way tie! Guess we're gonna have us a good-old fashioned run-off."

Laughs broke through the bewilderment. The gamblers wished they'd stayed for the conclusion and began to wonder how the match would be settled.

"What do we do now?" asked Balding Guy.

Skip replied, "Have a play-off. Nothing else to do, really."

"When?" asked another gambler. "In case you haven't noticed, there's fire and brimstone coming out of the sky."

The starter disappeared into the office.

"We'll just wait it out. As soon as it's done we'll go out and play one more hole," said Skip.

"You got to be crazy," said Nagga as he ended a phone

call. "You think you gon' decide that kinda money on one hole? If we go back out we goin' around the whole track one more time."

"What?" Billy yelled. "You smoke too much of your own stuff. There is—"

"You got one mo' time to say somethin' stupid to me," Nagga said. "Next time I'm gon—"

"Hey guys, settle down. Act like grown-ups, will ya?" Norbert said, walking between the two.

Billy continued, "Nobody in their right mind is gonna go back out there for another four hours and risk gettin' struck by lightning."

"I am," Joi said. "We've got a lot riding on this game and I can't just give it away for one hole. I vote for eighteen more." Norbert glared at his player, accepting her nod and realizing her strategy. Although she'd been the only one to put her ball in the fairway of the last hole, it was one of the longest par fours on the course. Any of the three men could have put themselves in birdie range with a good tee shot. At three to one, she knew her chances were better going around the horn again.

"No way," Billy insisted.

"I gotta agree with the lady on this one," Bob said, thinking he could lessen his mistakes with another shot at the entire golf course. Too much to be gained or lost here."

"That don't make no sense," Billy said, looking around the room for an ally.

"What do think we should do, split the purse?" Jeff asked. If a draw were declared he could beat Nagga without having to win for him.

"Ain't gon' be no splittin," Nagga said, staring only at Jeff. "In fact, somebody's stakes gon' get raised."

"Well...well," Billy was searching. "What if the rain doesn't let up? Then what are we gonna do? Come on people, this is ridiculous!"

"It'll pass and we can play lift-clean-and-place. No problem," Skip replied.

"He does have a point," Norbert said. "At this rate, we may get standing water on the greens and the grounds crew isn't here to take care of it. Although I agree that there's a lot on the line for just one playoff hole. Think about it—at the US Open, sudden death playoffs are eighteen holes," he said, nodding at Joi.

"Make up your damn mind, will ya?" Billy was belligerent. Then Kevin walked up behind him and placed a comforting hand on his back.

He whispered to Billy, "I need this match. Whatever it takes, however many holes. I need it." For the first time Kevin had asked a favor of his friend with a humbled head and shameful eyes. Billy sighed and saw only desperation in his man in need.

"Oh, what the hell. Do whatever you want. Who gives a damn?" he said to the crowd, then turned to Kevin. Quietly he said, "You just remember this when you're out there and things ain't going your way."

"Billy, if I don't get this money, things ain't gon' never go my way."

"We're all agreed?" asked Skip. "What do we do about the weather?"

"I'm not sure," Norbert replied. "We've got no choice but wait and see what happens."

"No need for that," the starter said, appearing from the office. He made his announcement with the diction and command of a platoon leader giving orders. "I've just consulted with another member of a local rules committee at another golf facility. He has informed me that the weather system is indeed large. It is slowing and it's coming from the east. Therefore, it is here to stay. My colleague informed me that the system which is stalled over us merely grazed by his location. My colleague has also informed me that the system's threat forced many players to cancel their recreational outings. Therefore, my colleague has informed me that his facility is willing to accommodate our match." Norbert wondered who the starter was referring to. "Lady and gentlemen, we have no other options as this system will be here for the remainder of the day. If we are to conclude this match we will do so...at Sugar Creek."

As if their next comment was orchestrated, synchronized, and harmonized, all four golfers said aloud, "Oh shit."

Leaderboard	
Jeff	-
Kevin	-
Bob	-
Joi	-

Chapter 22
Pushers Politicians & Presidents

Jeff dodged rain bullets and rushed to the car. He dumped his clubs in the trunk and jumped in the driver's seat when Nagga barged into the passenger's side.

"'Sup, J?" he asked. A sinister smile spread above his chin. "Damn shame we gotta keep playin'. Guess you finally woke up about yo' little brother, huh? Didn't I tell you he was a waste?" Jeff looked at the windshield, slaughtered with spears of water.

"Should have listened to you in the first place," Jeff said.

"You got that right. So, what, you just gon' let him die? See how long I let him live?"

Jeff stared and did not answer.

"That's cold, J. It's the right thing to do, but it's cold.

You ain't got nothin' to play for now, do you?"

"Guess not," Jeff said, using his attitude as a shield against reality.

"You guess wrong."

"Huh?"

"You guess wrong. We ain't about to go over to another course and lose or tie. You got somethin' to play for. I got my money on the line and you got you."

"What you talkin' about?"

"Oh, you don't know? You took your brother's place when you hung up the phone and stopped caring. It's all on you now, bruh. I ain't gonna lose no damn money to that punk. So when you get over there, you take yo' game, yo' best game. Maybe this time you'll play like you got SOME DAMN SENSE! Who you think you playin wit?" Nagga screamed and made forceful finger points at Jeff. His motions rocked the car. "This ain't no joke! You playin' wit *my* money! I'll kill you in this car right now! I don't give a damn about you or yo' brother! You lost my word when you started playin' like you was runnin' the show! I done changed the rules on you, now! So what's up, you want to dog it some more and save me some time!" Nagga grabbed Jeff's neck and shoved the nine-millimeter into Jeff's mouth. The windows had fogged and no one could see inside the shaking car.

"Let me know! Tell me right now and I'll blast you right here! Tell me! You wanna die, nigga?"

Fearful tears of failed misery for his brother's life fell down Jeff's face. He wanted Nagga to pull the trigger so he wouldn't have to make a decision, but he didn't know how long he'd feel the pain of a bullet piercing skin, shattering bone, splashing blood, crushing brain matter, and finally lodging into some lobe that would render him useless.

"That's what I thought. Crying like a punk," Nagga said, withdrawing the weapon. "Next time I talk to you is

gon' be on the eighteenth hole. After that, ain't gon' be no
mo' pep talks."

Kevin had been the first to run out of the Mystery Valley clubhouse when the announcement was made about
Sugar Creek. He'd been given a reprieve and the only thing
on his mind was the driving range.

Bob was a few minutes behind Kevin. He took the turn
into the entrance of the Sugar Creek complex. It was a
long, haunting road with an army of trees on both sides.
Long green oak arms formed a canopy overhead and covered vehicles riding through its narrow portal. The road was
threatening or relaxing, depending on the reason people
traveled it. For some it filled stomachs with queasy knots,
knowing the golf course was waiting to beat them into
oblivion. For others the road was a tranquil escape from all
things outside of the eighteen-hole vacation. But for the
foursome there was nothing to do here except work.

Bob entered the Sugar Creek clubhouse in hopes that he
might sneak a quick bite. He ordered a loaded hot dog and
a soda to ease its travel. There was a table in front a television where the weekend golf tournament was being broad-
cast. He sat and watched as the telecast went to commercial. Skip walked into the club house and saw Bob's face
transform.

An old woman sits staring out of a nursing
home window

A narrators' voice

Do you have an elderly loved one?

A young couple enters the room and the woman smiles

**Would you like to see them protected or
taken advantage of?**

SCENE CHANGE
A uniformed maintenance man comes
home to a stack of bills

Are you a hard-working citizen of DeKalb County?

*A group of men with big cigars are taking large clumps
of money from other men*

**Are you looking for an honest leader or someone
who just plays the game?**

*Camera focuses on well-dressed man standing on
courthouse steps as he begins monologue*

**It's time DeKalb County had a leader with real in-
tegrity. My opponent, Bob Berry, has literally robbed
senior citizens and taken dirty money from known
criminals. Blood money. It's time to wash our hands.
My name is Newt Dorsey and I want to be your next
state representative. I'm asking for your support in the
upcoming primary elections.**

*The candidate is joined on the steps by the elderly
woman and the maintenance man
Paid for by the committee to elect Newt Dorsey.*

Skip and Bob traded stares. Bob wiped his hand across
the table, slamming the food and drink against a wall.

"Bob, it's just..." Skip started.

The words were useless. Bob rushed through the front door, grabbed his clubs, and stomped over to the driving range with the temperament of a newly branded bull. He yanked a driver from his bag and started blasting tee shots into the cloudy sky. One after another, balls left his club and disappeared into a net at the back of the range. His practice became reckless abandonment. Kevin noticed the behavior and approached him.

"You're doing the wrong thing."

"What?" Bob snapped, his civil tone erased by the mudslinging.

"You'll only use that shot three or four times on this course. Wedges win out here. You all right?"

Bob looked at the net where his balls had been transported. He shook his head and turned to Kevin.

"Are you gonna help me or not?"

"What?"

"Look, I gotta make a decision here," Bob said in desperation. I have to do whatever it takes to win. I can promise you that *anything* you need, I can help you get it. Every one of us is out for something more than money. People don't just show up on a Saturday morning and dodge lightning and thunderstorms for a few thousand dollars. There's something else attached to it and don't tell me there's not. I don't need you to cheat for me. I just need a little insurance that it'll be easier for me if things gets tight down the stretch."

"You want me to throw the match? No way."

"I don't care what you do. Cough in somebody's back swing, drop your clubs during somebody's putt, it doesn't matter. But I need to win this match. Lives are depending on it, trust me."

"What makes you think I don't need to win just as bad as you? You don't think I have a life that depends on me winning?"

"Kevin, listen. Unless you have a bomb at your house or you need a miracle performed, I am telling you I can help with whatever your situation is. I mean...tell me what you need, what is it? Money, family problems, health, what? Doctor's appointment was it you said?"

All of the above, Kevin thought to himself.

"What makes you so sure you can help? If you need my help so bad, seems like you can't help yourself."

Kevin stuttered something incomprehensible and Bob plowed on. "Let's just say that I've got connections all over this county. Just about any area you're looking for, I know someone that might be willing to help."

"Might?"

"For instance, let's say you've got a mortgage issue and your house is about to be foreclosed. I've got associates who buy foreclosed houses. I can give them a call, ask them to buy your home after the bank takes over. My associates can sell it back to you at a lower price and we might be able to get you a lower interest rate."

"That's gotta be illegal."

"No, not at all."

"Then why don't people do it all the time?"

"Most people don't have associates who have the resources to buy houses with cash and the philanthropic spirit to help others in their time of need."

"And what's your need?" Kevin asked, sniffing out a hustle.

"That's nothing to be concerned with. I want to help you."

"I *said*, what do *you* need?"

Bob sighed and realized that he'd have to confess for Kevin's buy-in. He tapped his driver on the ground a few times, prolonging the inevitable.

"Let's just say, I need to defend my honor if I'm ever

going the help the world," Bob said finally.

"You need to tell me why you're here instead of answering questions like you're in front of a camera."

Bob was trapped. A common man fighting an addiction had cornered Bob with desperation. The political prowess that he'd worn like his own skin finally shed as he stood pleading for help.

"Friend, at times—"

"My name is Kevin, not friend."

"All right. You got me." Another hefty sigh. "It appears that I've been the victim of self-mutilation. I've cut myself up in more ways than I can imagine. Not literally, mind you, but politically. Most of my life has been spent trying to serve others and maybe I've tried to perfect my method of service instead of just serving."

"I'm not following you."

"I've tried too hard to be the best politician for the people instead of just being for the people."

"What's that got to do with what you need?"

"I've been set up, Kevin. And some of it is my fault. I was always working on my image and it made me vulnerable for attacks and sabotage."

"So the old lady with the checks thing is a set-up?"

"How'd you know about that?"

"Who doesn't know? People call you the Elderly Embezzler."

"Yeah I've heard that one."

"But why do you need all of this money?"

"All of my campaign fundraising is tapped out and I can't seem to get a dime from anyone, so I need this to start an investigation into—"

"Whoa, wait a minute. You can't get money from your people, but you can help me?"

"Sure. I've always been able to influence people to help others. But at this point, until I clear my name, I'm political enemy number one. If I had to I could get you a heart transplant, but I couldn't get anyone to give me CPR if I was dying in their living room."

"How could you get me a heart transplant?"

"I have associates on medical boards and non-profit agencies that help people every day. I recently worked with a health care management firm in order to establish an emergency surgery waiver. It's part of my plan to revitalize America's health care system. The way it's structured is that—"

"What about cancer?" Kevin said.

"Huh?"

"What if I needed surgery for cancer...or something like that?"

Bob looked through Kevin's eyes, trying to determine if it was a confession or simply a hypothetical test. Kevin grabbed his club and took a few short practice swings, disguising his concern.

"Well...if that's what you need, I can...uh...I can certainly do everything in my power to help."

"You don't sound too sure about it."

"Like I said, I've got lots of associates and they help people with less severe problems than cancer. I don't see why they wouldn't rally around a cause such as—"

Bob's promise was cut short by Nagga's arrival. Despite the sign that read NO CARS BEYOND THIS POINT, Nagga flew his shuttle through the gate and stopped in front of the driving range. He wanted to watch Jeff as he warmed up. Instead, he found only Kevin and Bob, chatting. The tinted window dropped and unveiled Nagga's face. He looked at both men and wiped a flat hand across his own neck, gesturing a cut throat. The window ascended and his face disappeared behind the black sheet. Nagga slammed the car in reverse and searched for Jeff elsewhere.

Bob shook his head and without hesitation thought of a

resolution for noise ordinances in public areas. His thoughts were interrupted by a voice. Nagga's gesture was the motivation Kevin needed.

"Bob, I'm in."

Joi had pulled into the parking lot shortly after Bob. She sat in the car for a while, trying to summon the spirit of her father. Joi replayed scenes in her mind when he would give her the valuable lessons. Their family jewels were not those of shining colors, but clumps of wisdom from which pieces could be extracted and consumed whenever spiritual nourishment was needed. As she waded through the voluminous record of her dad's advice, someone knocked on the window.

"Joi. How are you?"

A painful grumble pulled her gut when she saw the face. Unenthused, she replied, "Fine."

"Didn't think I'd run into you out here today. Some of the guys from work came out to practice before the big corporate outing next week. We didn't think the rain would hold off, but we got lucky." Joi didn't respond. "If I'd known you were planning to come out here, we would have invited you to join our threesome. There's still plenty—"

"What do you want?" Joi snapped.

"Excuse me?"

"Yesterday, you tell me that I'm going to either get fired or go to jail and now you're standing here inviting me to play golf. Are you crazy or are you just the devil?"

The president laughed, satisfied that he'd pierced her armor. "Little girl, let me tell you something. I'm whatever you want me to be, but I own you. And Monday morning

I'm trading you in for a better model. Who do you think you are? You don't come into my company and make up your own rules. You women have cried about playing in the Boy's Club for years. Now that we let you in, you're too good to play the game? To hell with you," he stormed on as Joi held onto tears. She'd rather poke her eyes out than let this monster see her cry. "When I asked you in front of my entire staff to play in my foursome, and you said 'Sorry, sir, I've got to get my hair done that day' you sealed your fate with me."

"I took that position to do a job. Not to be shown off like a trophy you'd won at a..." she turned her head quickly as her eyes moistened, ready to spill over.

"You know how many guys in that office would sell their firstborn to play in my group? And you slight me in front of everybody! Well, honey, we don't need your kind at our company. So do me and yourself a favor. Don't—"

A long Mercedes pulled up, gleaming with a fresh wax. The driver sounded the horn as the president turned on his grin and held an index finger in the air. He leaned back down to Joi's window and his executive smile flattened. "Don't even think about walking in that office Monday morning."

Chapter 23
Boot Camp

There was absolutely nothing sweet about Sugar Creek. It was tough, punishing, unforgiving, populated with narrow fairways, saturated with fast greens, lined with trees and bushes, intercepted by creeks—and those were the easy holes. The only salvation for the group was that it played shorter than Mystery Valley.

Eventually, the rest of banks made it over to the course and the crowd followed soon after. No one wanted to miss any more drama and they wanted to ensure that those who had to pay up didn't escape. When the money mob arrived in the parking lot, they were met by the Sugar Creek regulars, seasoned golfers who'd had love affairs with the game for many years. Through trials and triumphs, these men had found unconventional ways of mastering shots. They'd long ago traded the practice of hitting the ball far for hitting the ball close. Some of them spent hours smashing long tee shots on the driving range, but even more of them spent days on the putting green and chipping area. Most wise old men had figured out what mattered most in life, but the Sugar Creek regulars had learned what mattered most in golf.

The regulars used cross-handed grips, half swings, dispsy-do loop follow-throughs, and even a few sliding feet at the bottom of the swing. But also among the group were pockets filled with crumpled cash for regular games while in back pockets they had stacks of crisp large bills just in case a young and ambitious long-hitting visitor strolled through looking to put notches on his belt. As several young guns had discovered the hard way, Sugar Creek school was always open.

Like Mystery Valley, Sugar Creek was a breeding ground for junior talent. The courses were always hospitable to young golfers by hosting tournaments, conducting lessons, and allowing them to spend the day walking the course so that they might grow to love the game and one day give back. Today, however, nothing would be given away—it would be earned.

The regulars chewed the fat with the Mystery Valley mob and learned that there was no action amongst them, but there was plenty of side action on the foursome. They explained what was going on and what had transpired for most of the morning. Once the regulars learned who was playing and what kind of scores were made, they all joined and placed some back pocket cash on their player of choice.

The crowd was now a blob, consuming and swallowing every person it saw. The foursome, the banks, and the Suspender Starter were already at the Sugar Creek starter's booth. The blob rolled over in their direction. They were reviewing events of the last round when their murmuring became talking, and their talking became boisterous. Then they felt the wrath.

"Allll right!" said a man blasting through the door of the booth. You people back there, clam it up! This is a golf course, not a race track! We will have quiet and we will have order. Is that clear?" The man was a towering specimen with bulging biceps. His facial hair had been freshly harvested that morning, just as it had been every morning. A precisely trimmed hairline around his dark neck and over his ears showed the man's immaculate grooming. He stood before the crowd with hands behind his back as he inspected their faces, wondering who would give him trouble.

"You will remain quiet until my superior arrives. At that time he will further instruct you on conduct, order, and most of all, honor. Do I make myself clear?"

The banks and the foursome were confused. "Who is this?" Bob whispered to Skip.

"I don't know," said Skip. "I'm not sure if I should laugh or drop and give him twenty."

"Is there a problem over there?" the starter asked in Skip's direction.

"No. Not at all...sir." Others released a laugh as a golf cart pulled up.

"Lady and gentlemen," the Suspender Starter announced. "This is Mr. Ralph Jackson. I expect you to give him your full attention."

"Thanks." Ralph giggled at the starter's regiment. "How are you, Norbert?"

"Good, Ralph. Thanks for having us."

"I thought it was only one foursome coming over."

"It is. Here's the foursome right here. Those people are the gallery."

"A gallery? Are you kiddin' me? Is it that serious?"

"More than you know."

"Okay, we can handle it," he said, standing on the seat

of his golf cart. "Everyone, if I could have your attention for a quick second. For those of you that don't know me, I'm Ralph Jackson, one of the Sugar Creek golf professionals. We're pretty informal here," he said, noticing everyone turn toward the man who'd been barking commands. "Well, we try to be. Nothing special, just treat the course like it's your own and be respectful of the golfers. I'll just be here as an observer like you. It's been a long day for me, so the rules and decisions and marshalling will be handled by my trustworthy staff member to whom I'll turn things back over. So, if you haven't found out already, this man here...is Sergeant Starter."

"Thank you, Mr. Jackson. People, listen up. For this eighteen-hole match, we will invoke the rules of the United States Golf Association with myself and my counterpart from Mystery Valley as the local rules committee. In case you need a ruling, notify one of us. I have been informed that golfers will be walking for the duration of the round. For those spectators using golf carts, you will be restricted to the cart path only.

"Turn off your cell phones, pagers and other devices that might distract the golfers during play. Do not stand on the tee box nor the green while the golfers are present. Are there any questions at this time?"

The crowd was stunned and quiet. The regulars, accustomed to Sergeant Starter's military manner, simply nodded their heads and grinned. Sergeant Starter ducked into his booth and retrieved a Marine officer's hat turned upside down with four pieces of folded paper.

"I'm going to ask the players to each draw one piece of paper, which will determine playing order for the commencement of play." They all did as instructed and showed one another the papers marked one through four. Jeff was first, followed by Bob, Kevin, and Joi.

"Adhere to the rules I have just set forth and we will

have a good tour of duty. Good luck to you," he said, addressing the players. "Before we tee off we have one last order of business. If you would all please join me."

"The pregame show is longer than ride over here," Bob said to his opponents. "If I would have known we were going to—"

Bob's words were cut short by the Sergeant's blaring baritone voice hurling melodic words into the air. "Oooh say can you seeeee? By the dawn's early liiiight..."

Chapter 24
Jungle Love

The first hole at Sugar Creek was a deceptive tease, a trap door that lead to a haunting misery of holes yet to come, a peace offering for the human sacrifices that waited around the corner. It was straight-ahead 389-yard par four, no bunkers, fairway seventy-five yards wide, small creek to the left, no problem. Each player executed perfect tee shots. Jeff, of course, amazed everyone with a 305-yard drive while Kevin shocked the crowd when he rifled a dead straight shot down the middle of the fairway. Bob made a long putt for birdie and Joi chipped in for birdie, while Kevin and Jeff sank easy birdie putts as well. It was clear that each one had just stepped up the level of play.

An unseasonable cold front had made its way across DeKalb County and the passing thunderstorm crashed with the warm temperatures. The concoction of temperature turmoil began to push slight wind gusts through the trees and across the fairways. Everyone left the first green and began the trek to the second hole, around a corner and underneath an overpass, where eighteen-wheelers zipped by with heavy loads, oblivious to the burdens people walking underneath them were carrying.

"Nice chip back there," Bob said as he strolled next to Joi. "You play any college golf?"

Joi looked around to make sure Bob was talking to her. She said with suspicion, "Bethune Cookman."

"In Daytona Beach. Yes, I know it well. Didn't know they were making ladies as good as you."

"What's that supposed to mean?"

"Nothing. No harm meant. You're just playing beyond my expectations. In fact, I think you should be playing from the blue tees."

"What you trying to say?" Joi snapped. She stopped walking and the crowd passed around them.

"Nothing, nothing at all," Bob said with a coy smile, avoiding eye contact. "It was a compliment, really. Look, Joi...what's your last name anyway?"

"Why? What's with the interview all of a sudden?" Joi asked and resumed the walk towards the next hole.

"Just because we're all trying to beat each other doesn't mean we can't be cordial, does it?"

Joi strolled along as her eyes watched the repeated rise and fall of her feet. She was trying to decipher Bob's strategy. Joi, a master of game gimmicks, was cautious whenever an opponent began a conversation. *I'll play along and eventually figure him out,* she thought to herself.

"Okay, I'll bite. I'm Joi Trottleman."

"What?" This time Bob was the first to stop walking.

"Joi Trottleman. Pleased to meet you," she said, trying to trump the man's attack.

Bob's face was sullen. He was sorry he'd brought up the subject, ashamed that he'd even tried to inflict the mental joust upon her. He was sorry they were on the same course. He turned away from her and asked, "As in James Trottleman?"

Joi stopped. She saw the times of treasured years gone. She was transported to any place but this moment when the ghosts had returned. Then as quickly as the confused hurt came, it left. She replied with as much volume as a broken heart could give, "He was my father."

Bob shuffled his feet and tried not to trip over his own regret. He tried to hurry and catch up with the group, but Joi pulled at his arm. "You knew him?"

"I...I've gotta get to the tee box," he said, trying to look over the crowd. "Looks like Jeff is about to hit." Bob trotted toward the crowd and squeezed his way through them, offering *excuse me* and *sorry* along the way. Joi, knowing she would be last to tee off, took her time, once again wallowing in the revisited grief of her father's death.

The second hole of Sugar Creek was an official welcome to the jungle. A short par five, it offered just enough room for greedy golfers to blast a drive down the fairway and try to put themselves in a good position for eagle, if they could play a draw tight enough to escape the hungry hands of the tree brigade flanking the right side of the fairway, or if they could squeeze a fade by the kaleidoscope of woods and things that hid people, not to mention golf balls, as well as the creek running through it.

If the players could survive those pitfalls, then there was a slight chance that they could find the narrow fairway that eventually widened some 280 yards way from the tee box, which deceptively pointed toward the trees. If a shot survived the first stage of this golf ball torture, there wasn't much more to the hole, except an approach shot over a ten-foot-wide, twenty-feet-deep ditch. If the ball lived long enough to make it over the small canyon, it only had to clear a collection of dips and mounds covered in thick rough in front of a tiny green. Besides those minor obstacles, the hole was easy.

Jeff was on the tee, his tenacity returned. He wound up his steel driving club and ripped a shot straight down the middle. The new spectators watched in awe and proclaimed they had never seen a ball hit that far on this hole.

Bob remembered the blazing start Jeff had made at the beginning of the first round and knew that his first efforts would be his best, leaving much room for a late-round collapse. Bob started shaking, as usual, and eventually launched a fade that clipped an evil branch waving out over the fairway. The ball splattered a few leaves from the branch and lost some of its momentum on its way to a soft descent curling into the fairway.

Kevin's ball was already resting atop the tee before Bob's drive had stopped rolling. The crowd was turning to watch him swing, which he did less than a second later.

"That boy don't waste much time, does he?" a Sugar Creek regular asked. He was a dark gentleman with glazed-over red eyes. Eyes that had seen too little sleep and too many hours at the plant. His voice was deep and resonant. Having retired years ago, his new job was shooting low scores, playing for the occasional ten dollars, and helping out around the course. As always, he was adorned in his trademark purple shirt.

Everyone flashed their heads in the direction of Kevin's ball as it sped to the right for the trees. An instant gust of wind made the trees dance and bend. The wooden thieves reached for the ball. It seemed to take on a life of its own, a life that would be spared from the branches as it started to turn slightly to the left, riding the tail of a tight draw—tight enough to evade the trees and hit the fairway running with forward spin that would land it just ten yards short of Jeff's ball.

"Wooo hoooo!" Billy shouted. He'd seen Kevin warming up on the range and knew the secret formula had been concocted. "It's time to turn it on, brother!" The crowd offered a mixture of laughs and claps.

Joi grabbed a three wood and quickly drove her ball to the left side of the fairway. She put the club in her bag and waited for Bob.

"Did you know my father?" she asked as Bob tried to rush by.

"I...I knew of him, yes."

"What does that mean?"

"It means that...I uh...I knew him."

"How did you know him? Was he a good person?" Joi asked, seeking the repeated validation of her father's greatness.

Bob stopped walking, looked at her face and said, "Of course he was. Why would you ask that? Has someone told you otherwise?"

"No, I'm...you know, just curious."

"I thought I'd seen you somewhere before," Bob said, as he started walking up the fairway again.

"Me? Where? We've never met before."

"I didn't say we'd met. I said I thought I'd seen you before."

"Where?"

"At the funeral."

"You were at my dad's funeral?"

"Of course I was. I owe your dad a great deal. And here you are trying to beat me in a golf match."

"What? How did you know him? How long did you know him?"

"Don't step on your ball," Bob said, pointing to the

ground. He walked towards the creek, staying clear from where Joi would be swinging, and moved as far away from her as he could.

She pulled a five iron from her bag and gave Bob another look, which he did not return. Jeff had noticed the two conversing, as did Kevin.

After a practice swing, Joi hit an accurately placed shot five yards short of the ditch. She bagged her iron and moved towards Bob, who was starting his shake routine over his ball. Many wiggles later, he hit a high arching shot that came to rest at the one-hundred-yard marker. To avoid more of the inquisition, he hurried to where Jeff and Kevin would play their next shot. The crowd was still walking when Kevin swept the ground with a three iron, taking one of his rare practice swings.

"Ten-HUT! Quiet where you be, stand where you are!" yelled Sergeant Starter. "Move and you will be escorted from the premises." Eyebrows were raised and faces were twitched among the crowd, but no one dared move or talk.

Kevin drew his club back, struck the ball, and watched it take off, cutting through the air from left to right. Never rising high enough to flirt with trees or other impending dangers, his ball stayed below the wind's radar. It had plenty of speed and cleared the ditch and the mounds. Finally touching down at the front of the green, it bounced and rolled until it stopped ten feet behind the putting surface. The crowd cheered and Kevin's gamblers jumped with jubilation until Sergeant Starter gave them a glare.

"Damn," said Bucket Hat to no one in particular. "Is he gonna keep us in boot camp the whole round?"

"He'll ease up by the ninth hole," answered Purple Shirt. "He's always wound up real tight the first couple of hours of the day. Wasn't many people out here this morning, so I guess he's just now getting cranked up. He'll settle down...I hope."

Jeff prepared to match Kevin's feat. He took an unusually long stare at the target and finally splattered a large divot behind his ball, which launched high and long. The ditch and the mounds were no threat to Jeff. His only concern was the yardage he'd estimated. When the ball returned to earth, it made a pitch mark on the green and with a small bounce stopped eleven feet from the hole.

Again, the crowd erupted. They looked at the Sergeant, seeking permission to celebrate. The regimented regulator gave them a furlough by turning his head away as they whooped and hollered even louder. The banks of Jeff's opponents also offered light applause, except Billy, who remained as venomous as he'd been all day.

Bob was at his ball waiting, smiling at the marvelous shot and waiting for the crowd to calm. The Sergeant hushed them all with a command, this time less demanding, allowing Bob to shake away. He made a crisp sweep at the ball and heard his own cheers when the ball landed five feet from the cup. The skill level was increasing and so was the pressure. Joi responded with a half swing of her sand wedge over the ditch and mounds, two feet from the cup. The crowd was stunned. Four great shots on a hole that made most players throw their score cards away.

Bob seemed to rush off in the wind gusts as Joi turned to find him and finish the conversation. She saw him walking the bridge that crossed the ditch and led to the green. He and the other guys had begun their walk to the putting surface as soon as Joi hit her ball. She was the last to arrive. Then came the crowd, which watched in awe as Kevin chipped a shot that he would convert into a birdie. Jeff sank an eagle while Bob and Joi both dropped a birdie each. The Jungle had just been tamed.

Joi, focused on other matters now, shadowed Bob to the next tee box.

"Tell me how you knew my father. What'd he do for

you?"

Bob, frustrated with guilt, looked and Joi and relented, "You don't need to know and I really don't want to tell you."

Leaderboard	
Jeff	-3
Kevin	-2
Bob	-2
Joi	-2

Chapter 25
Treason

Each member of the foursome hit the fairway on the next hole. A par four that was a trip to Mars and back. They had shots scattered to different places in the narrow fairway, with the exception of Joi and Bob. She'd made sure that her ball would be near his, giving her an excuse to walk with him.

"How can you tell me what I don't need to know about my own father?"

"You're not gonna let this go, are you?"

"Why should I?"

"Because you're obviously out here for something your father did or didn't do."

"What's that supposed to mean?"

"What's your story? Owe somebody money? Gambling

debt? House in foreclosure? Everybody here's got a problem. What's yours?"

"What does that have to do with my father?"

"Everything, I'm willing to bet."

Joi watched Bob carefully. She tried to keep from tripping over her own steps.

"I asked you how you knew my father."

"I knew him the way most people knew him."

"Meaning?"

"He came into my life when I needed him and then he was gone after his job was done...or so I thought."

"Listen, don't you stand there and try to tell me that my dad helped you with some kind of scam 'cause I'll—"

Bob laughed. "A scam. You can't call what James Trottleman did a scam. That's a joke. Hit your shot," Bob said, as they approached Joi's ball. Hers was the furthest away from the green. The red tees were separated from the men's tees by only a few yards on this hole and Joi was left with more than two hundred yards to the green. The crowd stopped to watch and Joi's long turning shot brought nothing but silence as it bounced onto the cart path and disappeared from everyone's sight. Joi kept watching, hoping the ball would reappear and roll into the fairway. She never saw the white speck trickle into the green field and realized Bob was getting away.

"What kinda scam did you con my father into?" she asked, trotting up behind him.

"You've got it all wrong, Joi. I didn't con your father into doing anything. He did what he did of his own free will."

"Stand where you are, quiet all over!" the Sergeant shouted to everyone, but especially at Joi. Bob gave her a sly smile and gestured in the commander's direction.

Bob did his hokey-pokey for a while and then launched a laser-guided shot towards the green. The ball stopped a few inches short of the surface. Moments later, Kevin and Jeff placed well-executed shots to the middle of the green.

Joi was still tailing Bob. "What did he do? I need to know what he did," she said, almost begging. "My dad wouldn't have done anything wrong without good reason. What was it?" She grabbed his arm and lightly tugged him.

"Joi, trust me—you don't need to know. Now just—"

"I want to know! Tell me!" she yelled. Bob looked at the crowd and noticed that everyone was gawking at the disturbance.

Bob waved and smiled in their direction. "Little competitive banter going on over here," he said.

"You need to calm down, Joi," Bob said quietly.

"And you need to tell me what my father did."

"Go hit your ball," Bob said, pointing at the small cluster of men standing in the pine straw and looking at the ground.

"Tell me what I want to know."

"Joi, trust me, you don't need to know. Now, go hit your ball before you get a penalty. Then you won't be able to get yourself out of whatever trouble you're in."

Joi looked at Bob, then at the crowd waiting for her. She walked toward the gathering and glanced back at Bob to see if his expression had changed. She finally crossed the fairway and dropped her golf bag on the cart path before stepping into the pine straw to check her lie. One more look at Bob's face, which hadn't twitched or moved since she left him. She retrieved her trusty sand wedge from the family of clubs and flopped her ball out of the pine straw over a bunker and onto the green, leaving herself an easy par putt.

Bob was left with a forty-foot chip that skimmed by the hole. He tapped it in and headed for the next hole. Jeff followed suit while Kevin sank yet another birdie.

Bob was relieved that the next tee box was just a few feet away, giving him an opportunity to elude Joi's piranha press conference. Kevin continued his quiet attack. Billy was quiet. He recognized the focus and determination in Kevin's attitude. He had the same look and stride he'd possessed when he won the ACC championship. Kevin had come back from a five-stroke deficit to take the title. And here on this windy afternoon, he had the same swagger, the same gritted teeth, and was slowly approaching the same low score. Kevin quickly struck another perfect drive down the middle of fairway of the fourth hole, a long par-five dogleg, bending to the left three hundred yards away from the box. Had it not been for the bothersome breeze, his ball would have reached the corner of the hole, leaving him a straight shot to the green, which was protected by more of the snake-like creek and a sprawling tree older than the golf course itself.

Jeff matched Kevin's drive with a one iron. The low trajectory escaped the increasing gusts and hit the fairway like a rock skipping along a pond. Much to his gamblers' delight, Jeff's ball did reach the bend. After Bob and Joi hit drives, once again, to similar locations, the inquisition resumed.

"I wanna know what he did and I'm gonna make this match hell for you if you don't."

"You're James's daughter all right. He was a bulldog too."

"What did he do? Quit jerkin' around."

"Joi, I don't know what you're looking for. The man was nothing more than a volunteer."

The dip in her eyebrows disappeared and rushing blood slowed its tirade through her veins.

"Huh?"

"He and I were volunteers on a campaign for Johnny Isakson."

"Who?"

"Johnny Isakson. He ran for governor in 1990 against

Zell Miller. You've heard of Miller, right?"

"Yeah."

"Your dad and I worked for the other guy."

"Why?"

"You know...I'm not sure why I was there. I was young and energetic and Miller had all the help he needed. Guess I've always been an advocate for the underdog. Helping those who need it the most."

A whirlwind of dust and twigs bounced down the fairway. Everyone covered their eyes until the gust passed.

"Your dad was there because he was an absolute jewel. Your dad was a character. Every year up until that point, he'd voted Republican because your grandmother always contested that Lincoln freed the slaves. He ever tell you that?"

"No," Joi said, still afraid that Bob was about to besmirch her father's name.

"We talked for hours after we'd leave that office. You were away at college. Freshman year, I bet. We talked about life and politics, love and politics, money and politics. And that's when he dropped it on me."

"What?" Joi could feel the blood rushing again.

"He asked when I was going to run for governor. Saw right through me. He gave me ten reasons right there on the spot why I was supposed to help people. I mean, I knew all of them, but I'd never shared them with anyone before. In one week your father taught me how to fulfill my life and change the world. I'm sure he told you the same thing. God, that man was so brilliant. Every day he told me, *Sustain yourself by doing what you love—Love those who cannot do for themselves—Do what you're supposed to do instead of what you want to do.*

"How many times did you hear that?" Bob asked with a chuckle. "I can just imagine the wisdom he imparted in you. That's why I'm surprised you're out here. What kinda trouble are you in?" He waited for her response, but instead only received a face of internal defeat.

"Listen," Bob said and exhaled a huge wind of his own. "I want to help you." He began the same speech he'd given Kevin on the range. "Whatever it is that brought you out here, I can help you with it. I just need a little hel—"

"Hey!" Billy yelled at the two. "Are you gonna give her advice the whole round or just on the front nine? What the hell is this?" he said, giving Norbert a pointed look.

Joi quickly separated from Bob. She suddenly realized how she must have looked to the others, hanging on to Bob's coattails for the last three holes. As she dropped her bag and pulled out a club, she noticed Jeff's folded arms and lowered brow. Kevin's hand was on his hip and he os-cillated stares between her and Bob.

Her next shot was quick and unrehearsed. The ball floated too far past the bend of the dogleg and stopped be-hind the giant oak. Bob saw her mistake and avoided it by plopping a high shot with a soft drop one hundred yards from the green, away from the tree and a good distance away from the creek.

Jeff and Kevin continued to play like men possessed. They both placed approach shots near the green and missed the putting surface, but with a chip and putt, two more birdies were all but guaranteed. Joi and Bob were being slowly annihilated.

The words Bob had spoken numbed Joi's senses. *Do what you're supposed to do instead of what you want to do.* She sauntered over to her ball and stood there for a few seconds, wondering what to do. Not about the shot, but about her life, the money, and the remainder of the match. Her father, even in death, was trying to emphasize lessons she'd disregarded.

The shot was impossible but she wanted to try anyway. Her best option was to chip the ball near the front of the creek and then try to make another shot near the hole. She could then take one putt and escape with a well-earned par. However, if she hit the ball high enough to clear the towering tree, it would surely land on the green and give her a chance to make a birdie and get herself back in the game.

Joi yanked a nine iron from her bag and clipped blades of grass with practice swings. She looked up and estimated a distance that would clear the trees' highest point.

"Hope she don't think she gon' clear that tree," Purple Shirt said.

"Looks like she's gonna try," Bucket Hat replied.

"Never make it," said another Sugar Creek regular.

She made one more practice swing and tried to replace thoughts of her father's words with thoughts of her swing: keep the body quiet, don't rise up in the downswing, don't force the club, easy tempo, don't release wrists too early, and finally the worst thought possible—don't hit the tree. It was the mind's subconscious golf demon. If a negative thought could creep into the thought process of a golf swing, it would secrete the imposing vision through the brain, into nerves, and over the muscles. Ultimately, golf swing paralysis would set in. At that point, no matter how hard a person tried, the swing was ruined.

Joi knew the feeling and realized it was happening as soon as she started her back swing. Nothing felt right; the demon had taken over and would only be exorcised by a terrible shot. Her feet were moving, her hands felt awkward, her shoulders were turning too slow, her head was moving, her entire body was swaying. The back swing was destroyed and the downswing was hurting as a result.

Her wrists unlocked too early, she was standing up while trying to swing, her left foot slid to the front, her hips didn't turn. For a millisecond, Joi forgot how to play golf. It was just long enough to kill her already-ailing swing. As the inevitable meeting of grooved steel and dimpled sphere occurred, dirt exploded behind the ball and stole the momentum needed to clear the tree. Yet it still rose high despite her disastrous combination of physics and psychology. The crowd looked on as the ball kept climbing and rising. It scaled the sky with futile hope that miracles could happen without the proper prayer. The ball was halfway to the tree top when the sporadic breeze returned, collapsing curls of air pressure changes around the object, ballnapping it and whisking it away into the doom of leaves, branches, and bird nests. Within the confines of the tree, Joi's shot became a foster ball bouncing from one home to the other. It clunked around in the tree, falling faster every second and then emerging into sight, only to drop straight down and end its adventure in the creek.

"Didn't learn *that* from your dad," Bob said as he walked by Joi and headed for the bridge over the creek. Staring at the ditch that held the creek, Joi was delusional, hoping that the ball was rattling and bouncing on rocks and would soon spring out of the abyss and land safely on the other side. Eventually, she realized what had happened and what was going to happen. She was going to make a bogey at best and drop three shots behind the leader.

With two more birdies, a par, and a disastrous bogey, the group followed the crowd over to the fifth hole.

"Is that why you're out here? Because you didn't listen to your father?" Bob asked. He stayed behind with Joi as she slumped over, her golf bag increasing her burden.

"Go to hell," she mumbled.

"So I'm right, aren't I?"

"If you're right then why are you out here?"

"Because I listened to him. I don't know what he preached to you, but his message to me was always help people at all costs. It's what he told me I was supposed to do. Joi, your father put me on this path to change a county and a one day change a nation. Had it not been for your father, I'd still be waiting to turn 50 before I ran for any significant office. Your dad's mission on this planet was to guide people into their own mission. Problem is, he was damn good at it. Before this conversation started, my mission was to win this match and that's why I'm done talking to you."

"Wait. You said whatever I needed you would—"

"Who's in charge here? Or are we just changing the rules with each hole?" Billy was livid. "Those two have been yakking their heads off for the past twenty minutes and nobody's said anything. I'm about two seconds away from gettin' a lawyer on the phone and don't think I won't tie you up in legal fees for the next year. Somebody better get this circus under control and do it quick!"

Ralph Jackson, who was standing next to Norbert, asked, "Is this guy for real?"

"The prick has been crying all day," said Norbert. "His boy is starting to break away and he's still complaining. I'd keep him happy if I were you."

Ralph did so by giving Sergeant Starter a nod, and he walked over to Joi and Bob.

"I need to speak with your two privately for a moment," he said with crossed hands behind his back.

Joi began, "For what? We were just talking about—"

"Don't you eyeball me, young lady. Don't think just because you're playing from the heifer tees, I won't penalize you just as hard and fast as the bulls on this ranch. Now, I don't want to see you two so much as breathe the same airspace until we make it to number eighteen. I don't know what you've been talking about, but what I do know is that it ain't good for morale. And I won't tolerate any dissention in the ranks. From across the battlefield, I can't tell if you're giving each other advice or if you're trading war stories. Do I make myself clear?"

"Sir! Yes sir," Bob said with a mocking salute and sly

grin which the Sergeant did not return. Instead, he looked at Joi and reemphasized his order.

"Do I make myself clear?"

Joi answered with an irascible tone, "And what if I need to ask him something unrelated to golf?"

"Unless you wanna be disqualified, you'd better say it using Morse Code."

Sergeant Starter's commands hushed all four golfers and most of the crowd for the next three holes. The silence forced each of them to concentrate more on their individual play and less on strategy. The scores had not changed since Joi's debacle on the par-five fourth hole.

Fighting the wind, they'd begun missing fairways, hitting bad approach shots, and missing short birdie putts. Holes five through seven had been nothing more than a clinic of how to scramble to save par. Not one of them had played a flawless hole in the last half hour.

Jeff was fearful that if he continued this way, Kevin could easily take the lead—or worse, run away with it. Kevin was concerned that there was no way Bob could be held off if he turned into the putting machine he'd been in the first round.

Bob was hoping that he hadn't given too much inspiration to Joi, encouraging her to make a come-from-behind charge.

And Joi was concerned that she'd spent too much time building her father's legacy rather than learning from it. Over the past three holes, she'd made each shot without thought. Joi was simply swinging the way she'd been taught her entire life. For the first time, she realized, everything her father had taught about the golf swing was permanent. She'd already absorbed every possible lesson about the golf swing and that's when his last lesson, *Golf imitates life*, finally made sense. Joi thought to herself, *He gave me golf because it would be here to guide me after he was gone. Why am I out here losing to these...losers?* Then she mentally returned to the course, the match, and her destiny.

"What happened to your teammate?" Kevin asked Jeff after everyone hit tee shots on the eighth hole.

Jeff looked around for the field commander. "I should ask you the same thing," he replied.

"I'm not the one that's been playing with the enemy. And it looks like she's turned on you."

"If that's the case then your buddy has turned on you, too," Jeff said.

"Hell, that palm-greaser wasn't never on my team."

"So you admit you do have a team?"

"Huh...no I...er uh...How can we have a team on a individual stroke play match?"

"I don't know. I'm sure you and Bob worked out the details while you were warming up on the range."

"Huh?" Kevin said, surprised he knew about the meeting.

"Huh, hell. You think nobody saw that?"

"We were just talking about—"

"Well, why weren't you talking about it at Mystery Valley? Why did you wait until you knew how hard it was to win the match to talk about whatever you were talking about? Nagga couldn't wait to tell me that you two were in each other's face."

"Don't give me that. You've been chasing that girl's tail since this morning. You think I don't know the Two Strangers Hustle or the Guy-Girl Game. I made a living in Florida inventing hustles. So don't act like I'm the only one who's done some soul selling."

"Man, you bedda get outta my face. You talkin' to the

wrong person. Look at your partner. He's already left you."

"Yeah, he left with your golf hooker. She just goes along with whoever comes along."

"What did you call her? You don't even know that lady. You need to—"

"You fellas gonna play golf or do we need some boxing gloves?" Norbert asked, zooming up to the men in his golf cart. "If I were you, I wouldn't keep this up. Seems to me the Sergeant is looking for a reason to flex his muscle. At this point, nobody's taking up for anybody. Know what I mean?"

"Yeah, whatever." Jeff said, as he waved off the advice and headed for his ball.

Kevin said nothing, but looked at Norbert from head to toe and then walked away himself. As Kevin headed for his ball, he heard the familiar sound of rhythmic vibration inside his golf bag. It was the sound when he'd been on the course too long, or when he'd missed yet another commitment to have dinner with friends or make the nine o'clock movie.

Once, the vibration preceded a voice screaming that a mouse had invaded their kitchen and he was to get home immediately or call a realtor to sell the house. On another occasion, the vibrations bounced around in his bag for sixteen holes until he finally answered. To his surprise, the caller on the other end requested that he look behind him so that he could see her sitting in her car on the road behind the tee box. Unfortunately, it was the last tee box he'd stand on that day as Kristen demanded that he get in the car so they could make it to dinner at his mother-in-law's. They were already an hour late. Since that vibration, he'd always answered the calls immediately.

Sergeant saw Kevin answer the cell phone and yelled across the fairway. "What in God's name do you think you are doing, mister! This is a golf match, not a psychic hotline! You will turn that thing off or I will penalize you so hard, you'll think I was the marriage tax! Do I make myself clear?"

"It's my wife!" Kevin yelled back.

"I don't care if it's Jesus calling on the main line telling you where to buy front row tickets for the Rapture. You will turn that phone off, or I'll turn it off for you!"

Kevin waved off the Sergeant and disappeared into the woods with his phone.

"Why, that little bucket of worm piss," the Sergeant said to his suspendered counterpart. "That player will be assessed a one stroke penalty if he does not play his ball in two minutes."

"Hello," Kevin said into the phone.

"My tumor is malignant. I'm gonna die."

Leaderboard	
Jeff	-4
Kevin	-4
Bob	-2
Joi	-1

Chapter 26
Big Stupid Stakes

"What! Who told you that?"

"Does it matter? It's going to happen and my life hasn't been worth anything."

"Wait a minute. Why're you saying this? What's happened?"

"What do you think happened? The doctor called with the biopsy results."

"What did he say?"

"Kevin, did you hear what I said? I have a malignant tumor."

"Yeah, but what does that mean?"

"I have cancer, Kevin! What do you think it means?"

"I don't understand. I thought you could have a surgery or something."

"How in the hell can I have a surgery when you've pissed away all of our money and canceled our health insurance?"

"But I was gonna—"

"You're always *gonna* do something. Why don't you go—"

"No, honey. Wait. Listen. I've got something going right now. Just find out how much we need for the surgery. See if they'll let us pay a percentage or if we've got to pay it all up front."

"What does that mean? You've got something going? Are you gambling? Are you betting my life on a card game?"

"No, not at all. It's nothing like that. But if it pans out, we'll be okay. I swear."

"Kevin."

"Yeah? I need to go."

"You've killed me."

"What? No! Hold on! Wait!"

"What the hell is goin' on?" Billy asked as he sped up to where Kevin had entered the woods. "You're about to get a penalty stroke. Get your tail in gear and hit your damn ball!"

Kevin waved off Billy with the same disrespect he'd given the Sergeant.

"Hello? Honey, you still there?" Kevin looked at the screen of his phone. The word *wife* had been replaced by *call ended.* He was quiet for a moment, unable to move.

Billy leapt from his cart and walked toward Kevin.

"Don't forget that you came to me on this deal and it's my money on the line here, not yours."

"Do you wanna play the rest of the round or you gonna get out of my way?" Kevin replied. His eyes were watery and red. He marched past Billy and snatched a club from his bag. The Suspender Starter was looking at his watch counting down. He was the unofficial golf shot clock. The timekeeper held his hand in the air and bent his thumb towards his palm followed by the remaining fingers.

"Three—two—one," he counted.

Before his hand became a fist, Kevin's ball had already landed—in the creek. He rattled off a profane cadence of shouting. He cursed his wife. He swore at himself. He damned his game. Walking to the creek to take the painful medicine of a penalty drop, he began thinking of ways to cheat. His victory had been important before but now it was mandatory. Kevin thought of giving himself better lies in the fairway by rolling the ball with a tap of his foot when no one was looking. Maybe he could mark the ball on the putting surface and inch it closer it to the hole when he replaced the ball with his marker. *The risk was too great*, he thought to himself at first, but not as great as risking his wife's fate.

Each player made par except Kevin, who made his first bogey of the round. As Bob placed the flagstick back into the hole, the wind ripped through the vinyl square as the number eight flapped with the rhythm of fleeing wings. The crowd rushed to next hole ahead of the golfers.

"Everything all right?" Bob asked Kevin, who was sulking behind the group. Kevin answered him with a quick jerk of the head and crooked smirk. "Hey, what's wrong? You're still okay. Doing great. All we have to do is—"

"Screw you, I'm playing for myself," he snapped. Get that little chocolate bunny to help you."

"Huh? What is that about?"

"You heard me. Don't think I ain't been watchin'. Damn politician. Do you even know how to be honest anymore? I mean, have you always been a liar or did you practice it when you wanted to run for office?"

"I resent that."

"So what? You expect me to help you and I'm a few

strokes away from taking the lead."

"Don't get cocky. Just because you've have a few good holes doesn't—"

"A few good holes! Go to hell! I'm playing my ass off and my wife's at home with can—You son-of-a..." the watery eyes returned and forced Kevin to walk away before Bob saw him come undone.

"I'll help you!" Bob said to Kevin's back as he hurried to next hole.

At the ninth hole everyone stood around talking to each other, wondering what the Sergeant was saying to a maintenance crew member who was on the green when they arrived. He'd started twisting his hole-cutting tool into the green just before people had turned the corner. Ralph Jackson joined the conference, and after a short deliberation, they returned to the group.

"Folks, I'm sorry," Ralph yelled to the crowd. "It seems our crew member thought no one was on the course and wanted to get an early start on tomorrow's tournament preparation. He's plugged the hole for today and he's almost done with the new one, but he's got another fifteen minutes or so before the hole is playable. What we—"

"Nooo," grumbled the crowd.

"They'll be cold by then," said Purple Shirt.

"That's too long," yelled Balding Man.

"Unacceptable," replied Billy.

"Done lost yo' damn mind," Nagga added, awaking from his resignation of protests.

"Hold it. Hold on," Ralph said. "I was going to suggest that we move to the tenth hole and make this the last hole of play since it's just one fairway over from the eighteenth hole. Unless anyone has any objections, I'm sure the rules committee would approve."

The Sergeant and Suspenders both gave very royal and official nods with folded arms.

"Any objections?" Ralph asked.

Jeff led the way by placing a five iron back into his bag, throwing the straps over his shoulders, and pounding his feet in the direction of the tenth hole. Before anyone had time to think, complain, or debate, the other three golfers were on Jeff's tail.

Everyone crossed the first fairway and made it over to the tenth hole—a slight dogleg right with woods lining both sides. Jeff grabbed a three iron and hit his ball to the 150 marker. Kevin rushed behind him without a practice swing and whipped his club from right to left. He tried to maneuver the ball through the chute of trees and wrap the ball around the corner. It would have left him a short hundred yards to the green—if he hadn't turned the ball too far right. It deviated from Kevin's intentions and kept turning right until it disappeared just beyond the trees.

Joi's chest heaved with relief and Bob turned his head with raised eyebrows. *He'll need my help*, Bob thought to himself. They both followed the two previous shots with good drives of their own.

"I think it came back out," Joi said to Kevin as they headed to their drives.

Kevin's head jerked in her direction and he gave her a smirk before saying, "Don't even think about it."

"Huh?"

"You tryin' to get in bed with everybody out here before the round is over? Tryin' to cut our hair off like Delilah?"

"Excuse me?"

"You started out with Jeff. You did Bob a few holes back, and now it's my turn in the barrel, huh?"

"I don't know what you're talking about, but I'm just trying to help you by—"

"Everybody wants to help somebody out here, don't they? If there's so much damn help out here, why is everybody in trouble? What's your problem? Owe your pimp money?"

"I know you didn't just call me a ho', did you?" Joi stopped her stride. She stretched her neck, ready to roll it with virulent sass.

"I'm not the one that's been gettin' cozy with everybody in the foursome," Kevin said. He raised his voice and kept walking while Joi stood in shock. She thought of the epiphany about her father's teaching Bob had revealed and realized that her father had prepared her even for this.

"You know what?" she said, jogging and catching up to Kevin. "I oughta bust yo' head just 'cause I used to roll like that. But instead I'm just gonna get in yo' tail for the rest of the match."

"Please. If you weren't playin' from the red tees you'd be a bigger joke than you already are."

"Don't be mad at me because of the golf rules. Besides, from where I'm standing, we've been hitting the same shots into the green for most of the day and you were the one that got laughed at on the last—"

"Shut up, okay? Just shut up. I've got more things to think about than some slut who's out here for a charity case."

"Ain't nobody no damn charity case."

"No? Then shut the hell up and bet your own money. Five hundred for the best score on the next hole."

"Huh?" Joi said, stunned at the challenge.

"That's what I thought. Charity. A damn help-the-hookers golf-a-thon."

"No, prick. What I meant was why wait until the next hole? Five hundred on this hole."

"Done. Who gives a damn?" Kevin replied in haste. He walked down the middle of the fairway then quickly realized that his ball was in the woods.

After the last ball dropped in the cup, there were three pars, one bogey and a five-hundred-dollar debt.

"Cash only," Joi said as they walked off the green. A few people in the crowd overheard the remark and laughed, thinking she was gaining confidence and predicting a win. "I don't know you well enough to take a check and you seem a little shady."

"Screw you," Kevin said. "Double or nothing."

"What?"

"No confidence?"

"It's a par three coming up," Joi replied.

"And?"

"I've been killing them all day."

"So what. It's a grand or nothing."

"You sure?" Joi asked.

"Are *you* sure? If I hadn't hit the errant tee shot on the last hole, I would've been puttin' for birdie."

"If that's the case, you would've been puttin' for birdie on most holes today. That's all you been doing is hitting errant drives."

Kevin grimaced at the insult. "A grand for the hole and another five hundred for the closest tee shot to the pin."

"You've got a problem," said Joi.

"You're the one with the problem. I'm not giving you a dime unless you double down on the stakes. Take it or leave it."

"Not because of the threat, but because you're that arrogant and stupid enough to do it. I'll take your money. But if you—"

"What's with all this yappin'?" Billy asked. He met the two as they approached the tee box.

"Your boy's got a problem," Joi answered.

"Looks like everybody you talk to has a problem," said Billy.

"You just make sure he gets me my fifteen hundred after this hole."

"What fifteen hundred?"

"Ask him about the side bet."

Billy's neck twisted towards Kevin. "Tell me you're not that stupid," he said.

"Give it a rest, Billy. If I'd hit the fairway on the last hole I'd be—"

"Puttin' for birdie. I know. Heard that so many times I almost started believing it again. Don't think that I'm paying for—"

"Last warning!" Sergeant yelled. "This. Will. Not. Continue. One more slow play and somebody's dropping down and giving me a disqualification. Am I clear?"

Jeff laughed and wondered if Joi was still implementing tactics, or looking for other teammates. He picked some blades of grass out of the earth and tossed them in the air. The blades disappeared as soon as they were released in the swift wind. He decided on a four iron to fight the ghostly gusts. Bob did the same and the two were safely on the green.

Kevin hurried to his address position only to back away when the strong breeze floated debris across his ball and threw him off balance. He'd missed his rhythm pattern. There was indeed a routine to his jackrabbit play. While most golfers took time visualizing the shot, taking a few practice swings, aligning with the target, mentally making a good swing, and then finally swinging the club, Kevin's routine was to step to the ball, stop breathing, swing, start breathing. It was his way of committing to a task. First there was a quick death and the only resuscitation was achieving the goal. There was no time for wavering, thinking of other options, or changing his mind. When his impulsive ways took over, he couldn't stop himself.

After he'd been distracted from his routine, Kevin wasn't sure how to start over. He'd never done it. He took a step to the ball, but quickly backed away again. He tried to approach it from a different angle and walked away again. Then he took five steps back from the ball until he was out of the tee box. The others looked on with confused faces. Kevin walked up to the ball as if it were the first time he'd stepped onto the tee box.

Once over the shot, he held his breath, swung, and started breathing again.

"Wind's gonna get it," someone from the crowd said, as everyone watched the ball ascend and dance in the sky.

"Not enough club," another person said.

Kevin hadn't been paying attention when Jeff grabbed a bigger club to battle the wind. His ball continued to rise until it reached the only apex the elements would allow. It paused in mid-air as if it were being rejected. An invisible hand of blowing streams trapped the ball and slapped it from the sky. His dead-straight shot began hurling back toward the ground.

"Better hope that clears the creek," Purple Shirt said.

Kevin looked at the ball, then the creek. He tried to gauge the distance while fighting the discomfort in his stomach. The torture ended when the shot landed safely on the other side of the creek. But he'd missed the green by fifteen feet.

Joi gave a degrading *tsk, tsk, tsk* as she walked by him on her way to the red tees.

With delight and confidence, she pulled a three iron from her bag, teed up, aligned her body slightly to the left of the target, positioned the ball near her back foot, started her back swing, made a half shoulder turn, and cut through the ball with a steady tempo. The ball peeled through the air with a low flight teasing the wind.

"Knock-down three iron," said Bucket Hat. "Headed right for the flag."

Joi's accurate shot fell to the green and bounced its way back near the flag and rolled straight for the cup. The gamblers and spectators began yelling.

"Oh! Oh! Oh!"

"Go ball! Go ball!"

"Get in the hole!"

A protest of wind rushed through, blowing off hats and rippling through pants and shirts. It stopped Joi's ball five feet from the hole. The crowd cheered and clapped for the gale-fighting feat. Joi posed in her follow-through position, hoping the ball would roll further and disappear. It did not and she turned to the admirers. Joi waved, then winked at Kevin.

The hole had quickly become a useless fight for Kevin. Despite his pitch shot that stopped two feet from the hole for a tap-in par, Joi hadn't missed a putt shorter than ten feet all day and this hole would be no different. Jeff and Bob continued their par clinic, while Kevin's missed green and par save cost him fifteen hundred dollars in the face of Joi's superb birdie.

Everyone headed for the twelfth hole. Kevin was fiddling with the flagstick, waiting for Joi to walk by. She allowed a vengeful grin to invade her game face, which Kevin quickly wiped away when he gave her a cold stare and said without blinking, "Closest to center of the fairway and best score gets four grand on the next hole. Let's go."

Leaderboard	
Jeff	-4
Kevin	-2
Bob	-2
Joi	-2

Chapter 27
Golfer's Anonymous

"So that's your problem, huh?" Joi asked Kevin. They were walking the fairway of the next hole. Joi was walking to her ball, in the center, and Kevin's was near the left side cart path.

"Double up on closest to the hole for six grand. You in or out?" Kevin said, never looking at her.

"That doesn't make sense."

"What? You can't add?"

"No, you jerk. It doesn't make sense that you're out here trying to solve your gambling addiction by gambling."

"Screw you. I ain't addicted to gambling."

"Oh really? I'm sorry. Then what you really meant back there was four bags of crack instead of four grand? 'Cause you're addicted to something."

"Hey!" a voice boomed from behind them. They both panicked. The Sergeant had given his last warning and neither of the two could afford a penalty stroke at this point, or worse, disqualification. They tried to separate quickly, but bumped into each other.

"Hey!" the voice rang out again.

"When he comes over, tell him I was helping you look for your ball," Joi said.

"Hey! Stand back. He's punching out!" said Purple Shirt. "Wait, that's okay. Wasn't his ball."

Jeff's tee shot had clipped a tree and dropped into the woods near the creek that ran across the twelfth hole. When he vanished into the woods in search of the ball, Joi and Kevin had forgotten that he would be hitting his approach shot first. The two moved aside, uncertain where Jeff's ball could come out. They were so concerned about the side bets and side insults, they hadn't realized that Jeff could easily make a double bogey on this hole.

The twelfth hole was a long-ball hitter's dream—or nightmare, depending on how one was playing. It was a monstrous 417-yard par four. Short tee shots were rewarded with a free ball washing in the creek lying two hundred yards from the tee box. At its most generous offering, the fairway was seventy yards wide. To the right was a ball-sucking hollow that seemed designed for sliced tee shots or greedy fades.

If a player was long enough to get past the hollow, the ball still had to stay left to avoid the impossible bunker waiting on the right side of fairway. There was no sand in the bunker, just ball death. High walls and thick rough. That same long-ball hitter who was fortunate enough to make it past the hollow and miss the ball-killing bunker had to maintain a straight shot that wouldn't go too far left and risk getting knocked down by the ball-slapping trees or the small gorge on the other side of the cart path.

Jeff's tee shot had chosen disaster number one—the ball-sucking hollow. He hiked back into the area and took advantage of the five minutes he was allotted to search for a lost ball. A group of spectators joined in and even Nagga helped out. Kevin and Joi waited on the other side of the fairway.

"You need help," Joi proclaimed to Kevin.

"And that's your mission? To help us one by one?"

"How much are you in for?"

"In for what?"

"Gambling debts."

"Who are you?"

"I'm not the compulsive gambler that you are, that's who I'm not."

Kevin snickered with contempt "And what makes you think that? Slept with one before?"

"Why do men think that because you're a woman you're a whore? Is your wife a hooker?"

Kevin's eyes blazed. His jaw smashed teeth together. "I've never hit a woman before. But I'll beat you down right here if you say anything else about my wife."

Joi squinted her eyes, straining to see the real person behind Kevin's threat.

"Does she know you've got a problem?"

Kevin stared into the woods, hoping that play would soon resume and Joi would stop her painful inquires. "Does she know that you're a compulsive gambler?"

"I ain't compulsive."

"You know, you're right. The reason you're into me for four grand is because you make rational, conscious decisions. Just like the way you think through each one of your shots. I don't mind you being an arrogant prick, but at least be an honest one."

"You're a funny one to talk about honesty. That's what

you're telling the other two, right? Be honest and play with integrity? Damn hypocrite."

"Get mad if you want. You're the one that's about to fork over four large. I'm in the middle of the fairway. How about this? You lost the fairway bet, right? Good chance you're gonna lose the hole too. How about we both lay up to the front of the green and see who can chip the closest for another five grand. Round the hole off to an even ten large. You game?"

"Hell, yeah," Kevin replied quickly.

"Next hole we'll do center of the fairway for five hundred. Closest to the one-hundred-yard marker for a grand, closest to the hole for fifteen hundred, best putt for another five hundred, and best score on the hole for five large. How's that?"

"I'll take all of that. No problem."

Joi watched as Kevin salivated and panted like a dog waiting for the Frisbee to go out again. Kevin's face transformed from elated to skeptical to uncertain to guilty.

"But you're not a compulsive gambler, right?"

Joi had exposed to the man to himself. "Look, I don't need the extra action. Doubt you could've paid up anyway. I'll cancel our side bets if you show me some damn respect as a golfer and especially a woman. And give some to your wife while you're at it."

"Hey! He's got it. Heads up," a voice shouted from the hollow. Kevin looked up for Jeff's ball and watched it curve out of the abyss and into the middle of the fairway. He looked back at Joi to make a remark about the good shot, but only found an empty space where she'd been standing. He looked around and found her walking toward the 150 marker. Kevin's face flushed with relief. He knew there was no way he could have won the hole.

He quickly calculated that had he taken all of the bets Joi dangled in front of his face, he stood to lose close to twenty thousand dollars in less than twenty minutes. For the first time ever, Kevin felt sick because of his illness. He stood over his ball, stopped breathing, started his back swing, uncoiled his torso to strike the ball, and stopped in mid- swing. A second later, after staring at the object that had consumed so much of his life and led him to his detrimental habit—he stepped away.

Kevin walked behind the ball, visualized his shot, took a moment to align himself with a target. He took several deep breaths while telling himself the shot would turn out okay. Then he struck the ball with a firm, quelling blow that stopped just short of the green. It was an awkward feeling, thinking things through. Joi made another par on the hole and gave Kevin a wink after his putt to save par rolled around the entire perimeter of the hole before losing the fight to stay above ground. Jeff wasn't able to save himself from the ball-hollow fate and made his first bogey of the second round. Bob drilled another par.

Instead of playing wise on the punishing thirteenth hole—a brutal par-four dogleg right with an approach shot over the creek—Jeff tried to make up a shot by swinging for the moon. The tee shot required perhaps the longest drive on the course, with a slight fade to work the ball close to the hole. And if anyone could hit a three-hundred-yard fade, they'd be in a laboratory getting tested as a mutant. When Jeff's fade kept fading, he found himself ball searching again and ultimately fighting for another bogey. His second of the day while the consistent Bob, confident Joi, and overhauled Kevin parred the hole with no problem. Jeff sulked over to the fourteenth hole when Nagga tapped him on the shoulder.

"Uh, homeboy? Do you need some motivation?"

Leaderboard	
Jeff	-2
Kevin	-2
Bob	-2
Joi	-2

Chapter 28
Campaigning

"You've been pretty quiet up until now. Everything okay?" Bob asked Jeff. They'd both hit identical tee shots on the fourteenth hole. Bob whacked a driver 270 yards and Jeff did the same with a three iron. The wind had danced around and pushed in the direction of their tee shots, helping with the distance. Joi and Kevin were on opposite sides of fairway. "Isn't that always the way with supporters. Love you when you're at the top and on your case when you're down?"

"Can I help you with something?" Jeff asked with a biting tone.

Bob returned the snap with an offensive look, wondering why he'd responded in such a manner.

"No, not really. Just making conversation. Is that okay?" Bob smiled, more from reflex than genuine emotions.

"Guess what? I'm not one of your supporters and this ain't a campaign."

"Whoa. Take it easy, big fella," Bob's damage control went into autopilot. "All I'm trying to do is have a civil conversation."

"Is that all?"

"That's it. I swear."

"Then what was your next question?"

"What do you mean?"

"After you asked was everything okay, what was your next question?"

"Oh...well...uh... I was going to ask where you where from?"

"And then what?"

"Probably...uh...how long you've been living in Atlanta?"

"Then what?" Jeff machine-gunned another response.

"Where you went to school?"

"Humph." Jeff smirked at the man and turned back to watch Joi hit a shot that bounced onto the green. Her ball stopped twenty-five feet from the hole. The crowd watched Kevin as he struggled to make himself slow down and think through his decisions. He walked up to the ball, backed away, told himself to slow down, yelled at himself for taking too long, calmed himself for having yelled at himself, stood over the ball, backed away and approached again. Eventually he hit the ball, which rolled into a bunker.

Jeff played next and just barely missed the green. Bob's preshot routine lasted longer than all the others combined, but yielded the best result.

"So that's why you won't get elected, huh?" Jeff destroyed Bob's good-shot grin and headed towards the green to try and save himself from another bogey and more aggravation from Nagga. Bob bagged his club and caught up with Jeff.

"What's that supposed to mean?" Bob asked.

"I wouldn't vote for you."

Bob pulled from his book of ready-made answers "And that's the great thing about this country. Every citizen has freedom of expression and can vote for whosoever they chose. My hope is that every American exercises his or her right to—"

"You believe yourself? I doubt anybody else does."

Bob searched his bag-o-responses. "You sound like a proud citizen who's concerned about the issues."

"I gotta be concerned about the issues. 'Cause you ain't," Jeff said, walking away. Bob was stunned and out of canned responses.

Kevin was in the bunker twisting his feet to get a better stance. He began another conversation with himself, complete with conflicts and resolution. After he'd made up with himself, he splashed his club through the sand. His ball popped onto the green and rolled ten feet past the hole. His followers shouted, hoped, then finished off with a collective and descending *ooohhhhh*. Two putts brought him a bogey and a few *mumbles* while Joi lined up a putt that stopped three feet short. As her three-footer dropped, Jeff was preparing to chip from the fairway. Bob was standing near the back of the green leaning against his putter with one foot crossed in front of the other—the classic putter pose. Jeff chipped close enough for small applause, and he too finished off with a short par putt. Bob's ball was sitting ten feet above the hole with a downhill slope waiting for a chance to add to the ball's momentum.

With the thoughts of Jeff's sentiments fresh in his mind, Bob hit his ten-foot-downhill putt with the speed of a ten-foot-uphill putt. The ball just barely missed the right side of the cup. It was off and running, eventually reaching the bottom of the green—thirty feet away from the cup. Two putts later, Bob walked off the green with a gut-wrenching bogey.

The spectators and banks formed a chute with people standing in two lines that led to the fifteenth hole; a straightaway par-four 324 yards. Long hitters practically putted for eagle after a smashed tee shot. Aggressive players went for the green, while conservative golfers played for the hundred-yard marker, leaving themselves a full swing instead of the often miscalculated three-quarter or half shot. Kevin and Bob chose the proven method and landed near the hundred-yard marker.

Jeff, who was anxious to gain his lead on the group, tried to quickly take advantage of the dead wind. He rushed through his practice routine and rushed through his shot even faster. Jeff hooked his drive left into the trees. He listened for the plunk of wood and waited for the ball to roll out in the fairway. He heard only groaning from the crowd and saw Nagga's eyes widen with rage.

"Should be all right down there," Purple Shirt said before the mob rushed off, sensing the drama building for the last few holes.

"I don't know," said Bucket Hat. "Looks like Alcatraz to me."

"We've got another player to hit. Stand please," commanded the Sergeant.

Joi placed her drive to the right and it settled under a tree.

"People startin' to come undone," a spectator said.

"Come on, Joi. Just a few more holes, now," one of her gamblers yelled.

"Jeff, don't worry about that shot. Punch out and stick it close," someone added.

The group headed off to their respective shots backed

by encouragement and cheers. They marched down the fairway like soldiers heading for an unknown doom. As if enemy guns had just launched a shower of shells, the whole group stopped abruptly. The sprinkler activated and began spraying cannons of water over the fairway and green. Ralph Jackson and the Sergeant looked at one another, wondering what could have happened. They both reached for their radios like guns in a high-noon showdown. They couldn't raise anyone and the Sergeant sped off to a control box while the others waited.

"What makes you think I'm not concerned about the issues?" Bob asked Jeff. He'd been walking towards Jeff before the sprinklers attacked.

Jeff grinned. "Because you've got all the questions before you hear the answers."

"Huh?"

"You told me back there what you were gonna ask before you even heard what I would say. You're too rehearsed."

"I don't get it."

"I know you don't. And that's because you're too rehearsed."

"Rehearsed? Rehearsed for what?"

"Everything. You've got the right answer for whatever needs to be said. I ain't mad at cha though. You're a politician. That's what you're supposed to do, right?"

"Well, actually we're here to serve the people, make public policy, preserve the values of the country and—"

Jeff's burst of laughter disrupted Bob's speech. "You're joking, aren't you? You don't think you *mean* that, do you?"

"Why, yes, I—"

"Serve the people, huh? What chu doin' about teenage boys in the streets with no motivation?"

"We have afterschool—"

"Wrong. What chu doin' about abused kids in the welfare system?"

"I myself can attest to serving on—"

"Wrong. What about guns and violence in schools?"

"There's a police officer assigned to every—"

"Wrong again! See that's what I'm talkin' about. How can you possibly know the answers to problems you've never seen? You know what? I've never heard a politician say, 'I don't know, but I'll find out.' Why is that? You scared of being incompetent? Hell, most of y'all incompetent without even showin' up. I mean, when was the last time you hung out on a corner and asked somebody what they needed? Have you ever gone into a super ghetto house and seen kids doomed for life 'cause their parents are ignorant and the parents are ignorant 'cause even their parents didn't have the tools to get out of the cycle? You even hang out with the people in other communities?"

Bob's face was turning shades of red he'd never known. He erupted. "Don't you dare stand there and lecture me about knowing people and getting out on the corner. I'll have you know I was doing just that when someone put an envelope of money in my hand and took my picture as a setup."

"That's probably because somebody knew you would take it. They anticipated what you were gonna do because you're too predictable. If you keep rehearsing all the time, people know what your show is gonna be like and they say the punch lines before you do. You always been like this?"

"Like what?"

"Like an automated phone service." Jeff began imitating Bob's polished speech. "Press one to hear my views on crime. Press two to get a firm handshake. Press the pound key to get a pat on the back, then the star key if you'd like me to wave and smile simultaneously." Bob was not smiling.

"What are you doing about the issues?" Bob said sternly.

"Going to work, obeying the law, contributing to society, voting for write-in candidates, paying taxes that pay politicians."

"What does a write-in candidate have to do with anything?"

"They're not a Democrat or a Republican."

"So you have no party affiliation?"

"Why do we have political parties? I mean, what is the logical reason and benefit for citizens? We know it helps y'all get support from your buddies, but why can't I go and vote for who I think is the best candidate without getting a label across my forehead?"

"Actually political parties date back to—" Jeff shook his head and smirked when Bob answered. "What I meant was, I'm not sure, but I could probably find out."

"Yeah, right. Don't rehearse that line too much. Let me ask you something. What is it you really want to do? I mean why did you get into the political game to begin with?"

"Honestly?"

"Yep."

"I wanted, well I still do, I want to help people."

"How high you plan to go?"

"How do you mean?"

"What office? Mayor, governor, what?"

"You really want to know?"

"I asked, didn't I?"

"All the way."

"President!"

"It could happen," said Bob. Jeff giggled with disbelief. "What's so funny? You know something I don't."

"How are you gonna get there? What's your claim to fame?"

"It's complicated. World changing, really."

"I hope so if you're dreaming like that."

"It's difficult to explain but it addresses the needs of every person in this country, all within the parameters of a system based on three key areas of concern. When all three things are addressed, the rest of the issues fall into place. I've tried it in smaller organizations like college fraternities and church committees, and it worked every time. It's totally kewl," Bob added, having abandoned his formal language.

"Sounds like it. If you're so excited about it, why aren't you concentrating on that instead being the billboard politician?"

"Because that's what it takes sometimes. You can't go door-to-door shaking hands and asking for support these days."

"Why not? You tried it?"

"By the time I shake the hands at two houses, a TV commercial could have reached the whole county."

"That's true."

"It seems crazy, but sometimes a person has to give the right image, say the right things, and kiss the right babies in order to get elected. Once we get in, we can forget about that and get to work. But it's two jobs. One is getting elected and the other is getting things done. You can't do the second without the first. And the first one has to be done any way you can."

"I feel ya. I still think you should go door to door."

"As much as I want to, it's just not the best way to get elected anymore. But you could be a supporter and go door-to-door for me, passing out literature," Bob said, jabbing Jeff in the side.

Jeff gave a sincere smile and replied, "No, no. I stay away from politics. I'm just a voter."

"We'll see about that. Wait until I get in office and start

addressing some of those issues you rattled off," Bob paused for a moment and checked to see if anyone was watching their conversation. "I can help you. Whatever it is that brought you out here for this match. I can help you."

"No you can't. It's too late. I needed help years ago. It's too late and I should have cut him off long before now. You can't do anything now."

"Well...uh I could always use your help."

"I don't think so. You need to help yourself. I told you I don't do politics."

"I mean, I could use your help in this match."

Jeff squinted and turned his head. He looked at Bob out of the corner of his eye. "Ain't nothing I can do for you. I'm gonna try and slit your throat on these last holes." The sprinklers' assault of rhythmic water stopped and the crowd headed for the fairway. Jeff winked at Bob. "Don't take it personal, though. Good luck."

Sergeant Starter came barreling down the path in his golf cart.

"What happened," Suspenders asked.

Sergeant replied, "I forgot we're experimenting with a wireless network to operate the sprinklers. This one was set and I forgot to bring a key to the override switch."

"Wireless remote. Everything's on 'puters now, aren't they?"

"You got that right. I heard on the NPR there's a guy out in California who controls the lights in his house by a computer jacket he wears."

"You're kiddin'."

"I swear it does. Must have a heck of a dry-cleaning bill."

"Reminds me of the time we were working the Bell-South Classic and that fella tucked that camera in his jacket," said the Sergeant.

"And you told him to either take the film out of his

jacket or you'd take him to the one-hour photo shop in your boot," Suspenders said. "What about the time that guy kept using his cell phone and you made him go in the portable toilet to make a call and locked him inside."

"Wouldn't been so bad if it wasn't one that hadn't been emptied all day," said Suspenders. "I don't think that beats the time when you told that fella to get behind the ropes."

"You mean the guy that told me he lived in the big house right next to the tee box," Sergeant said.

"And you said, 'Good. You won't have far to walk when I kick you off the course.'" The two snickered at the war stories.

"Let's not forget that you were the one that told that lady Tiger was on the tee box somewhere on the course and all she had to do was wait for him."

"Well, he was. I didn't say he was on *that* course. She should have known he stayed at home to practice that week."

"Poor lady—she probably stayed there every day," the Sergeant said, grinning.

"Oh, I know she did. I saw her the last day when I was leaving."

"Did she say anything to you?"

"Asked me did I ever see him."

"And what did you say?"

"Nothing. I just showed her the picture I took with the life size picture of Tiger," Suspenders said, holding an imaginary portfolio in front of him.

"Dirty son of a gun."

"And I get muddier with old age." They slapped backs and loosed a short roaring laugh that made heads turn in their direction. The two chums looked up and saw the four-some walking off the green. Bob's head was lowered and Kevin was mumbling to himself. Joi and Jeff charged ahead of them with heads held high.

The Sergeant and his buddy hurried to catch up with Ralph Jackson for an update.

"Sorry about that, boss. What'd we miss?"

"Getting tense out here. Everybody made par," Ralph answered.

"You mind holdin' it down?" Billy said to Ralph. "Don't know how in the hell my player's supposed to concentrate with the circus in town. Why don't y'all make up your mind who you're gonna protect and who you're gonna screw up."

"Tell 'em again!" shouted one of Kevin's gamblers. "Just 'cause we're almost done don't mean you guys can throw a party."

"Aww, hush it," a Jeff gambler replied. "Don't blame somebody else 'cause your man is choking down the stretch."

"It ain't right," one of Bob's supporters added. "And if this thing don't come out fair in the end, there's gonna be a problem."

"Ain't gon' be no problem, long as you don't try to reach back here for no money," said Purple Shirt.

"Don't you—"

"Ten-HUT!"

"Oh lordy," Bucket Hat mumbled.

"We will maintain order!" the Sergeant yelled. "We will not turn the civility of this environment into barnstorming anarchy! Anyone wishin' to do so can fall out of formation, forfeit your wagers, and have a safe trip home. We will be more than happy to use your money for rations in the clubhouse at the conclusion of this exercise. Do I make myself clear?"

"Sir. Go to hell, sir!" Billy yelled. Gasps and giggles followed his insult, then faces became stone.

Sergeant Starter headed for Billy. The crowd and the golfers were watching. Ralph and Norbert positioned themselves to pull the Sergeant off Billy's chest or head or wherever he would choose to attack. The two men stood in front of each other, breathing the other's air, increasing the other's pulse. The Sergeant smiled and spoke softly.

"Son, you better hope your man flies right for the rest of the way. If he marks his ball on the green and misplaces it by one blade of grass, if that man so much as plays one tenth of a second too slow for my liking, I'll penalize him and I'll do it so he won't have a chance at winning bingo at a church social."

Leaderboard	
Jeff	-2
Kevin	-1
Bob	-1
Joi	-2

Chapter 29
Death by Debacle

Hole sixteen was another short par four with a severe dogleg bending to right like a disfigured boomerang. The trees were too high to even think about going over. Shoe-vanishing rough grew from the front of tee box to the fairway. And of course the ever-present creek continued its role as golf ball graveyard on the left side of the fairway and fifty yards in front of the green. Drives too straight died in the ditch and drives too long headed off for the woods.

Jeff easily hit a five iron to the white marker. Kevin, realizing he was running out of holes, wanted to turn the ball around the corner and leave himself a few yards for an easy birdie chip. His tee shot formed an elbow instead of a boomerang and his ball disappeared underneath a shaded area near the bridge used for crossing the creek. Before Bob hit, the Sergeant raced down the cart path to find

Kevin's ball. He looked back at Billy and smiled. Billy smashed the accelerator, taking off after him.

"What's that about?" Bob asked before he began shaking over his own ball. Bob's drive veered to the left, turning into a nasty hook heading for the left side creek. He'd chosen a four iron and luckily the tee boxes were set far back enough for the ball's momentum to dissipate on the very edge of the creek.

Joi pranced down to the red tees and smoothly whipped her ball to the one-fifty marker. Jeff caught up with her before she began walking.

"We got 'em," he whispered as he walked by.

"We got who?"

"Bob and Kevin. They're falling apart. I've been getting in Bob's head and you got Kevin, right? You jacked him up good."

"We don't have anybody. I didn't intentionally distract him. He just pissed me off."

"Whatever. It worked. Ain't no way they can beat us both. I mean the last hole we'll go our own way to see who wins, but the rest of the way in, we got these clowns."

"I thought you didn't care anymore."

"I...er...uh...I don't care that much, but damn as long as I'm out here I may as well try to win."

"That doesn't make any sense."

"So what? What makes sense is that we can close this thing out. You the one that got me into a team format anyway."

"I was wrong and I can't keep it up."

"What?"

"Watch out for my ball," she said. They'd reached the shots and there was a group underneath the shade where Kevin's ball was heading.

"Bob knew my dad."

"And?"

"And I can't do him like that."

"Like what? You let him hustle you?"

"Nobody hustled me. He just told me something that make me look at him differently."

"Are you kiddin' me? You got hustled, Joi. What the hell is wrong with you. How you gonna let him use a dead man to get to—"

"You need to get outta my face, right now."

"Oh so now you mad, right?"

"Get outta my face."

"What you say to Kevin? He know yo' daddy too?" Joi was silent. "All somebody got to say is *yo' daddy* and you give in?"

"Jeff, don't mess this up."

"You already messed it up when you—"

"I'm gon' ask you one more time for your own sake to get away from me."

Jeff waited for something. A nine iron to the jaw, an outburst, a stepped-on ball. Joi's face was turned away from him.

"You trippin'," he said as he gave her the distance she'd requested. Jeff dropped the bag from his shoulder and kicked it, causing it to fall over with a club-clanging crash.

"That ball is in an area marked hazard and if that player touches a twig on the ground with the club, he's penalized," the Sergeant said.

Kevin had arrived at his ball to discover it barely resting against a pine cone and a red line painted on the ground. He'd asked the Suspender Starter for a rule clarification, but the Sergeant had gladly stepped in.

"You may attempt to move the pine cone, but if the ball

moves you will be penalized," the Sergeant said, smiling at Billy.

"How far does it have to move for me to get a penalty?" asked Kevin.

"As far as a fly fart," that Sergeant answered.

Kevin shook his head and whirled a heavy sigh. He took a few moments to simmer and then punched out into the fairway. His ball landed near Bob's. Bob had also hit a small punch shot out of some gook lining the top of the ditch leading down into the creek.

Joi spent little time playing another tempo-controlled shot that landed in the center of the green. Jeff followed her with an awkward shot that stopped twenty feet from the hole. Kevin quickly walked up to his ball and without hesitation slashed his approach to the back to the green. Bob's attempt landed a few feet from the green and the bogey twins made another startling performance, upstaged once again by the pars of Jeff and Joi.

Supporters for the bogey boys were grumbling and the others were holding on to erratic heartbeats and cotton-mouths.

Jeff swung around the crowd to meet Joi, who had gone out of her way to avoid him.

"You tryin' to tell me you don't want to help me nail the coffin? Your dad would have wanted—"

"Get away from me! Do you hear me? Get away! I don't want to do that anymore!"

No one moved. No one even thought about talking. Eyes shifted, waiting for more. Only the beginning of a re-turning breeze was heard, followed by the sound of Joi's golf spikes crunching up the cart path. No one followed.

"Is there a problem?" the Sergeant asked.

Jeff was still watching as Joi's bag, straddled on her back, moved up and down with each step.

"Nawh," Jeff replied. "Ain't a damn thing wrong."

The wind pushed the herd back as they tried to walk the hill leading up to the seventeenth tee box. The 167-yard par three had just been hijacked by a cross wind and the elevated green made guessing the right club a miracle.

Jeff sauntered up to the tee, as red as his dark skin allowed. He pulled a seven iron from his bag and slowly placed the ball upon a tee. His practice swings were weak and lazy. No one noticed or cared when he dragged his club up to the ball and made a jerking motion in his back swing. Jeff's shot elevated high like most of his iron shots, but the crosswind stole it and swept it to the left, where it crashed down into back side of the green side bunker. Jeff's head dropped and he threw his club at its cousins in the golf bag, as if they were to blame for letting the wrong club come out to play.

Bob seized the opening and made a smooth, crisp swing that threw his ball to the right side of the green. Kevin rushed to tee his ball and then stepped away to give his new routine another try. Heads in the crowd snapped from the tee box towards the sky, following Kevin's ball as it dropped and stopped twelve feet from the flag stick.

Billy yelled, "That's what I'm talkin' about, Kev! Show 'em, baby!"

Kevin's gamblers jumped and cheered and others made grunts and noises praising the shot.

Joi waited for the crowd to calm before strolling to her box. No one had noticed that her play had been the most consistent. She was collecting pars like stamps. Again, she nailed a shot to middle of the putting surface.

Jeff saw his ball and his stomach churned. It was buried in the sand in the back of the bunker on a downward slope six inches from the edge of the sand trap. He had no room to stand, no room to swing his club toward the hole. The cup had been placed on the left of the green, three feet away from the bunker.

"Come on, Jeff," someone shouted. "Nice thump in the sand, good putt and we're outta here for par. Take it to the house, baby."

"You got it, Jeff," said another anxious soul with bill-paying money on the line.

He didn't respond to any of the encouragement, only walked around his ball and tried to find a position from which he could make an attempt at anything remotely resembling a golf swing. Jeff couldn't get a good stance by standing in the bunker with both feet. He tried turning his back to the green hoping that he might be able to chop it, but realized he wouldn't have enough power to splash enough sand behind the ball and make it pop out. Jeff put one foot in the bunker and one foot outside the bunker to give himself the most room behind the ball. Even that left a small opening for the club to swing down into the bunker.

He took several fake swings, careful not to let his club touch the sand before making the shot. The foot in the bunker kept sliding forward with each movement and his legs spread further apart, stretching his groin. Jeff readjusted his stance and readied himself for whatever happened. The crowd was quiet and the brutal breeze that had brought him to this place subsided as though the world was waiting to see the outcome. Jeff picked the club up with a short back swing, cocked his wrists early, barely turned his shoulders, then dropped his club for the downswing.

His front foot began sliding in the groove of sand it had made during the practice movements. Everything was wrong: rhythm, balance, ball position, Joi's exclamation, and finally the impact. Jeff had aimed for a spot inches behind the ball, but his forward movement made the club descend closer to the ball than he wanted. Just before impact, a thought of decreased power passed through his conscience and invaded his arms until it manifested through the club as Jeff tried to execute the shot. Thinking the sand would splash in his face, Jeff closed his eyes. The sand wedge's blade fell straight down on the ball and the powerless swing didn't move it forward, but instead buried it deeper into bunker with an avalanche of sand.

When he looked on the green for his ball, Jeff saw only the three balls that had been there before. He scanned every bit of the green for another ball and then looked exactly where he'd hoped the result would not have been, at his feet. Onlookers offered condolences with *Ooohs* followed by murmurs.

Jeff jumped out of the bunker and slammed his club against the ground. He placed a hand on his hip, looked at the hiding ball, and jumped back in the bunker. Without evaluating the shot again, he took the same awkward unbalanced position and swung as hard as he could. His ball pushed out of its cubbyhole and bounced against the other side of the bunker and back to his feet. He didn't think but swung again. The descending blow hit the ball again, but this time on the club face. Jeff wanted to hit the sand first, but he made the shot so quickly he didn't bother to aim. There was an explosion of brown particles behind a white sphere that seemed to launch out like a wayward comet leaving behind a planet it would never see again. As the sand splashed down on the green, the ball kept flying on a straight trajectory headed across the green and into the crowd. The people parted to avoid a painful collision as the ball whizzed by them and settled in a gnarly clump of bushes on the other side of the cart path.

Jeff felt sick. He could feel urine boiling in his bladder trying to make an uncontrolled escape. His bowels felt like revolving doors and his chest was burning from the increased energy pumping cells through stretched arteries. His eyes widened and then watered.

Jeff's feet and brain were the only logically functioning parts of his body. With his sand wedge dragging behind him and his shoulders slumped, Jeff walked over to his next shot like a lobotomized Neanderthal.

Joi, Bob, and Kevin all did things to keep their minds off Jeff's catastrophe. They cleaned balls, took practice strokes, read the line for their putts, anything that would keep them from watching the suicide.

Jeff saw his ball resting on a stick. He stooped down to move the impediment when someone in the crowd coughed a thinly disguised *Nuh uh*.

Jeff stopped a few inches away and set up over the ball before striking it. The stick raced in the air behind the ball and they both landed on the green, thirty-five feet from the hole. There was no need to read his putt, no need to think about where to hit the ball—he'd given up. Jeff yanked the putter out of his bag and hit without aiming. The golf gods had tortured him enough and his ball stopped seven inches from the hole. He received obligatory applause for his role in the slaughter. His opponents all headed for the next hole with routine pars as Jeff recorded the first quadruple bogey of the day.

The crowd rushed for the eighteenth hole, leaving Jeff to sulk behind. A cart drove slowly behind him, coming closer with each step. When the golfers, banks, and gamblers were all out of sight, the golf cart tapped Jeff from behind.

"You dead yet?" Nagga asked.

Jeff moved from the cart path to the grass so Nagga could pass by. Nagga turned the cart and followed Jeff onto the grass.

"You dead yet? You hear me talkin' to you? Hell nawh, you ain't dead 'cause I ain't killed you. How you want it? Want me to run you over? Bat to the head? It don't make me no difference. But you gon' die, you hear me, fool?"

"Whateva."

"What! Who you think..." Nagga jumped from the cart

without setting the brake. He rushed Jeff and grabbed his collar, then pulled the gun. It seemed to be a natural extension of his arm.

"What did I tell you before?" Nagga asked, twisting the barrel against Jeff's temple.

"I'm gettin' tired of you puttin' that gun in somebody's face all the time. You gon' do somethin'? Do it."

Nagga shoved Jeff away with both hands and reached in his pocket for a phone. "Yo, ya'll come to the seventeenth hole at this other golf course. Bring a bag." Nagga pressed the end button and reached in another pocket for a cylindrical tube and began screwing it onto the end of his nine-millimeter.

Jeff dropped his golf bag, held his head high, sucked in his gut, and pushed his chest out. He felt around in his pocket for something and Nagga saw him searching and screwed the cylinder faster. Jeff kept searching his pocket but couldn't find what he was looking for. He remembered he'd tucked it into his golf bag. Jeff bent down as Nagga began to struggle with the gun. The thin pointed item was just where he'd put it and Jeff pulled it out. Nagga saw it and froze. Jeff lifted his shirt, removed the cover from his object, and drew a circle in the middle of his chest with the marker he'd retrieved from his bag.

Jeff, fueled by arrogance, said, "Aim right here."

Leaderboard	
Jeff	+2
Kevin	-
Bob	-
Joi	-2

Chapter 30
Near Win

"Jeff!" Joi yelled from the crest of the hill on the cart path. Both he and Nagga looked at her. "We're waiting for you! Come on! Here he comes now," she said, yelling back at the group she'd just left.

"I'll holla at chu in a minute," Nagga said.

Jeff grabbed his bag and walked backwards up the hill, watching Nagga the whole way.

"You all right?" Joi asked.

"Why you wanna know?"

"Jeff, I'm sorry. A lot's been going on today," she said with a hand on Jeff's arm.

"Whateva," Jeff said, snatching his arm away. He took another look over the hill for Nagga and rushed to the tee box where Bob was gyrating through his routine.

The par-five eighteenth hole was a crap shoot. Short

enough to reach in two shots, but dangerous enough to ruin what could have been a good round. Two hundred fifty yards out, the ever-present creek awaited and was twenty yards wide. Players had to hit a tee shot a good 270 yards in the air to make it over. The hole turned slightly to the left, which forced anyone trying to drive the ball over the creek to hit a strong draw. And if the tee shot didn't turn from right to left, it was headed for either the creek, the woods, more woods, or deeper woods. Once on the other side of the creek, jail-cell pine trees sat to the right and the creek began on the left where more trees ended.

Bob and Kevin, like most players, laid up twenty yards short of the creek with four irons. Jeff stormed to the tee, pulled out his driver, and hit the ball as hard as he could, unconcerned about where it would land. After a quick glance at Nagga, he forced the driver back into the bag and shouldered his clubs.

"Whoo wee!" one of his gamblers yelled.

"He made it over!" another supporter shouted. "That boy's gonna get on in two!"

"I know I made it over," Jeff said to the crowd, but still looking at Nagga. "You must think I have fear in me."

The wind rushed back when Joi headed for the tee box. She could easily make it over the creek from the ladies tees.

"Real easy, lady," one of her gamblers said. "Par this and we're home free. You can do it." She put her bag down as supporters clapped and encouraged.

"Stand please, quiet!" Sergeant yelled.

Joi blocked them out and started her smooth practice swings a few times before she stepped up to the ball. She looked up at the tops of the trees and tried to gauge the wind. Joi took a glance around and in back of her. She caught Jeff in the corner of her eye. He gave her the same bulldog glare he had given Nagga.

As the club went back and coiled around her body, the

wind ripped through the trees and swept across the hole. Joi swung and saw the ball shoot up into the gust. The blowing force pushed her ball to the right where its stolen energy slammed it into a wavering tree branch before it dropped into the ditch. Joi dropped the club and threw her hands on top of her head.

"Can you believe that?" Balding Guy said.

"Bad break right there," Purple Shirt responded.

The herd moved towards the creek where Bob and Kevin played iron shots to the white marker. Bob nodded and Kevin shrugged his shoulders.

Joi pulled a new ball from her bag, held it out from her body, and dropped it in front of the creek. She took a few breaths to recover and aim her body towards the right side of the fairway. She tried to hit a knockdown shot, ridding her herself off all chances of getting caught up in the wind. The ball began turning from right to left and turned even further left when it hit the ground, heading for the creek.

"Sit ball. Sit!" she commanded as the white speck disappeared into the rough adjacent to the creek.

"Joi, just hold on. We're not out of this thing," a supporter yelled.

"Let's do it, Jeff!"

"Come on, Kevin!"

"Bob, good approach and a putt and we got this!"

Shouts and advice rang from the group when they walked over the bridge covering the creek.

Jeff ignored them all with a tenacious walk to his ball. He pulled a three iron out and took several practice swings—half swings, full swings, three-quarter swings, and knock-down swings. Throwing blades of grass in the air, he watched them dance away to his left. The golf gods owed him and he came to collect by standing over the shot, never looking at the hole again until he smashed the ball as firmly as he had all day. The wind picked up, but Jeff didn't move, knowing that the forces were on his side. The three iron would have been too much for him on a normal day, but a left-to-right cut into the wind was a perfect match for the club. The white streak rode powerful wings of perfection and hit the left edge of the green, spinning and rolling to the back right side of the green, one foot from the cup.

"Yeeeahhhh!"

"Whoooo hoooooo!"

Hands clapped and slapped and missed and shook and raised for the best shot of the day while the other three shook their heads.

"Don't know how much more of this I can take, Kevin. All this excitement is too much stress," said Bob.

"He'll miss it. Been missing those eagle putts all day. I'm gonna birdie here and collect my money. Been nice playin' with ya."

"What about the help? You said you'd—?"

"Bob, you're a nice guy, but the day I start believin' politicians is the day I give up action."

"Quiet, please!" Suspenders yelled.

Joi was nestling her feet in the rough behind her ball to save her bogey. When the noise left and the wind floated off to haunt someone else, she sliced through the grass, but lost her power when the miniature forest choked her club. The ball squirted out, but missed the green by an inch.

Kevin prepared to make good on his birdie proclamation by reverting back to his old ways. No practice, a rushed shout, a ball fifteen feet from the hole.

Bob's wiggling held up the mob's procession to the green. Twenty seconds later, he whacked away and watched his ball plunk into the sand.

Jeff reached the green first and marked his ball while Joi held a wedge and a putter. She decided on the putter, thinking that the gamble could pay off if her long putt dropped. Bob twisted into the bunker. Ten practice swings later, he plopped the ball eight feet from the cup.

Joi knelt down over the ball and walked around the green, eyeing her shot from every possible angle. Finally returning to the ball, she looked down at her putter and re-solved not to raise her head in search of the ball for a full three seconds. Her putter went back and she brought the pendulum stroke back with a strong push. She wanted to make sure there was enough speed to make it through the small section of grass and make the uphill climb through to the hole.

One, two, three, she counted.

"Whoa ball, whoa!" someone yelled.

Joi saw the ball speeding for the hole. If it slowed down it would drop, if the flag stick had been taken out of the hole it would have banged against it and stopped five feet away, if she'd chipped the ball it would have stopped by now, but the extra force she gave it carried it passed the flagstick, by the hole and to the back of the green, leaving her a downhill putt to save bogey.

Kevin hurried to his ball, putted the way he was accus-tomed, and missed the birdie the way he'd done that morning. Joi was walking around the green like a vulture again. Looking for bumps and spike marks and unforeseen problems that would derail her putt. The group waited in silence for her to address the ball. She stood over the putt, waiting for the wind, waiting for a cough, waiting for dis-tractions, waiting for a miracle. She released the putter, tapped the ball, and didn't move. She held her position and resolved not to move her head until she heard one of two sounds: the ball rattling in the cup or—

"Awwwww!" the crowd grunted. And Joi knew that when she moved her head she would see her ball still out-side the hole. Her two-shot lead was gone. She saw the white piece of misery resting a few inches from the hole. Joi walked up to the ball, pulled her putter back like a meat cleaver, dropped it down with a swift haste, and stopped just before knocking the ball into oblivion. She tapped the ball into the cup and spit profanity into the windy air.

Bob made his short putt without thinking about it and the crowd prepared to watch Jeff suffer over his eagle putt. They all had visions of the holes at Mystery Valley and the breakdowns he'd suffered all day. They thought he'd take as long as Joi, if not longer, to pontificate on how to conquer his task. His opponents had taken their putter poses and began cursing themselves silently when Jeff walked up to his ball and hit it without aiming, thinking, or worrying. He heard the sounds, the ball rattling in the cup, the crowd shouting, and hands colliding. His supporters rushed to the green to hug him. Nagga folded his arms and smiled as he headed towards Billy.

"What you say now, huh? Tiger who?"

"Get out of my face," Billy replied.

The green was covered with people shaking Jeff's hand, patting his back, while confused faces were standing off the green.

"What's their problem?" Bucket Hat asked the Sergeant. "You need to do something about that."

The Sergeant walked to edge of the green and stood erect with hands behind his back.

"Hey!" The crowd continued to celebrate as Jeff tried to squeeze out. "Hey, you maggots! What in God's name do you think you are doing? Get off that putting surface and I mean get a move on!"

"Sure thing, Sergeant," a supporter said. "Who's holding the money? I'm buying Jeff's first beer."

"What the hell you wanna know about money for? Y'all didn't win any money. Get off of my green."

"What!" the bouncing men deflated. "What's goin' on here? Our man just eagled the eighteenth hole."

"So what does that have to do with a man pissin' in a

rice field?"

"He won, that's what."

"Like hell he did," one of Kevin's gamblers said. Jeff had slipped off from the crowd.

"Where's the scorekeeper? That put him at one under," the man said.

"You wish," Purple Shirt exclaimed.

"Well, what the hell was the score?"

"Ladies and gentleman," Suspenders announced. "As of the eighteenth hole, we have Joi at even par, Kevin at even par, Bob at even par, and Jeff at even par."

Shouts and comments burst from the crowd.

"What!"

"Another tie?"

"Not again."

"No way they're gonna play another round."

"Playoff hole or you give me my money back."

"Ain't gonna be another round or a playoff hole," the Sergeant said.

"Well somebody better give me my money."

"Ain't gonna be no refunds either," said the Sergeant.

"Why the hell not?"

"Because," the Sergeant replied, pointing through the woods at the foursome walking across a fairway, their banks riding behind. "They gotta go back and play the ninth hole."

Leaderboard	
Jeff	-
Kevin	-
Bob	-
Joi	-

Chapter 31
Kiddin' a Round

The greenskeeper had long ago completed the task of cutting the hole into the ninth green and was somewhere else, cutting and raking, oblivious to the lives that would change or end at the cost of his handiwork. He would travel home after working and talk about geese on the course and an ailing back, while others would have to deliver bad news and decide how to survive the week.

Joi sulked over to the tee box, the lessons of the day and the double bogey holding her brain for ransom. She'd beaten them all. A two-stroke victory in her palm and the money to alleviate her problems practically in her bank account. The advice and life of her father finally put to rest and good use. She reached the tee box with a lowered head.

Kevin was alive again. Having died several times during the day, and often by falling on his own sword, he'd been reincarnated as himself plus rational thinking and judgment. Kevin smiled with optimism that he'd been given one last shot. One time to get it right, forever.

Bob's smile, for the first time, was inverted. Skip Breiser, having stayed away from Bob for most of the Sugar Creek round, saw his friend's face painted with emotions. He walked towards his player and friend, but was stopped by Bob's stretched palm and a shaking head. There were no more speeches; negotiating was over. Bob could only hope his true intentions would be seen by anyone needing his help.

Jeff walked to the tee box as though he were casually beginning a practice round by himself that meant nothing to anyone. The eagle on the previous hole was another roller coaster of controlling Nagga. Jeff had lost his brother long before the round had even begun. There was only the matter of staying alive, but he wanted to make Nagga think he didn't care if the gangster's SUV would become a hearse after this hole was played.

Nagga stood behind the tee box, waiting for Jeff's glare. He tapped the iron bulge in his pants, knowing his player would look one last time.

Billy was pacing, thinking behind the tee box. He wanted to pat Kevin on the back or kick him in the pants, whichever would make him win the hole, but he dared not break what seemed to be a mandatory silence.

Norbert swayed from right to left, watching the trees match his motions. The breeze was coming for its curtain call. Having performed the brutal cameos during this round, it wanted to be in on the final act.

Ushered over by the Sergeant and Suspenders, the crowd arrived at the tee box. Some of them were still in disbelief that they'd forgotten about the skipped hole. The golfers were all staring at the green, tuning out sounds and movement around them.

Jeff was first. He teed his ball up and a gambler yelled, "You da man Jeff!" Heads jerked towards the man who'd desecrated this sanctuary. The Sergeant extended his thick arm, pointed at the man, and then pointed to the parking lot. It was a warning to him and all others thinking of disturbances during pre-shot routines.

Jeff took two identical practice swings. The ball was positioned in the middle of his stance as he looked down at the object. He thought of his brother. Thought of the times he'd gotten him out of trouble, rescued him, protected him. And he thought of the boy beaten, bruised, near death. He thought of Nagga's gun barrel pointed at his own head, the cold tip prodding him like a cow going to slaughter. He thought of life and swung. The wind tried to interject its intentions on the ball, but the crisp iron shot rose just high enough to stay below the dangerous swirls. Jeff's body, in the follow-through position, was a statue of perfection.

Along with the others he watched, waited, and hoped, as the ball never wavered from course. Finally, the downward travel of the arch began, the uncertain behavior of ball flight when one can only hope the calculations, the assumptions, the mechanics, the good fortune line up with destiny. They all watched and the ball thumped the green and stopped eight feet from the hole. The crowd freed itself and shouted,

"Yeahhh!"

"You got it, J! You got it, baby!"

"It's your world!"

Jeff was unmoved by the accolades and the shot. *All putts can be missed*, he thought grimly.

Jeff's gamblers smacked hands and hugged. There would be no explanations to inquisitive wives why there was no extra money to have dinner and see a movie, or why they would have to wait longer for the overdue shopping spree.

The Sergeant held up his hand and the people were silent again as Bob placed his ball on the ground. He took five practice swings, each one different and strange. It was as if he were trying on different outfits, hoping the one he decided on would fit the occasion. Bob approached the ball, stood over it, waggled his club once, adjusted his grip, shuffled his feet, and shrugged his shoulders, waggled the club again, grip, feet, shoulders, waggle-grip-feet-shoulders, wagglegripfeetshoulders. He stopped moving and saw the old woman on the mud-slinging commercial, the picture with a known criminal, his Tri-Factor program.

Bob swung the club in a way unlike any of his practice swings. The club took a path away and out towards the right and the ball sprang from the club in the same direction, raced for the right-side bunker and suddenly began turning to the left, heading for the green. Bob leaned his body to the left as though he could tilt the earth in his direction and have the ball fall captive to the influence. It was physics instead of Bob's body that was turning the ball on a precise collision course with accuracy. The wind futilely tried, but could not steal the flight of Bob's shot as it was sucked down out of the sky by gravity's greed. It bounced near the right side of the green and did not rest until it was five feet from the hole.

The shouts were louder this time.

"Oooooh!"

"Yeeeesssss!"

"Wooooo-hoooooo!"

"That's what I'm talkin' about!"

Bob looked as if his shot had landed fifty feet away from the hole. The polished smile was gone, the cordial nod had vanished. *Short putts are the hardest*, he thought.

Suspenders held his hands high and the hush returned before Kevin stuck his tee in the ground. He backed away from the ball and stood a few steps behind it. The flag, the ball, and his body connected to form an earthly constellation. Kevin stood erect, his head high and shoulders back. He was proud and confident regardless of the circumstances he faced. It was the moment in his new pre-shout routine where he would take a controlled practice swing, but he remained behind the ball, looking. The flag was fighting the wind, shaking and waving with an impulsive ferocity, flapping to the right, falling with the wind's sudden change, and then dancing to the left. Kevin watched as the indecisive banner designating the position of the final resolution, decided to drop as the surrounding elements stopped and allowed it to remain still in its own comfort. Kevin approached the ball and was motionless. He thought of his wife's discomfort, her vulnerability because of his own illness. There was one last look at the peaceful flag and Kevin swung with ease, poise, and prudence. He'd thought of the shot, the swing, its intentions, its priorities, and its course.

The ball split the air with a low projectile, tracking the flag. Kevin made pushing motions with his club, urging the ball to keep going. Onlookers were confused, wondering why he'd taken such an easy swing with the three iron. It was as though Kevin had taken a long chip shot. He kept urging the ball, demanding that it keep going. It prematurely fell to the ground, but bounced and skipped to the front of the green. Kevin kept yelling. The ball kept listening. Its relentless momentum for success remained strong as the ball pushed further onto the green still connected to the constellation of Jeff and the flag. Everyone saw the potential, the path of the ball, the distance. Their voices avalanched into a roar as Kevin's shot rolled to the hole with plenty of speed to drop in.

"Get in the hole!" someone yelled.

As if the ball had been frightened by the command, or distracted, it zipped by the edge of the cup and stopped three feet behind it. Kevin's eyes were inoculated, his veins overdosed with adrenaline. He was waiting for the wind to blow the tiny white speck back and for it to disappear. It didn't move, not even with the group screaming, jumping, and running in disbelief that the balls were landing so close to the hole.

"Sergeant, what are we gonna do? Go back and play the eighteenth if they tie, or come back tomorrow?" Purple Shirt asked.

"We ain't playin' tomorrow. I'll tell ya that right now," Billy said. "Better play until this thing is broken or give me my money back."

"Quiet please!" Norbert said. His player was walking down to the red tee, preparing her shot. "Take your time, Joi. There's no pressure," Norbert added.

Joi felt nothing. She'd lost her swing on the last hole. She'd run into the brick wall that lurks around the corner of every golfer's psyche. The moment when a person forgets, mid-swing, what golf is. No matter how she walked to the ball, or what she told herself before swinging, her mind would repeat the same thought until impact—*this will be a bad shot*. Joi, like all golfers, had lost her swing before. Once when she suffered her first and only boyfriend break-up, and then again after her father's collapse. Somehow, she recovered and managed to finish out those rounds and find her swing within a week of hitting five hundred golf balls a day. But there was no round to salvage here. There was no time to figure out where the glitch was. And there was certainly no chance to hit five hundred balls. She had three shots left, two if she wanted to stay alive and remain in the Boys' Club.

Joi was standing over the ball, taking more time than Bob, thinking faster than Kevin, wishing she could hit as far as Jeff. She started to shake. Her body wanted to swing, but her mind kept telling her it was useless. Golf was imitating life—things had become impossible and she needed to explore other options.

She could tell her boss that she didn't know where the money was and had no way of knowing. Then she'd wait for the outcome. She could resign and not give them the satisfaction of firing her. She could change her resume to reflect that she'd never worked for her soon-to-be former company. How would she explain the lapse in work? Her body was trembling fast now. She'd either have to hit or withdraw. Maybe she would pass out in a few moments and be given a continuation. She'd have to hit. Her body was screaming, while her mind rejected the notion. Joi's arms started back while her brain asked what the hell she thought she was doing. Her shoulders didn't move as her arms began turning around her body and her brain demanded an explanation. Joi's hips shifted with weight and her arms continued to rebel while her mind called for backup and made her head rise from its initial position.

Her body was in perfect form—to chop wood. A golf ball could never have been hit well with this contortion. She tried and her brain sent *I told you so* messages through her body when she yanked her arms down and across the ball. It was a soft slice and Joi knew it before impact. The crowd saw the ball and groaned with sympathy. Joi watched the ball sail into the air and out of control.

"Jesus Christ! Agggh!" Joi yelled and tossed her club into the trees. Her eyes welled up and acid boiled in her stomach. She was going to cry, vomit, and die all before the ball touched the ground.

"That's way to the right," Balding Guy said as the crowd watched the disaster head for the bunker. The other members of the foursome stomped out of the tee box, headed for their birdie putts before the ball dropped. Each of them reciting swing thoughts in their minds. *Take it straight back and through. Keep your head down. Trust the read.*

All thoughts stopped a second later when Joi's ball crashed into a plastic rake lying on the outside of the bunker. The collision halted the group and caused a few giggles until the impact of the ball with the hard plastic object sent the ball ricocheting onto the green. All eyes followed the movement from rake, to rough, to fringe, to green, past Jeff's ball, closer to the cup, heading for the flag, and finally to the bottom of the hole.

The crowd was berserk, shocked, and angered.

Cries and questions came from everyone.

"Are you kiddin' me?"

"You're friggin' kiddin' me!"

"You gotta be kiddin' me!"

Joi was just walking off the tee box when the eruption occurred. Spectators cheered and shouted as they turned to applaud Joi, who hadn't seen the ball drop.

"Joi! You see that?" yelled Norbert. "You won! You did it, honey!"

Joi's wrinkled eyebrows lifted. She looked up at the green and saw only three balls, turned to Norbert and said, "Stop kiddin' me."

Chapter 32
Generosity

"Joi, what a pleasant surprise. Didn't expect to see you until next year."

"Good to see you as well, Mr. McMinville. Sorry to drop by unannounced first thing Monday morning, but—"

"That's no problem. Don't give it a second thought. You're always welcome here."

"I am?"

"Of course," Mr. McMinville said, ushering Joi into his office. "Have a seat. Can I get you some coffee or something?"

"No, I'm fine thanks, but what I wanted to talk you about, and this may seem a bit unorthodox, but I think—"

"I'm sorry, Joi. Let me stop you right there. I'm sure

you knew I was gonna bring this up so don't be surprised. But I really need you to tell me something."

Joi's early morning make-up was being penetrated by stress-induced sweat. She'd been fighting the feeling all morning, dabbing more foundation on her cheeks and forehead while sitting at a red light and again in the parking lot. She'd eaten off all of her lipstick with nervous lip biting before her car was even in drive. Now she just had to figure a way to sell Mr. McMinville on taking the check as a project savings refund without calling her boss.

"Yes?" Joi asked.

"I desperately need to know why I'm not getting enough distance from my irons. Everybody knows you oughta be playing on tour. Just give me this one free tip. What do ya say?"

"Huh?"

"I'm getting desperate. We played Sugarloaf this weekend and I swear I couldn't get more than 140 yards out of my seven iron."

"Well...uh. What's your handicap?" Joi asked, thrown off by the man's interest.

"Nowhere near yours, but I play to about a fifteen, twelve on a good day."

"That's not bad. How often do you get out?"

"Once every two weeks, but much less in the winter."

"I wouldn't worry about those few yards you're missing. Could be your shoulder turn, how soon you uncock your wrists. Lots of things. I'd spend more time working on the short game if I were you. It'll save your life more than you know."

"Aw, hell, Joi. There's nothing fancy about the short game. Boomin' it out there and hitting irons into the green is where the thrill comes in."

"Maybe. But I think the thrill is collecting money at the end of the round," Joi said, then joining the man in a rumbling laugh.

"Touché. Now, what can I do for you?"

"Sir..." Joi took a deep breath, trying to fight the skin-slamming pulse. "It's about the project audit."

"Yeah! I've been meaning to call your boss about that. That was the damnedest thing I ever saw."

"I don't know how it happened myself. And it was just recently brought to my attention so I—"

"I'm no bean counter, but when there's a huge surplus credit one month and then it becomes an expensed line item the next month, my flag goes up."

"Excuse me?"

Only reason I didn't make a big stink about it is 'cause you guys were thirty percent lower and fifteen percent faster than all the other bidders, so I didn't make anything of it. But I am gonna call your boss just to bust his chops about it. Don't know how you did it, little gal, but you got it done cheaper and faster."

"Wait," Joi said, holding her hands out. "So from the audit you saw what?"

"Like I said, there was surplus and then it was gone. You knew that, right?"

"Yeah...I...uh. Sure. That's why I came by. Just to make sure you were okay with it. Gotta keep you happy," she replied, clutching the envelope inside her suit pocket.

"We're thrilled with ya. Companies like Hisco, SPE, Mar-Tec, Gammer & Dietrich, and yours keep us running."

"That's great...this is good to know. Really good. Okay, I'll let you get your week started and thanks again for seeing me."

"Don't mention it," he said rising from his chair to give Joi a departing shake. "Give the old man hell over there for me. Will ya?"

"Sure will," Joi said, leaving the office and drawing her cell phone for the showdown.

"Mr. Berry?"

"Speaking," Bob said into the phone. His voice was lifeless. The fountain of optimism and hope had gone bone dry.

"This is Joi, from the golf match."

"The miracle worker herself."

"I got lucky, that's all. Really lucky."

"Luck counts, doesn't it?"

"Mr. Berry, I want to make a campaign contribution."

"What?"

"You plan on running in the primary, right?"

"I had been, yes. But I need that—"

"Money from the match?"

"How'd you know?"

"I'm not stupid. Besides, I saw the commercial. Is it too late?"

"No, no. 'Course not. How much did you want to donate? And how soon? Timing is everything."

"My dad used to say that. Depends on how much you need to make it happen. First, there's something I need to take care of at work. I can deliver the cash to you this afternoon, if you'd like."

"No, no, no, no! No cash. No personal deliveries. I need you to make a check out to the committee to elect Bob Berry and deliver it to Skip Breiser. You got a pen? I'll give you the address. What made you do this? And is there something I can do for you? I mean, legally that is."

"I need you to help somebody. I mean really help somebody. The way my dad helped you."

"It would be my honor."

"Remember that thug that framed you with the picture?"

"I'd rather not think about those days."

"Just thought you might have some connections. I need
to get in touch with Nagga."

"The guy that was harassing Jeff during the match?"

"Yeah can you put me in touch with him? Phone number or something? You know cops and people in that world,
don't you?"

"Joi, your father would not—"

"My father's dead and I'm living my own life. I can
take care of things myself. If you could just get me that info
and I'll pick it up when I drop off the contribution to Skip
Breeze."

"Breiser."

"Whoever, just get it. I need it as soon as possible."

"I'll see what I can do. I might be able to have someone
give you a call tomorrow."

"No, I don't think so. If I don't get that information today, I won't be in a position to give you the maximum
contribution. Got me?"

There was silence.

"Are you hardballing me? I can't afford to be in com-
promising situations anymore."

"You tell me. You knew my father, right?"

Bob sighed. Satisfied that she'd come from virtuous
stock.

"All right. I'll get it for you. If I get right on it, I can
have someone call you back in the next few minutes."

"Then I think you'd better get on it."

"Ever think of working for the people? You've certainly got the nerve to do it. Once I'm elected, send me
your resume. I might have a job for you."

No thanks. I'm about to start a new one," Joi said,

pressing the end button and stopping the car at a light. She popped the trunk, jumped out of the car, and fished through her golf bag. The light changed and cars were blowing at her, building the first stages of road rage. She knew it was in there although she'd thought of throwing it away. It was underneath a pile of tees. Joi grabbed the crumpled paper as more horns blew.

She jumped back in the car and slammed the door just as the light turned yellow and middle fingers began flying in her rear view mirror. Joi waved her hand, offering the best apologetic gesture she could during the emergency.

A call came through on her cell just as Bob had promised. Pounding the phone's buttons, she hoped there was still time. There was plenty of time and also a cooperative collector ready to take her money. She ended the conversation, sighed with relief, and made one last call.

The phone stopped ringing, but there was no response.

"Hello," Joi said. "Hello!"

"Who is this?" a disguised voice asked.

"I must have the wrong number. I was looking for Jeff King."

"Who is this?"

"It's Joi."

"Oh, hey, what's up," Jeff said with clear diction.

"Bill collectors callin' your cell phone too?"

"Something like that."

"Hey, I got a job for you."

"What?"

"A job. You know, where you should be right now."

"I got a job."

"This is a better one. It pays well if you work hard."

"Don't need it."

"Really. How long you think you can keep your job if you stay away just to hide from Nagga."

"What chu talkin' about?"

"It's obvious he's after you...well, he *was* after you."

"That ain't none of yo' business."

"It is now."

"How you figure that?"

"'Cause I'm paying your debts to him."

"Whateva."

"No, the word is thank you. And I'll pick you up tomorrow for work at seven o'clock."

"I'll be on my way to work then."

"Right, working for me."

"How are you gonna call me and just demand that I do somethin'? Who are you supposed to be?"

"I'm the person just paid your debt to Nagga. Just finished workin' out the details. I own you. So do me a favor and wear comfortable shoes in the morning."

$$\mathcal{S}$$

"You're in awfully late this morning, Joi. Long weekend? Lots to think about?"

"No sir, things were great," she replied, looking through her desk drawers.

"Did you give any thought to our conversation on Friday?"

"Nope. Not really." She hadn't looked at him yet, nor had she turned her computer on.

"Joi, why don't you step into my office for a minute so we can get this over with. Don't want to make this embarrassing for you."

"Why sure. I'd love to," she said, following her boss into his office and plopping down in the first chair she saw.

"Have a seat, why don't you."

"Don't mind if I do."

"Now listen here. I don't know what drugs you're on,

but you either tell me where that money is or I'll pick up this phone so fast it'll—"

"What did you do, get a new boat?" Joi asked.

"What?"

"Got a membership at Sugarloaf or something?"

"I don't have time to play games with you."

"Your daughter's tuition? Is that it? Remodeling? New truck? Where did it go?"

"Fine, if that's how you want it. I'll just call right—"

"Make sure you call Mr. McMinville while you're at it."

"What do you mean?"

"Nothing. He said he was gonna call you, so I figured you could call him first. You could thank him for the thirty-five thousand dollars you stole from him."

"You're out of your damn mind!"

"That's what I was thinking. I said 'Joi, girl, you done lost yo' damn mind. How could you miss an expense item like that?' And Mr. McMinville was kind enough to clear things up for me this morning. You stole the surplus from their project's account."

"What? That's ridiculous...I...uh...that wasn't stealing," he said, his skin turning red. "It was a business loan that I—"

"Loan my ass! That *loan* was gonna get me fired! You were gonna try to put me in jail for embezzlement. How the hell is that a loan?"

Her boss rose from his seat and pleaded. "Joi, look. Calm down. This is all—"

"Don't get up! Don't get out of that seat. I'll defend myself if you come across that desk and I will bust yo—"

"Joi, wait. Wait. Just listen. There must have been some misunderstanding. Let me take the day to go over the reports and I'll sort it out. I'm sure it will come out favorably. In fact, you may even get a bonus for your hard work and dedication."

"Nope. Try again. I've got a copy of the original audit and so does Mr. McMinville. Any changes and you're gonna get investigated. Let's try again. Start at the part where you tried to tell me that your funny accounting was a personal unauthorized loan. Okay, your turn."

Her boss fell in his seat, checked a closed window, and sighed.

"Cut through the crap, will ya? Just tell me what you want. We're all grown-ups here. Raise? Promotion? What the hell? I've got enough to buy you," he said, tugging the lapels on his jacket and hooking his finger between his neck and tie knot.

"No, you've got me confused with someone that works here. Today is my last day."

"Good. How big a severance you blackmailing me for? Or BlackFemaling, I should say."

"No severance package."

"What it is then? Don't even think you're getting shares."

"Wrong again. Not looking for ownership. You'll get me sponsorship."

"For what?"

"You'll provide me with travel, lodging, meals, fees, and daily expenses, plus a monthly allowance."

"What for?"

"I'm trying out for the LPGA tour and you're gonna sponsor me."

"Great, you idiot. That'll work out fine. We'll love advertising our logo on your shirts and hat. You got me up against the wall," the man said, spitting with arrogance.

"Uh, I don't think so. You're gonna be my silent sponsor. As long as you keep the sponsorship coming, I'll be silent. But the first month I don't get my allowance, travel, or whatever, I'm gonna drop a copy of the McMinville group audit to every client you've ever had. Wonder what'll show up after all those years. So, for you, my little buckaroo, I'll wear a one-inch image of the company logo embroidered in white thread, sewn on the back side of my underwear. That way every time I play you'll be kissing my ass."

Chapter 33
The Beginning

Joi and Jeff entered Jimmy Mozley's driving range and were greeted by Mr. Mozley himself.

"Howdy. What can I get for you?"

"We'll be needing three hundred balls a day, five days a week, for the next few years," Joi answered.

"Really! Plan on joining the tour?" the greeter said, laughing.

Jeff looked at the man with a stone face and replied, "Yep."

"You serious?"

"Very."

"Okay then, Let's get you started. If you need—"

"Shhh, look," Joi said, pointing to the television in the corner.

This is a WSB newsbreak.

*From his DeKalb County home, Newt Dorsey has offi-
cially pulled his name from the upcoming primary election.
Speculation here is that there was a massive private investigation into campaign irregularities. The investigation was
supposedly initiated by Mr. Dorsey's opponent, Bob Berry,
who people may or may not remember because he has been
doing virtually no campaigning. Mr. Berry is holding a
press conference right now. We take you there live.*

*Thank you all for coming. First of all, let me say that I
appreciate the fighting spirit of my opponent. It has made
me stronger than I ever thought I could have been. There is
indeed a detailed report that will be distributed at the end
of this press conference. In the report are the findings of a
private investigation, clearing me of several false accusations and listing the sources by which these accusations
were made. However, I am not here to call attention to the
finger pointers. Rather, I am here to make you aware of the
Tri-Factor system for improved government. One that will
address all the needs and benefits of every DeKalb county
citizen. The Tri-Factor works and is working. As an example, I'd like to introduce one of the first participants in a
series of preliminary tests.*

The camera shot goes wide and shows two men and a
woman.

Joi shouted, "Hey, that's Kevin and...Skip!"

*This is Mr. and Mrs. Kevin Tanner. Mrs. Tanner is in
need of emergency surgery so that a life might be saved
and a life might be made. Doctors and other supporters
who are taking part in the preliminary Tri-Factor tests
have made it possible for families such as this who have
health care and health insurance issues to get the necessary care they deserve and desperately need. Before I open
up for questions, just let me say the Tri-Factor will work.
It's not just something we want to do. It's what we're supposed to do.*

"Oh my God. He did it," Joi said.

Jeff nudged her from the hypnotic glare. "We need to get going, if we're gonna get everything done. We don't want to get behind on our first day."

"Huh? Oh yeah. You're right. Wow. Good for them," Joi said, giving another look at the tube.

"So all I have to do is coach and caddie and travel with you and I get paid?"

"That's it."

"How much?"

"Depends on how much I win. And that, of course, depends on how well you coach and how well you caddie in the tournaments."

"What you're saying is I get out what I put in."

"Exactly."

"So I gotta basically be with you all the time."

"You got it."

"It's like we're gonna be married."

"Hey, golf imitates life."

Dear Readers,

Golf is quickly becoming immensely popular. For those non-golfing readers who have yet to fall in (and out of) love with the game, I have included this golf glossary in hopes that it will make The Big Money Match more enjoyable.

Written With Warmth,
Brian Egeston

Golf Glossary

Ace: Hole in one. A golfer makes one swing from the tee box and the ball goes in the hole.

Approach Shot: The shot made from the fairway into the putting green.

Birdie: One stroke less than par for the hole. If the hole is par four, a score of three would make birdie.

Bunker: An area of sand in the fairway or around the putting surface.

Cup: Another name for the hole. The goal is to hit the ball in the cup.

Dogleg: Layout in which the fairway is angled to the right or left.

Driver: Largest golf club a golfer will carry. Used to hit the ball the greatest distance possible.

Driving Range: Area where golfers can practice hitting balls to different targets and various distances.

Eagle: Two strokes less than par for the hole. If the hole is a par five, three strokes makes an eagle.

Fairway: The optimum area where the ball is normally played. Areas outside of the fairway are generally out-of-bounds, hazards, or poor places to play a golf shot from.

Fairway Metal: A large club, smaller than a driver, but used to hit a golf ball a long distance.

Gimmie: A putt in which the distance from the ball to the hole is so small it is rarely missed. The golfer picks up his or ball instead of putting.

Green: Also known as the putting surface. An area on which only a putter is used to strike a ball. This is where the hole is located.

Hazards: Any obstructive or difficult feature of a golf course, such as lakes, ponds, fences, molehills, or bunkers. Often marked by yellow or red markers.

Hole: See cup. Also note, the term "hole" is used to individually label each of the eighteen layouts on a golf course. Example: The eighteenth hole implies the collective sections of the tee box, fairway, and putting surface on the eighteenth layout of the course.

Hole-In-One: See ace.

Honors: The privilege of teeing off first on a hole, usually given to the player who scores the lowest on the previous hole.

Irons: Clubs which are not fairway metals or drivers. Used to make accurate shots. Irons are numbered 1-9.

Lob Wedge: An iron used to hit the ball a short distance with a very high trajectory.

Par: The standard score in strokes assigned to each hole on the golf course. If the hole is a par four, a golfer should get his ball in the hole using four strokes.

Pin: A thin, tall flexible stick with a flag. Placed in the hole of each putting surface to designate the hole position from far-off distances.

Pin Placement: Designated place where the hole is cut into the green. Usually changes every day.

Provisional: A ball after a bad shot when it's assumed that the previous ball will not be found.

Punch Out: Term used to describe a short shot played from the woods or place not conducive to a normal golf shot.

Putting Green: See green. Also called the putting surface or the dance floor.

Read: The act of looking at the putting surface in order to determine which way a putt will roll.

Rough: Thick grass off to the side of a fairway.

Shank: A shot struck by the club's hosel that travels dead right (for a right-handed player). Considered the worst possible shot, other than missing the ball completely.

Short Game: All shots that are made less than one hundred yards from the hole.

Short Grass: Fairway.

Starter: Person at a golf course in charge of sending golfers off to start their round.

Starter's Booth: Area where most starters are stationed.

Sand Trap: See bunker.

Sucker Pin: Very difficult pin placement. Often used to entice golfers into making a bad shot.

Wedge: Term to describe one of three typical short irons: Pitching Wedge, Sand Wedge, a Lob Wedge. Used to make accurate shots from the fairway towards the hole.

Carter-Krall Publishers

Literature that lasts forever

Books By Brian Egeston

☐ **Whippins, Switches & Peach Cobbler**
$13.00 Trade paperback ISBN-096755021
Please send   copies.

☐ **♣ ♠♠♣♠♠**
$13.00 Trade paperback ISBN-0967550580
Please send   copies.

☐ *Catfish Quesadillas*
$13.00 Trade paperback ISBN 0-9675505-5-6
Please send   copies.

☐ **The Big Money Match**
$13.00 Trade paperback ISBN 0-9675505-6-4
Please send   copies.

Available at your local bookstore or use this page to reorder.
Make check or money order payable to: **Carter-Krall Publishers**
GA residents add 6% sales tax.
MAIL TO:
Carter-Krall Publishers Order Fulfillment Dept.
P.O. Box 1388
Pine Lake, GA 30072

Please send me the items I have checked above. I am enclosing $ _____
(please add $2.15 per book for postage and handling).
Name _____ e-mail _____
Address _____
City/State _____ Zip _____
Please charge my Visa/MC/American Express # _____
Exp. Date _____ Signature _____

Carter-Krall Publishers
Literature that lasts forever

Books By Brian Egeston

☐ **Whippins, Switches & Peach Cobbler**
$13.00 Trade paperback ISBN-096755021
Please send ____ copies.

☐ **♣ ♠♠♣♠♠**
$13.00 Trade paperback ISBN-0967550580
Please send ____ copies.

☐ *Catfish Quesadillas*
$13.00 Trade paperback ISBN 0-9675505-5-6
Please send ____ copies.

☐ **The Big Money Match**
$13.00 Trade paperback ISBN 0-9675505-6-4
Please send ____ copies.

Available at your local bookstore or use this page to reorder.
Make check or money order payable to: **Carter-Krall Publishers**
GA residents add 6% sales tax.
MAIL TO:
Carter-Krall Publishers Order Fulfillment Dept.
P.O. Box 1388
Pine Lake, GA 30072

Please send me the items I have checked above. I am enclosing $ _____
(please add $2.15 per book for postage and handling).
Name _____ e-mail _____
Address _____
City/State _____ Zip _____
Please charge my Visa/MC/American Express # _____
Exp. Date _____ Signature _____

Carter-Krall Publishers
Literature that lasts forever

Books By Brian Egeston

☐ **Whippins, Switches & Peach Cobbler**
   $13.00 Trade paperback ISBN-096755021
   Please send _____ copies.

☐ **♣ ♠♠♣♠♠**
   $13.00 Trade paperback ISBN-0967550580
   Please send _____ copies.

☐ *Catfish Quesadillas*
   $13.00 Trade paperback ISBN 0-9675505-5-6
   Please send _____ copies.

☐ **The Big Money Match**
   $13.00 Trade paperback ISBN 0-9675505-6-4
   Please send _____ copies.

Available at your local bookstore or use this page to reorder.
Make check or money order payable to: **Carter-Krall Publishers**
GA residents add 6% sales tax.
MAIL TO:
Carter-Krall Publishers Order Fulfillment Dept.
P.O. Box 1388
Pine Lake, GA 30072

Please send me the items I have checked above. I am enclosing $ _____
(please add $2.15 per book for postage and handling).
Name _____ e-mail _____
Address _____
City/State _____ Zip _____
Please charge my Visa/MC/American Express # _____
Exp. Date _____ Signature _____

The Brian Buy-Back

Dear Readers,

If you purchase any book that I've written and you don't enjoy the story, I'll buy it back from you or give you another one of my books for free.

All you have to do is send me a letter or an e-mail stating what about the story you did not enjoy, a receipt showing the purchase, and the book.

It's not a gimmick, but a gesture of confidence and the ultimate offering of reader appreciation. This offer is good for every book I have written and every book that I'll write for the rest of my life.

Written With Warmth &
Sincerely Scribed,

Brian Egeston

Brian@brianwrites.com
Send books to:

Carter-Krall Publishing Order Fulfillment
P.O. Box 1388
Pine Lake, GA 30072